Pizza Pie and Politics

How Mitchell Moon Lost His Childhood

By
Troy Place

PublishAmerica
Baltimore

© 2007 by Troy Place.
All rights reserved. No part of this book may be reproduced, stored in a retrieval system or transmitted in any form or by any means without the prior written permission of the publishers, except by a reviewer who may quote brief passages in a review to be printed in a newspaper, magazine or journal.

First printing

All characters appearing in this work are fictitious. Any resemblance to real persons, living or dead, is purely coincidental.

ISBN: 1-4241-5426-X
PUBLISHED BY PUBLISHAMERICA, LLLP
www.publishamerica.com
Baltimore

Printed in the United States of America

To Nicole

Acknowledgments

The author would like to thank Laura and Ron Place and Judy and Don Burrill, who gave him the time he needed to finish this work.

Chapter 1

It had been drizzling for an hour, and suddenly a crack of thunder came down on us and shook the building to its anchors, making our torsos resonate as if they were empty barrels. The lights and the TV went out, and the refrigerator and radio stopped for a second, as if God needed to give a defibrillator jolt in order to put the world's heart back on rhythm. The straining clouds finally released a downpour that sounded like a million leaves rattling in a forest of trees; lightning pulsed through the little pizza shop's windows; fluorescent lights flickered back on; the refrigerator began to hum, and someone on the radio began to sing. The TV screen lit up again in a blizzard of static, and then, as usual when it rains, the phone began to ring.

I wasn't about to lunge for the phone in a lightning storm, but Neil picked it up anyway and began to take orders. There were five in a row. When he hung up, he said, "I'll roll, Charlie makes, and Mitch watches the oven and delivers."

"No way, I'm not going out in this."

"Somebody's gotta deliver, and you always put too much damn cheese on," Neil said.

"I'll roll and you deliver."

"You're too slow," Neil said.

"I'm not slow; I'm quality oriented."

"Bullshit. They want their food in thirty minutes."

He had a point. We had to compete with the chains more often since we started working there in high school. Although, the fact of the matter is the only reason Drew could stay in business despite those chains is because the shop stood north of the Battle Creek city limits, and we delivered to customers on all of the back roads of which a lot of people, except EMT's and firemen, were not aware. And these places were precisely where I was headed on that gloomy night after pulling the pies out of the old, blackened, front-loading pizza oven rescued from a junkyard fifteen years prior.

I placed the food—pizzas in the red, vinyl warmers, salads in white Styrofoam containers, and subs in aluminum foil—in the back seat of the delivery car, a 1982 grey, five-speed, Dodge Omni, which I did not drive well and which didn't run well regardless.

Frigid Michigan rain poured down on my back as I opened the front door and slid myself into the driver's seat. I started the car, which brought alive the song we had been listening to inside.

I backed out onto the right lane of M66 and took a right onto Pennfield Road, the windshield wipers frantically keeping time with the music. My first stop was at the duplex on this road. I dropped off a sixteen-inch with mushrooms and GP's (green peppers) and didn't care about getting a tip because I was drenched and pissed off. Then it was on to Clear Lake Road about three miles to the end of Pennfield, a right onto Pine Lake Road and then a right into the middle of nowhere. On Clear Lake Road, I dropped off two taco salads and a large order. Then I was off to Little Clear Lake Road, which is a dirt road, twenty yards down from the former delivery and which ends in a forest. Here the house numbers are not marked, so whenever I deliver there, I have to rely on my fabulous memory: "Now 17775, is that the place where the parents are never home and the seven- or eight-year-old always pays me in dime rolls, or is it that big putty-colored cottage that sits way down by the lake and whose driveway I can never seem to do anything but back out of (up hill on a fifty-five-degree grade) because they always seem to have so much damn company?"

"I'll take a shot with the dime roll kid," I thought, fooling myself.

With a sixteen-inch P&M (pepperoni and mushroom) and a two-liter of Coke in my hands, I pounded on the screen door, granite paint chips shattering onto my right arm. A little boy with mussy hair and a red Kool Aid mustachio answered. With a face as bright and beaming as Christmas morning, he immediately recognized me as the pizza guy.

"Is that for me?"

"If you ordered it."

He turned away and shouted, "Kelly, did we order pizza?"

"No," came a reply that brought the Kool Aid monger and me back to reality.

Immediately, he asked if he could have it anyway.

"Maybe next time," I said, reluctant to explain my mistake.

By this time I might as well have jumped in the lake and swam to the putty-colored cottage's back door because I was thoroughly soaked from my head down to my Rods (Rod Laver Adidas), and I was late.

I speed walked to the running Omni and drove down to the cottage. As usual cars lined the driveway and filled the circle turnaround so that my only way out would be to put the stick on "R" or drive straight into the lake and see if it was an amphibious vehicle, which I was sure it wasn't after the way it handled in the thunderstorm.

Met with a red-faced retiree with a snifter of brandy in his hand, I dropped off four sixteen-inch Royals (sausage, black olives, mushrooms and green peppers), received a generous tip (retired folks don't care as much about delivery time as others unless they have to come out of retirement to become drivers themselves) and proceeded to imagine a way that I would get myself up that grade, which was as slippery as a river bottom by then.

The only way I could see myself gaining enough momentum was to mash the accelerator and ball the jack. My tires spun for a couple of seconds and then gained just enough traction for me to get it halfway up with no problem. There the Omni began to peter out, front wheels kicking silt that covered the car in a film that I imagine stretched from fender to fender. I pushed the gas to the floor again, and caught some gravel and slipped into a rut, which hurtled me toward a brand-new BMW. For an instant I thought of squashing the brake pedal, but then I would have lost momentum, so I threw the wheel back the opposite way, nicking the truck's bumper with my fender. After that the grey ghost took to the middle of the driveway, and I spun my way up and over.

Once onto Little Clear Lake Road with eyes forward, I realized that the window wore a sweater of fog, and the defroster never worked. Daunted but not defeated, I sat dangerously close to the windshield and drove with my left hand while my right continuously cleared the glass in front of me with a rag

My next stop was Burrows Road (a wet burrito, a two-liter of Dew and a twelve-inch green olives, green peppers, thin crust, extra cheese).

Three miles of serpentine roads through the remains of a dense deciduous forest brought back visions of some archetypical, fairy-tale induced nightmares I used to have after my mom would read Hansel and Gretel to me before bed when I was little. The storm made what would usually be a nice Sunday drive into an experience in gothic horror. I was just waiting for some sort of highwayman to run out in front of me, causing a chain of events that would leave me stranded in a place that Roosevelt's New Deal forgot.

Seeing imaginary outlines of creatures all along the unshouldered road, I finally dropped off food to a boy and his sister or girlfriend who laughed at my saturated appearance and gave me three quarters for my trouble. I'm sure I could have coaxed a dollar fifty out of them had I worn a yellow fisherman's jacket and a matching sou'wester, singing a sailor's song and doing a little jig on their front stoop.

I imagine I waddled like a duck back to the car, and it was off to Lynch Road for my last delivery.

The rain began to let up; I gained some visibility and turned on the radio. The singer for Sad Paradise seemed to scream at the remaining clouds, and I began humming along and tapping on my steering wheel. Soon I would be back at the shop in time to close, finish my beer and accompany Neil and Charlie to the bar. Lost in my thoughts, I forgot to bypass the infamous S curves on Lynch Road.

I don't remember thinking anything else because, somewhere down that road, a buck bolted out of the swamp on my right. He was frightened and galloping swiftly, and I swerved right to miss him, but I clipped one of his legs, sending him sprawling into the other lane. The next thing I saw were saplings being mowed over by the front of the Omni, which dashed headlong into a swamp. My head bashed against the steering wheel, and I saw the most glorious constellations.

After that little bit of ecstasy, I decided to look around myself to see exactly where Will-o'-the-Wisp had led me. I wasn't really in too deep. I was only up to about the axles in muck, but with the road five feet above me, I knew I would have to leave the car and hike about a mile down the road to my cousin Brad's house, and I decided to carry the last pizza of the run, which was supposed to go to the Sportsmen's Club.

I grabbed the pizza from the back seat, opened the door, stood on the floorboard and scaled my way over the Omni and onto the very edge of the swamp where the ground was only a bit marshy. Once onto the road, I looked for the buck, but he was long gone into the cover of the woods on the other side.

After sloshing back down Burrows Road and up the hill in my waterlogged shoes, I spotted the Leopolds' farmhouse, with white clapboard siding and all of the windows on the bottom floor lit up. I walked up the driveway and rapped on the side door.

Aunt Cathy's chubby face appeared in the door's window almost immediately, and her usually smiling eyes dimmed with suspicion.

"It's me, Mitchell," I said.

The door swung open, and her gaze fell on me very critically.

"I didn't hear you come up the drive and, and you're bleeding!"

(I didn't realize this.)

I touched my forehead and said, "Oh, I had an accident down the road. Is Brad here?"

"Let's get that cut cleaned up," she said, taking the pizza, warmer and all, and turning to place it on the kitchen's island.

"Could I call back to Drew's and tell them what happened?" I asked.

"Sure," she lifted the phone from its hook on the wall, dialed the number, gave the phone to me and vanished into the bathroom.

"Drew's!" Neil answered, probably sitting back on the counter during the seventh-inning stretch.

"Hey, I'm not gonna be back for a while."

My uncle came into the kitchen to get a can of Coke. He looked at me, nodded, and pointed at the red pizza warmer. I shook my head no, and he scowled at me.

"What happened? Where've you been?"

I told him, and he said, "Oh shit!" I could tell that he covered the speaker and laughed. I hung up and called Hercules, a towing and auto service across the road from Drew's, whose number I know by heart.

"Hercules."

"Hey, Bubba?"

"Yeah. Who's callin'?"

"This is Mitch from Drew's. I'm off the road, about a mile east of Burrows. Yeah, it's on the right, in the swamp."

"All my guys are out right now. I could get you in about two hours."

They constantly towed and fixed our delivery car for free in exchange for free lunch, so I said two hours would be great. Aunt Cathy came back with cotton balls and peroxide, and, after cleaning my forehead, found that the cut wasn't deep at all. The bleeding had stopped.

I explained my delivery and towing situation to her. She said that Mr. Leopold or Brad could drive me back and asked if the Casteele and Waters boys still worked with me.

"Yeah, Neil and Charlie are there tonight as a matter of fact. We all decided to come back here for one more summer before we go our separate ways."

"Oh, that's so nice. I love how you boys have always stuck together. That's rare these days; everyone's out for themselves you know."

"Oh, yeah."

"Well, what will you do after this summer? You all have degrees from Michigan State now?"

"Yeah, well, Neil has a job lined up in Washington, D.C., and Charlie's going to music school in New York City."

"And what's your degree in?" she asked.

"Political science, just like Neil." I intentionally did not state what I would be doing at summer's end.

"Now, you boys are going to be in Bradley's wedding aren't you?"

"We're planning on it. Where is he by the way?"

She hustled up the stairs. I heard some bickering whispers, and she returned with Brad.

"Bradley's going to give you a ride to the Sportsmen's Club and home."

In high school Brad always had a girlfriend, not the same one all four years, but one every marking period. He didn't have many other friends; he just had short, seemingly monogamous relationships with one person at a time. Regardless, he was as good of a friend to me, Charlie, and Neil, even though I don't remember ever doing anything with him after school. He couldn't go out with us for one reason or another, and he hadn't visited us in East Lansing since our junior year when he began dating Gretchen, a girl from South Bend. But he never fell out of touch with us, or we with him. The problem was that whenever I met him by myself, it was difficult to think of anything to talk about anymore. So once we got into the car—me sitting on a towel as if coming home from the beach in my bathing suit—it was almost as if we were strangers.

Despite this I talked about myself more than I usually do because I was grateful for the ride, and I was nervous about returning to the shop to face Charlie and Neil. (We couldn't wait for each other's competence to flag.) It

PIZZA PIE AND POLITICS
HOW MITCHELL MOON LOST HIS CHILDHOOD

was a joyous occasion to be celebrated with mockery, condescension and satire, as though the greatest farce of all time had been executed with methodical expertise.

As Brad pulled his car into the muddy side lot of Drew's, I realized that I would be the scapegoat for all of the weekend's inconsistencies when Andrew got back from his vacation.

As I opened the door to step out of Brad's Ford Escort, he asked who was working with me that night.

"Charlie and Neil. You wanna come in and say hi?"

"No. Well…" he paused for a moment. "Have you guys been fitted for tuxes yet?"

"Sure. Why dontcha come in for a minute?"

Charlie and Neil had come to the back screen door and were clapping from inside. He waved at them and laughed.

"I'd like to, but Gretchen's supposed to call at 10:00."

I looked at him with pity as held the steering wheel and stared forward. After thanking him I walked across the back yard to the door and stepped inside where I would be taking the stand at my own trial where there were only jesters turned prosecuting attorneys.

Charlie sat on the freezer close to the doorway to the back room I had just entered, and Neil was leaning against the stainless steel prep table in the middle of the room with his back to the TV. As soon as I reached the doorway, Charlie looked around and said in a very confidential tone, "You just put Drew's car in the swamp," as if I had just awakened, hungover and oblivious to the crimes I had committed during a three-day drinking binge.

"Let's close up and go see if the buck's still there," Neil suggested. "We'll have venison all summer."

I looked at my Rods, not being able to hide my smile. "It ran away into the woods."

Visceral laughter.

"I never said I hit it." (I wasn't even about to mention that I had just clipped it a little. That would have reeked of dishonesty and given them the certain victory.) "If I had hit it, the car would have been totaled."

"You can't stick with that story," Charlie advised. "The Grey Ghost can't be totaled."

"And no one's ever put it into a body of water. That definitely qualifies you for the Pantheon, Mitchell Moon," Neil replied.

(The Pantheon of Derelicts was a hall of fame for the characters who had

13

done the stupidest things in Drew's history, and it existed only in Neil's mind.) I tried miserably to justify my claim that it all could have been worse. When that didn't work, I tried to blame it on Neil, who thought he was in charge while Drew was on vacation. Then the phone rang. Neil answered, scribbled things down and hung up. He slapped his left fist into his open right hand, as if prepared to shag a fly ball and said, "A sixteen-inch pepperoni to the crack house. I roll. Charlie dresses, and you cruise in your own car, Swampy."

Sunday night's business ended at 10:00, and we mopped, washed dishes, set the alarm and headed off to Rikki Tikki's Tavern for some cricket and pints.

The bar inside of Rikki Tikki's fills half of the room. The other half is two booths, three circular tables, a jukebox on the wall in the very middle, a pinball machine in a corner under the TV, and a pool table with black cigarette burns speckling the green felt and an upside-down skillet propping up one of its broken legs. We were never welcome here, maybe because it's a blue-collar bar across the street from a cereal factory where we smelled Boo Berries baking that night. So we were met with the usual suspicious stares from men who might have thought we were hooligans or who just thought we looked too damn young and stupid to be fooling around with a pastime they took seriously—"Rookies, amateurs," their eyes said. We ordered three hamburger baskets for $2.50 a piece and three pints of Bells beer, which only made everyone but the bartender all the more uncomfortable. A request for Pabst Blue Ribbon might have made us some friends.

As we turned from the bar and looked into the right-hand side of the establishment's narrow parlor, we saw Mandy and her two friends sitting at a round table by the jukebox on the far wall, opposite the door we entered.

Mandy's companions were two girls we had never seen before, so after a quick gaze at what they were drinking, Charlie ordered two White Russians in order to contradict any statements Mandy had made about us previously. Although I dated her for three months in ninth grade, she harbored some suspicion of me after she and Neil began dating, which was also in the ninth grade—she dumped me for him—and I thought she hated me and Charlie after we talked Neil into working at Drew's one last summer. She worked as a waitress part-time and pretended to go to school part-time so that her parents would let her live with them. She used her credit cards for various novelties such as cell phones, a jet ski, a down payment on a slightly used sports car, tickets to see every pop band that came to Michigan and a boob job to beat the bands, all because she believed Neil would take care of her once he finished college and started his career in politics. When he decided to come back to Drew's instead of taking his first job offer in D.C., she panicked and threatened to kill herself if he went through with it. Of course she didn't blame him for long because she didn't believe he had a mind of his own; it was all our fault.

By the time Charlie had received his cocktails, and we had bellied up to the table, she and Neil were already in an argument:

"Why didn't you call me at 7:30?"

"We were busy as hell…" etc. etc.

Charlie handed the drinks to the White Russian aficionados and said, "Hi, I'm Charlie, this is…"

"We know," the black-haired girl with a barbed-wire tattoo on her bicep said.

"I'm Howk and this is Lane." These introductions were given as if we didn't really need to know, since we wouldn't be seeing them ever again. Mandy had obviously poured all of her troubles out on the table for these people she had probably met at work the day before and who were her best friends during happy hour.

As a formality, I nodded my head at Lane, a wiry blonde wearing black mascara and a grey slip she tried to pass off as a dress.

"So what do you do, Lane?" I asked. I always felt like Johnny Carson upon meeting Mandy's jaded friends, overly polite, nervous and patronizing all in one breath.

"I do guys like you for money," she turned to Howk, and they both giggled

I laughed as long as they, but I also turned to Charlie and raised my eyebrows in my most concerned tone.

He looked at me and smiled. He got up without saying a word, put money in the jukebox, and played "She's Like the Wind." This began shortly after he returned to his chair. The girls, including Mandy and Neil, began to giggle as if they had us pegged. After a moment of silence from Charlie, he began to sob violently, blubbering about his days as a dancer in New York City and his ACL injury that prevented him from becoming a Broadway star. Real tears dribbled down his face, as he concocted tales of his trials and tribulations as a performer.

Mandy and Neil continued to laugh, as Howk and Lane, unaccustomed to anything but sly indifference to all things human, began to shift in their chairs and reach for their purses.

"I thought you wanted to dance," Charlie called to them.

They grabbed their purses and scurried from the bar without a word.

"I wanna show you something!" Charlie screamed as they walked out the door. We polished off their White Russians for them.

Mandy had a sense of humor about all of this buffoonery and laughed and let Neil make up with her. They began cuddling and kissing each other's necks. This meant that Charlie and I would be playing cricket alone and that we, in three hours hence, would be listening to their love making in the bedroom next to ours in the glamorous Crimson Rouge Apartments.

Chapter 2

Charlie and I woke up early on Monday morning (Memorial Day) because we all had a field hockey game to play at Potter Park. Most people thought it was strange that this was our sport of choice. (My dad used to think it was an excuse to go and get stoned, until he followed me to a game one afternoon.) However, it's fast-paced, inexpensive, and you can play anywhere. Also, since we couldn't find any referees, there was plenty of contact for the aggressive types. Charlie started this as a joke one night, shortly after high school, at his own house party. His mom still had some equipment from her college years. At about 1:30 in the morning, something possessed him to drag all of his mom's old equipment out of the garage. Neil and I started smacking the ball around the side yard, and Charlie tried to organize an actual game when others joined in with brooms and bats and such. (I believe one person used a croquet mallet while riding a lawn tractor.) We all had a blast, and everyone at that party plus several more groups organized an informal summer league in Battle Creek.

Anyway, after a bowl of Corn Flakes and Gatorade, I politely knocked on Neil's door, and I heard them getting out of bed seconds later.

"You didn't tell me you were going to play with your friends," Mandy said from inside, astonished.

Feeling another fight coming on, I told Neil we'd be waiting in the car. But it was a clear day, and we lay on the hood of my car, sunbathing. At ten to nine, Neil and Mandy emerged from the building, kissed goodbye, and the three of us were off.

Sometime during the second period, Neil asked me if we were still supposed to be in Brad Leopold's wedding, probably because Mandy had already made plans for them on that day. I imagined that it was already entered into her PDA/written in stone, so I began to wonder if I would actually have to talk to her about letting Neil be a groomsman, wondering if she knew that she was automatically invited.

After losing miserably to a team comprised of eleven deft ladies from Olivet College's team, we headed to Drew's for lunch. I hoped the whole way that Drew slept in and would not be there, but, as we pulled into the lot and up to the big front window, he scowled at us with his arms crossed.

"What the fuck, bud?" he said to Neil as we entered. "I come back from vacation, and there's a message on my machine from Bubba sayin' that my car's gonna be in the shop for three days and he thinks it's gonna cost me eight hundred bucks."

"Don't look at me," Neil said.

Charlie rolled his eyes toward me, and the three of us tried to hold back laughter.

"Oh. Don't tell me," he rubbed his temples as if he were a great Swami. "You hit a deer."

"No, he missed it," Neil said enthusiastically.

"It was a buck, a big one. It would be worse if I hit it," I mentioned.

"I haven't seen a buck around here for years," Drew argued.

"The Omni crashed in order that father deer should live," Charlie chimed in.

"Fuck you guys!" Drew said. He went on a short tirade about the way everything is in shambles every time he tries to get away for a weekend and how it cost him more to take care of our blunders than it costs to run the place, and he also mentioned that, from then on, we were to pay for every lunch we ate when we weren't even scheduled to work.

He stormed out of the building and walked across the road to Hercules, probably to negotiate a deal. While he was gone we made and ate three dagwoods. As we were wiping our ungrateful chins, he returned smiling and recounting the adventures he had in Chicago and to buy us three Busch Lights with which to wash down our lunches. It wasn't long before he was calling us our old nicknames, Charlie Hustle, Neil the Deal, and Seven Year Mitch, and he invited us over to put the pontoon in the lake later that afternoon.

At around 5:30 we pulled into the steep, blacktop driveway that led down to Drew's house on St. Mary's Lake. He had already pulled the pontoon, on its trailer, around to the shore. He came out of the house and onto the porch in back as we were walking down to the lake, saying, "Time ta put the float boat in, boys."

After pushing and tugging it from the trailer into the water and mooring it to the newly painted white dock, Drew asked if we wanted to take it out, saying:

"Might as well. Not a cloud in the sky. Call Mandy," he said to Neil, handing him a cellular phone. "Hell, I'll go out with ya. Let me just call the pie house and make sure Kenny's holdin' down the fort."

"Order a case of beer and two sixteen-inch Royals," Charlie yelled as Drew was entering the house.

"I've got some beers in here," Drew said.

"We'll drink those too."

The three of us sat down in lawn chairs set up on the artificial grass, which covered the pontoon's deck. I wished that it had no canopy so I could burnish the tan I had earned in the two weeks since I graduated. Charlie got up and went to the car to get his guitar.

"So are you gonna call Mandy?" I asked, hoping Neil would get her over because, despite the fact that they always spent the night either fighting or cuddling and cooing to each other, she always ended up drinking too much and getting naked when we went out on the lake.

"Yeah, later on," he said. "You know I knew we were going to officially move in together after this summer, but she's been hinting about getting married." He paused and looked me in the eyes. "I'm thinking about going to look for rings." He paused again and looked at his shoes. "You wanna come?"

"Hell no," I said. "It's the ultimate cop-out, the ultimate give-in. You shouldn't marry her just because she's ready. You're still in denial about what you want, Neil. How can you commit to anything important right now if…"

"…Because I'm sick of this shit already. Call it denial or call it reality, but I'm not gonna to do what we did today every day of my life. It's gotta end sometime. We're just gonna get real drunk tonight just like we have for the past two weeks."

"I thought that's why we agreed to do this for one last summer. That's why you didn't take the internship; that's why Charlie didn't join that band; that's why…"

"...What, to get drunk? Fuck that! I'm broke and I'm beat, and I'm not doing anything. We did it because it's all we're comfortable with; it's all that you're comfortable with anyway."

"You're a dick! We're twenty-two years old. This is all we *can* do: drink beer and be poor and enjoy it."

"That's stupid. This is all we can do? That's stupid."

"Oh no. What's stupid is marrying somebody out of some sense of duty that you seem to have only when she's around. You're always worried about how things appear, and you never care about how things are. *That's* stupid. You should marry someone out of passion, not because you're tired of living off of Corn Flakes and raw hotdogs."

"Passion and blah, blah, blah," he mocked. "Where the hell did you hear that, Mr. and Mrs. Right's school of bullshit? You talk about reality and truth and all that shit, but you've never even had a relationship that lasted more than six months. You've never been laid. You don't know jack shit about what to do when passion fades, and you think anything intimidating to you is unreal. And then you think you can control everything because you're afraid life might not be the way it is in your head."

"I don't know what the hell you're talking about," I said.

"You and Charlie are looking for the perfect girl because you're too arrogant to commit to anything. Commitment means bending a little to someone else's will. You're afraid to do that, so it's safe to pretend to be longing for the perfect girl because if something is perfect to begin with, there's no reason to commit yourself; there's no reason to change your little ideas about what things are really like," he spat.

"That's bullshit!" I exclaimed.

"True bullshit. *True* bullshit," Charlie was yelling to us from the middle of the yard, while Drew set down a cooler on his deck and closed the sliding-glass door. After they boarded, Neil pushed us off, and Drew stood behind the wheel. He maneuvered the pontoon onto the lake encircled by houses with their glass porches reflecting the sunlight into our eyes.

He navigated around the lake and into a cove, far from the torque of jet-ski engines and speedboats towing children on inner tubes. This niche was thick with water plants, and Drew and Neil began to cast bass lures that looked like armored bugs rescued from the Mesozoic era. They cast far into the underwater garden.

I reached into the cooler and brought out four cans of Busch Light and distributed them. Charlie began to reach for his old six-string Gibson covered with Dave Matthews Band stickers, but Neil shook his head, scowled and nixed the idea.

In the cove the four of us finished off the beers, and Drew drove us to the far side of the lake by the landing to wait for Kenny to show up with more straw from the fire.

Charlie was already getting rowdy. On sliding past another pontoon full of young men who were holding up cocktails and yelling "Party" at us, he retorted with, "Why don't you get a job…and when you find one put a good word in for me, will ya?" As we motored to the landing, he sang his tribute song to Nelson Drebik, our old music teacher:

Sit down Steve Rupp.
Shut your mouth and get that trumpet up.
What the hell are you playin' Jay?
Have you been listnin' to NWA?
Kim, when's the last time you cleaned that flute?
Looks like you found it in a garbage chute.

Kenny was waiting for us at the landing outside of his red low-rider Chevy S-10. We could hear the bass line from his stereo thump at the pavement. Drew waded in to fetch our provisions, and everything turned bleary about an hour after that.

I do remember that we picked up Mandy, who wore a bikini that had to have been two sizes too small for her. Also, Drew's fiancée Jenn, and her friend Keely, who always looked as though she were hanging around a country club in Palm Springs, joined us. I remember thinking that I really had to kiss her before the night was over. The catch is that I didn't want it to be over. I never do.

Supposedly, sometime during the night, shortly after we ran out of beer, Keely took the wheel of the boat, and Jenn and Drew slipped off to check the pizza shop. Charlie told me that I tore off my Michigan State University shirt and threw it in the lake, saying that I had spent enough money there and I wasn't going to be a walking billboard. Apparently, that triggered a stripping trend, as Charlie took off his clothes and jumped in the lake with a naked Mandy following. I can imagine her little pink nipples erect, the skin around her areola becoming pimpled from the cold, and the blue moonlight glimmering off from her perfect bottom as she disappeared into the lake.

I believe Keely took us home, and I also recall going to bed upset with

Charlie because he made a lame pass at her before she let us out of the car, which resulted in a long kiss for him.

Upon waking up in the morning, feeling aroused from either an erotic dream or the carbohydrate charge from the beer, I began to wonder what it was like to kiss Keely. Charlie was awake, propped up on pillows, and reading my copy of *Wolf*. A few days prior, I retrieved it from behind the toilet in our filthy bathroom, and the paper was yellowed from drowsy misfires in the middle of the night. I meant to throw it out, but Charlie didn't seem to mind. I looked at him for a minute and asked, "Did Keely really kiss you last night?"

"Yup, right on the lips," he said without lifting his head from the book. "I think it was a mercy kiss more than anything though. You know how drunk we were last night?"

I shook my head and lay back, trying to figure out why I didn't kiss her first and thinking about why Charlie always got the affection, although it never seemed like he wanted it.

Chapter 3

Brad's bachelor party began very miserably. Charlie and I had to bribe Kenny and Craig to cover for us on Wednesday night. That cost us fifty dollars each. Then after picking up Brad at the farmhouse, the stark reality of the fact that he wasn't completely comfortable with us revealed itself again. We played the radio.

I said, "Hey, is this station all right?"

"It's all noise to me," he said.

"That it is," I replied, thinking that I never should have agreed to this party. It was an inane tradition in the first place, and the fact that he didn't even know we were going to a strip club made it seem even more awkward. It was Neil's idea, and he wasn't even going to show up until eleven o' clock because, inevitably, he was trying to appease Mandy. However, I took the night off from work to see some girls, and I was driving, so that much was settled.

Charlie turned off the radio and said, "Hey, Brad, do you know where we're going?"

I wished I could retract his question, but I decided that maybe it would be a good idea to involve the groom in the plans for his own party.

"No," Brad replied.

"We're goin' to Sirens, dude," Charlie said nodding his head.

"Cool. Are you guys gonna open that beer or not?" He pointed to the brown bag under Charlie's legs. (We bought a twelve-pack in case we were at the club later than two o' clock when the stores stop selling alcohol, but I hadn't even thought that he might want one.)

Charlie handed him a road beer and asked about Gretchen and wondered if her bridesmaids were "hot."

He smiled sheepishly, raised his eyebrows and nodded. Charlie opened a beer for himself, and I heard their cans bump together for good cheer. We were on our way to Kalamazoo.

As we entered Sirens and paid our cover charge, we were accosted by the guitar riff of an ACDC song, and six strippers slithered on a runway that stretched about one quarter of the distance to the end of the room. Even though I don't think it had changed, the club wasn't what I remembered it to be. Only a year and a half ago, just after I had turned twenty-one, I had the same feeling there as I had when my parents took me to see *Return of the Jedi*. (I didn't know such things were possible.) This time I wished that I had taken a wrong turn on Kalamazoo Street.

I hesitated. I wanted to go back down the street to Bells where we could have much more fun for less money. (We would easily blow three hundred dollars that night.) But Brad marched past the doorman and up to the bar to order three Bushmills straight, two pitchers of Budweiser and thirty one-dollar bills. On his way back to Charlie and I, who had found a table at the end of the runway, he set down the tray he was carrying, slipped a bill into a passing stripper's underwear, said, "Keep up the good work," and gave her a thumbs-up.

A dancer named Lotus walked to the end of the runway and said something inaudible to Charlie. She had black hair, blue eyes and wore a white g-string so tiny that she would have had to shave everything. As the song ended, she suspended herself upside down from the top of the brass pole, spread her legs toward Charlie, looked back and smiled at him. Brad, transfixed, set the end of his tray down on the table, almost spilling everything on the floor, and I felt like Odysseus, wondering where I had led my crew.

Shortly after Lotus exited, the six girls began carousing around the floor asking for dollar dances. Charlie and I alternately paid every one of them to do their thing for Brad, telling each of them that he was a groom-to-be. The first one told him to pull his chair out from under the table and spread his legs;

PIZZA PIE AND POLITICS
HOW MITCHELL MOON LOST HIS CHILDHOOD

she then rubbed her crotch on his for a minute and put her behind up as high as it could reach, thumping her thighs against his chest. She turned around and rubbed her perfumed breasts against his face and asked why he was there if he was going to be married. I got so nervous for Brad that I downed my Bushmills in one swallow and poured myself a beer, which didn't last quite as long. Finally, Lotus was approaching our table, and I decided that Charlie and Brad needed a dance from her. While I held up my two bills, another dancer had given her bra to Brad, and he attempted to try to tie it around his neck Windsor style.

After dancing for Brad and Charlie, Lotus took a seat between Charlie and me, and she lit one of Brad's Marlboro Lights and blew the smoke my way. I introduced myself and made sure to look into her blue contacts despite everything else she was showing. We talked for over an hour while Charlie and Brad occupied themselves at the bar and the catwalk. I had cavalier dreams of taking her out of that place and really showing her the world. Then I learned that she made more in three nights than I did in two weeks, so I dreamed about how she could show me the world, until Neil came rushing up to our table, introducing himself to Lotus, pretending to look for Charlie and Brad and sitting in for a beer. (He was supposed to be our designated driver.)

For about an hour after that, I listened to Neil's conversation with Lotus, and Charlie continually tried to explain to the waitress why Brad was sitting in a trance, staring at his own reflection in the brass pole at the end of the stage. After another hour Charlie and I fell into Brad's trance as the DJ made last call and Neil and Lotus, hand in hand, walked toward the door without saying goodbye.

I could not drive home. I asked the waitress, who had been our friend for the last three-and-a-half hours, to call a cab to take us to Battle Creek.

The cab driver didn't quite trust me when I told him that we were headed for Battle Creek and that he should take 94 East to the 66 south exit and wait for directions. He got us home anyway, and as I watched Brad enter his parents' farmhouse that I had delivered so many pizzas to before, I wondered what happened to me from the time we used to play on the swing set in his backyard to the time when we became absolute strangers.

Charlie could have been thinking this too, but he was in wonderful spirits. He believed that those who controlled their own destinies were absolute failures, and he chatted with the driver about all of the other ways that he might have driven us home, and the driver laughed and laughed at the things that came from his imagination.

Chapter 4

    Partly because we had to sit through a fight between Mandy and Neil (She wasn't going if he wasn't staying.), partly because we had a two-hour drive to a small town on the lakeshore close to the Indiana border, and partly because Neil drove separately, we arrived at the rehearsal twenty-five minutes late that Friday. Everyone in the little Lutheran church acted relieved to see us, but Brad didn't have time to do any of the introductions because the minister had another rehearsal after ours and hurried us into a little room behind the pulpit and explained to us where we would be standing when the ladies came down the aisle. We heard some organ music, which was our cue to come out. The girls walked in, the minister briefly went over the vows, and we receded. I walked with Bethany, the tallest of the bridesmaids, who looked smart wearing glasses and her brown hair in a bun. Charlie walked with Chelsea, a petite girl with black hair and green eyes, and Neil escorted Hannah, who had loose wavy curls in her blonde hair and a dark tan. Then we said hello to Brad's family and met Gretchen's family, two members of which were Bethany and Chelsea (Gretchen's younger sisters), and drove off to the rehearsal dinner at a very large German restaurant off of I-94.
    The wedding party sat at one large round table, and the elders sat at

another in a back room set off for our party. There was a vacant fireplace with a large oaken mantel ornately carved with what looked like a picturesque version of the book of Genesis. The dark paneling and arabesque wallpaper made the room somewhat gloomy, but we did have our own busboy and waitress, which was a first for me. They kept us satisfied with homemade meatballs and crackers with cheese spread made with their dark beer. For dinner we ate rack of lamb, also a first for me, but Gretchen and her sisters had vegetarian meals, and the staff kept our glasses full of water, then homemade brandy, then table wine, and finally champagne with our dessert of cherry tarts. Through dinner Brad and Gretchen looked scared and nervous and hardly said more than a few quiet words to each other. By the end of dinner, there wasn't much room for conversation as Gretchen's father and Grandpa Leopold were getting loaded and loud.

Charlie tried to talk over them, asking Chelsea, who had just graduated from high school, where she was going to college and what she was majoring in, etc. etc. Chelsea perked up and said she was following Beth to Purdue.

"Oh, that reminds me," Charlie said, waving to the busboy who stood by the fireplace. "A round of Boilermakers, man."

The busboy looked doubtful that we needed eight of these concoctions, but he went to order them anyway. When he brought them back on a tray, Gretchen's father said, "Oh, no you don't, gentlemen. My daughters are staying sober, thank you very much," as he moved the beer and the shots to his table. Charlie and I had two apiece as Brad and Gretchen waived theirs, and Neil also had two because Hannah didn't want anything to do with them.

My belly started to warm, and the storm clouds that still filled my head from Wednesday night began to break up, letting in the sunshine and high pressure. I knew what was coming: I tend to run my mouth a little too much when this feeling comes over me because I want to share it with everyone, but I checked myself in a room full of strangers and asked Bethany if she wanted to go for a walk before I joined Gretchen's dad and Grandpa Leopold in their bear dance.

We walked down to a pond that had Canada geese in it, and I tried to listen more than speak for the half hour that we were together. Then, while we trudged up the hill to the back entrance, she held my hand. I opened the door for her, letting the darkness and cool air out of the restaurant, and she gave me a wink of hope before silence was broken by a rumble of voices and the clatter of dishes and silverware.

Brad's father wanted all of the drunkards to pile into his minivan so that he could take us back to the hotel. During the ride Grandpa Leopold suggested that we continue our drinking binge at the hotel bar, so the five of us, he, Neil, Charlie, I, and Gretchen's father had cocktails and talked about all of the Notre Dame/Michigan State football games we could recollect. After an hour or so of this, Brad's father and uncle came down to have a beer. After the old-timers went to their rooms, Charlie, Neil, and I went up to our room to drink Heinekens from the mini bar and order a porno. The movie was less than entertaining, so Charlie and I spent an hour making prank phone calls to other rooms until we were hoarse. Then, at about 2:30, we called Bethany, Chelsea, and Hannah, and eight of us soaked in the hotel's Jacuzzi until the fourth time the security guard threatened to call the police.

When we woke in the early afternoon, we ordered scrapple and chorizo breakfasts, which I found to be as good for a hangover as Gatorade and Corn Flakes, and we spent about two hours floating around the pool. At around 3:30, we were back in our hotel room, shaving and changing into our tuxedos. We walked out of the hotel and drove toward the church, overdressed and sweating like mad on a ninety-degree, eighty-percent-dew-point day. I wanted to feel all afternoon the way I felt in the pool with the buoyancy and serenity of the water pushing away all of the aches and uncertainty that I had gained from another night of drinking.

Either I sweated off my hangover on that ride or I finally realized for one of the few times in my life that I owed a service to someone other than myself. Regardless, I felt completely sober and ready to go by the time we reached the church. The minister wrangled us into his office and offered to all of us some last-minute advice on marriage, which was do not fear it. He told Brad that all of the pomp and circumstance is for the guests and for the church; it's not to influence his way of thinking about marriage.

"That's between you and Gretchen, and the Lord," he said. "This is one of the largest weddings we've had here, and it might be intimidating to you, but remember that the church and its congregation was never meant to control marriage; the church and these people are here to nurture a marriage. On the same note, you can't make a marriage something that it's not, but you can make it as good as it gets by believing in yourself, believing in Gretchen, and believing that you can do better things for the world together than you can apart from one another."

I had never heard anything like this before because, naively, I always thought ministers were despots who only told people what they could not do and showed them an impossible example by which to live. As if to confirm that I was a rube, Aunt Cathy came in after the minister left, checked us all over and discovered that I had folded the blue handkerchief in my breast pocket in a square instead of a triangle like the others, and she offered me some make-up to cover the razor bumps, which she called blemishes, on my neck. I said no, but I realized that if a fifty-five-year-old lady who had worked on dairy farms all of her life was worried about a blemish on my face, it should be an important day to everyone.

Besides the dirge-like songs during the wedding and the fact that the minister really couldn't get to the heart of the matter with the dogma as well as he did in his office, Brad and Gretchen were married. Once again, I walked with Bethany, who had her flowing brown hair down that day, (Charlie with Chelsea, and Neil with Hannah) to the greeting room and waited for Brad and Gretchen, whereupon we lined up to shake hands with the congregation. After this we endured an hour of pictures. By then I had forgotten why I was there and had lost perspective; I didn't handle the posing and overexposing very well. This made me crave not only a Bushmills, which I drank in the limo, but also a trip inside of myself by the time the limousine arrived.

At the reception hall, which was on the ground floor of the hotel, we had to wait outside until we were given the signal to enter because the DJ had to introduce the wedding party and the new bride and groom. He played an energetic dance track and announced our names as if we were the starting lineup for the Lakers while laser lights and strobes flickered around the hall. We sat down at an elevated table on the west wall of the building, and everyone clapped for Brad and Gretchen and began tapping on their glasses with their spoons so that they might kiss. While they did Charlie stood up from his chair, threw down his napkin and pretended that he was going to kiss Chelsea, as if it were about time. Everyone encouraged him to proceed, so he did and carried off a counterfeit kiss with his neck and shoulder hiding the lack of lip contact. He held up his arms in victory, but everyone gave him a thumbs-down for bad acting. He sat and ate some cheese and crackers as if nothing had transpired, and the guests began clanking their glasses again for Brad and Gretchen. After about a half an hour of Kenny G, hors d'oeuvres and guests coming and going to and from the bar, the DJ handed me the mic so that I could make my speech. I hadn't thought of making a speech, and I almost made a motion to refuse what the DJ offered. Then I noticed the expectant look on Aunt Cathy's face, so I knew I had to go through with it. I had never spoken into a microphone before, and I had never spoken to a group of more than fifty people. My stomach turned, and the whiskey that I had consumed burned in my throat. I swallowed hard and decided to open my mouth to speak.

As the room waited, I realized that I had nothing to say. So I said, "I've never had someone special in my life."

Charlie yelled, "His room number's 225."

As I waited for everyone to stop laughing, I realized that I was off on the wrong foot. While the last few snickers tapered off, I decided that I should quit digging and go for the surface quickly. "There are a lot of different reasons why we're all here today," I said. "Some people are here because they love their family. Some people are here because they love their friends. Some people are here because they love a free chicken dinner," I stared at Charlie for a moment. "But it's no mistake that we're all here, brought together by the love of Gretchen and Brad. So, despite the fact that some of us might not know each other, and because of the fact that some of us might never see each other again, let us make the most of our time together in this world, and let us make this a night that Brad and Gretchen might cherish until the days when they are old and grey, poring over pictures that have documented this very day."

I sounded like Edgar Guest, but everyone clapped. (I found out that summer that one of the only times a man will not be judged in this world is when he is delivering a speech at a wedding.), and my aunt grabbed her handkerchief and began to wipe her eyes as I sat down, which was worth more than the three hundred dollars I had blown on the bachelor party at Sirens.

We ate acorn-squash bisque, spinach salad, honey-roasted chicken, prime rib or vegetarian lasagna, steamed broccoli, and cauliflower, and we drank the wine that Bethany and Chelsea had stockpiled before the bar closed for dinner. I asked the DJ to play John Coltrane and Charlie Parker during our meal, and he said he would but continued to spin Kenny G. About half way through our meal, Neil told Hannah to make the same request that I made, and he played some jazz right away, after making sure to get a good look at her ass while she walked back to the table. I thought this music was a little more stimulating, and it felt to me as though people began to energize even before it was time to cut the cake and open the bar. Brad did not shove the white cake into Gretchen's face, nor did Gretchen accost Brad with the dessert, as I had seen newlyweds do before. It's an unfortunate way to begin a marriage, a passive-aggressive way to show the public that the power struggle has begun before the wedding is a day old.

Three songs meant to be poignant were played for the dance of the bride, the dance of the bride and her father and the dance of the wedding party. Bethany and I, disregarding the tempo of Lionel Ritchie's "Easy Like Sunday Morning," danced a fluid but very formal box step as though we were dancing to "The Emperor's Waltz" instead. When the song was ending, we did several elaborate spins and a dip. I wanted to kiss her because she surprised me with her endearing silliness, and we held hands and walked back to the table and drank until we were giggly. I asked her if she wanted to cut a rug to "Jessie's Girl."

Although I didn't wear a tight dress like Hannah, I walked up to the DJ to try another request, one for Rick Springfield this time. Gretchen's father blustered up in front of me, slapped down a five-dollar bill and requested some polka music. Almost as fast as he could slur out his orders, "Beer Barrel Polka" was blaring through the hall to a very positive reception from the two families. Gretchen's father opened his arms to the guests and sang in a very exaggerated baritone voice, "Roll out the barrels" and told everyone to come to the dance floor with his hands, as if he were helping someone back up a truck. Ladies and gentlemen of all shapes and sizes skipped, walked, waddled and limped to the dance floor, formed a circle and sang with Gretchen's father and clapped and stepped to the left and stepped to the right, and Grandpa Leopold danced into the middle of the circle and shook a leg and shuffled his feet and swayed his shoulders and began clapping his hands and slapping his knees to animate the oompah rhythm of the song. After a minute he danced back into the circle to meet enthusiastic applause and thrown-back faces enlightened with laughter. Then a grey-haired couple took to the center and executed a rigid little fox trot. Everyone cheered and made cat calls.

All of the sudden, Charlie came out of nowhere, slid into the middle of the circle as if rushing home plate, jumped up without using his hands and began to maneuver around the perimeter lifting alternate legs and clapping under them as he hopped. Then he slid on his knees back into the center and swung himself into the helicopter (A hip-hop move that made him look like a spider at the mercy of a toilet flush.) He got out of this with a hand stand and flipped himself backwards onto his feet, just as Neil came in with his wobbly-leg dance which made his legs look artificial, the way a pencil appears to be made of rubber when it is shaken between the index finger and thumb. Then he clapped his hands, jumped into the splits and bounced from the floor back onto his feet just in time for me to put my drink down on the DJ's table and join him in the middle to do what was something like the Charleston. The song ended, and everyone cheered for another polka and pushed Charlie back into the middle to join Neil and me. The three of us, soon to be joined by Grandpa Leopold and Gretchen's father, danced the best we could to the capricious clarinet, the oaful tuba and the popcorn snare until we had to catch our breath and belly up to the bar. The bartender saw everything and laughed with us and gave us beer and Jagermeister. Someone said, "Hey, you guys!" and snapped a photo of the three of us giggling our faces off. When the flash in my eyes disappeared, the woman behind the camera stunned me.

She was tall and slender and had faint peanut-butter freckles, dark eyes and long dark hair with highlights that reminded me of drinking iced tea with a twist of lemon after mowing the lawn on a hot July afternoon. She smiled at us with her eyes and a mature mouth that had the slightest half-moon wrinkles parenthesizing her full lips. Charlie told her to vamoose; he didn't need the paparazzi always trying to catch him red faced and half in the bag from drinking with his low-down cronies. She said, "You guys are a trip," and walked back to the party. Although I thought that she must have been someone's date, I followed her and asked her name and if she wouldn't mind putting that camera around her shoulder so that we might dance.

Ilo was her name, and we danced to a song called "My One and Only Love." With her heels on she was almost as tall as me, and she looked into my eyes, and I looked into hers, and there were sparkles in her dark pupils like a herd of white horses roaring over a far hill at midnight.

Ilo gave me a hug when the song ended, and we went back to the bar to sit with Neil and Charlie, and the bridesmaids had taken seats too. I sat next to Ilo, not in the reality of dim lights, half-full champagne glasses, lilting love music, muffled voices in the reception hall, or the well-drink liquor canon above the head of the bartender who wanted to go home two hours ago, but in a state of bliss where I could sense nothing but a different kind of blood pulsing through my body, where all of my veins and arteries tingled. I had no idea what to say to her.

I was shaken from my foggy world when she said, "What's wrong? Why are you so quiet?"

I reacted a little too slowly to comfort someone I had just met. I began to open my mouth to speak when she turned from me.

"What's wrong with him?" she asked Charlie.

"He's in deep thought."

She looked disconcerted by this, and Neil asked her to dance, maybe to keep her from leaving as quickly as she had entered our lives, and they disappeared.

PIZZA PIE AND POLITICS
HOW MITCHELL MOON LOST HIS CHILDHOOD

If I were sober, I would have taken this for what it was. But after they decided to stay out on the floor for three more songs, I was hurt and disillusioned, and I wasn't drunk enough to handle reality after returning from the place I had been two minutes before this.

I left the banquet bar without saying a word to anyone and walked down to the hotel's cocktail bar where I met Ted Dreisbach, a cousin of Gretchen, and his fiancée for the first time. In a different state, I suppose I might have thought it awkward that they were not in the reception hall. As it was I plopped down next to them as if I had been with them all night. The last thing I remember is giving him unsolicited advice about his campaign strategy. (As it turned out Ted had been on the Chicago city council since he was a freshman at the U of C and had been campaigning for senate since January, shortly after his twenty-sixth birthday.)

When I woke up in the morning, I had a perma grin of my face because I, retroactively, felt good about meeting Ilo, and because I hadn't yet remembered exactly what happened. I scanned the hotel room without moving my head. Bethany lay beside me; Charlie lay in the bed next to us, reading Gideon's Bible with a sleeping and fully clothed Chelsea beside him. Hannah, wearing only a white half shirt and light blue underwear, lay on a blanket at the foot of Charlie's bed. I wore my full tux with a very large Michigan State Spartans basketball T-shirt over my jacket. I also had a pack of Lucky Strikes and a pack of Marlboro Reds in my front pockets. I don't smoke, but there was a cigarette butt in a plastic cup beside the bed. I realized upon pulling the crushed packs out of my pocket that both were otherwise full.

Bethany wore her bridesmaid dress, which was as wrinkled as used tissue paper. I noticed this because we slept on top of the bed cover, as though in our own coffins.

The first thought that crossed my mind is that I did not see Neil, and I remembered that the last time I thought I saw him was on the dance floor with Ilo. I was angry with him; then I was miserable with myself when I remembered that I had run away from a situation that deserved all of my patience and humility. I lay there for a long time and decided to deal with it in my own bullheaded way: if Ilo were the one I wanted, she wouldn't have danced with my friend; she would have given me a chance even though I was self-absorbed and distant; and she would have known, without asking, that I was thinking of her, before she assumed that something was wrong with me. Then I got out of bed and grabbed a little bottle of wine out of the mini bar because the beer was all gone.

"Where's Neil?" I whispered.

"He's on his way home. He has to work lunch," Charlie replied, somewhat annoyed that he had to stop his reading to give me an answer he thought I already knew.

I saw Bethany began to awaken.

"Where'd he sleep last night?"

He shot me a puzzled look, pointed to the foot of his bed where Hannah lay and said, "I didn't think you were *that* fucked up last night."

"Then what happened to that Ilo girl?"

"I dunno. She came around and asked for you, and I didn't know where you went. Then she left."

"Bride or groom's side."

"I dunno, man." He put his book down. "Do you remember Neil getting in the shower with his tuxedo and shoes on?"

I shook my head no and took a sip of bitter wine.

"Oh, dude. It was hilarious. He came out here carrying about twenty pounds of water in his clothes and pretended to towel off, and you laughed for about fifteen minutes until everyone was laughing at *you*. This morning his tux looked like crepe paper thrown away after a Halloween party. Ah! That was a good night, Mitch. When do we do this again? Doesn't Brice get married later this month?"

"June twenty-fourth."

"Oh man, we danced for an hour and a half after you left. Nonstop. Everyone was just trashed, and one of Gretchen's aunts kept pinching my ass. It hurts; I think I have a bruise or somethin'." He put his hands on his head and looked at the ceiling. "Oh! and when the party ended we all decided to go to the cocktail bar for some karaoke, and there you were wearing that T-shirt, yelling at that Dreisbach dude and everyone else who would listen about the demerits of the two-party system. You were really putting on a show; Everyone was watching you. It was hilarious; Neil was crying."

By this time Bethany was sitting up trying to get her bearings, and Chelsea and Hannah were awake but trying to go back to sleep as if hoping the whole thing were a bad dream.

"Was Ilo at the cocktail bar?"

"No. I told ya. She left after she asked for you."

Chapter 5

When Charlie and I got home from work that Sunday night, Neil told me, "There's a message on the machine for ya, jackass!"

I pushed play, and it said, "Hey, Mitchell Moon. Ted Dreisbach here. I'm just wondering if you were serious about bein' my best man in July or if you were just talkin' shit 'cause you were drunk. Give me a call back, buddy."

I was kind of relieved that he called when we were out because I had obviously made an empty promise to the guy.

"What's that all about, buddy?" Neil asked.

"Dude, *call him back*. He's runnin' for senate; can you imagine the party?" Charlie added.

"Maybe later."

"It's always later with you," Neil said. "You're such a puss; You're just gonna leave the guy hangin'?"

"No. I'll call him back. Just let me sleep on it."

I went to bed with no intentions of ever talking to Dreisbach again.

That Monday morning was the first time in three weeks that we didn't know what to do, mainly because Drew had not scheduled any of us that day, which was a first for the summer break. To make things better, Mandy was infuriated at Neil for leaving her alone all weekend, even though it seemed to be a mutual decision when we left on Friday, so she wasn't around that day.

At ten o' clock in the morning, Charlie walked out to the storage closet, appeared at the sliding screen door with a stepladder and announced that he was going for a jog. The next thing we heard were thumps on our ceiling, and we walked out to see him running around on the roof of our L-shaped building. A few people came out to see what the trouble was but only shook their heads and went back inside before they were noticed by the shirtless troll on their rooftop. When he came in, we played songs from the '80s: "Cum on Feel the Noize" and "We're Not Gonna Take It." We thumped on the furniture with our field hockey sticks and jumped on the couch as we did when we were in fifth grade on a Saturday morning after a sleepover.

Charlie, breathless, threw a towel over his shoulder, grabbed car keys and proclaimed that he was going to Lake Michigan, and we could come too if we so desired. Taking just enough time to slip flip-flops on and grab a Frisbee, we piled into his '88 Sunfire, which screeched like a hawk when he turned the ignition the first three times, and we drove to South Haven.

After a couple of hours on the beach, Neil suggested that we visit the Idler, an old steamboat turned bar and restaurant that was permanently anchored in the channel. I was still reeling from a weekend of drinking. Charlie was all for it, so we spent the rest of the afternoon watching cigarette boats, yachts and sailboats from places as far as Ashepoo, South Carolina, and Goose Cove, Newfoundland. It was very much like sitting in an airport terminal watching hundreds of people enter or exit our world, except these ones waved at us and said hello.

Toward evening Charlie took one of the sails on a toothpick that adorned his Blue Motorcycle and spread it so that it looked like a mask with eyeholes, as the sail had two finger-sized windows in it. He held this to his face, and we didn't know what he was up to until two girls wearing string bikinis and sashes around their waists walked by. He said, "Excuse me, miss. Am I late for the ball?" They thought he was cute and sat with us until the sun was going down, and after they drilled us several times about where we were renting a condo or a boat slip (it takes money to stay in South Haven in June) we had to leave them to take a long embarrassing walk in order to be fit for driving home. We walked to the beach, and Charlie swam while Neil and I chose to sober up to a mauve and powder blue sunset.

On the way home, I had a recurrent urge to ask Neil if he knew anything more about Ilo than I did, but I couldn't stand the notion that he would tell me to forget about it; she's just another bitch, as he had so many times before. I couldn't stop thinking of her, replaying the few words she spoke and trying to piece together exactly how she looked after she had taken that picture and brought the camera from her face. I was jealous that she had a picture of me but I had nothing of her. I thought I could try to memorize the shape of her nose, cheekbones, eyelashes and chin so that I could create a complete picture of her in my mind. I wanted to remember her face well enough to put each faint freckle in its appropriate place. What a fool! What a fool! I knew it, and that's why I didn't ask Neil a thing.

It was easier that way because once my passion was revealed, I either had to act upon it or forget that it was ever mentioned. I had no idea how to act upon it; I never did, so I was content to fall asleep in the back seat of the car, thinking about the weekend's events in the easy and uncomplicated way in which I thought they had occurred.

After I arrived at Drew's on Tuesday afternoon, Mr. Leopold stopped by during his lunch break to give me an envelope for Charlie. I opened it immediately, and there was a note inside that read, "Charlie, I found these in your tux before I took it back. Hope you don't mind me going through your pockets but all of you forgot to take things out. –George [Mr. Leopold]." With the note there were fifteen dollars, cheese pincers, and a cocktail napkin on which there appeared to be a Battle Creek phone number written in red lipstick. I immediately called Charlie to tell him that I had some things of his. He didn't ask me what they were, he just said, "Oh, this is too cool. I love it when I find things that I forgot in my pocket. I'm comin' in."

I thought that he was kidding me, but fifteen minutes later, he came in and asked where his stuff was. I threw my thumb in the direction of Drew's office, and he came back with his envelope. He stuck the money in his pocket and sniffed at the silverware. "Classy," he said.

"Whose number is that?"

"Oh, you remember that Ilo chick?"

"Yeah."

"She told me to give this to you." He gave me the napkin.

"Thanks a lot, Charlie," I said and tore it from his hand.

He looked surprised and said, "Sorry…forgot." Then he put his pocket surprise up in the air and rapidly pinched the tiny tongs together about ten times, as if it were a minuscule mouth, and he left.

I enjoyed approximately two and a half hours of elation over this napkin before Neil came in at three o' clock to take over.

Before the screen door even banged behind him, he asked, "So have you called Dreisbach yet?"

"No, dammit! And I'm not going to."

"You're a sissy." He picked up the phone. "Call him. Right now."

I tried to end this intimidation by using a little fabricated confidence between him and me.

"Neil, the guy's weird, okay? I'm not gonna repeat it, but he said something to me that just made me think he wasn't quite right. I think he might be in the mob. And you saw the way he stayed in the lounge all night, away from his own family?"

"You jackass. It's obvious that his family can't accept the fact that he's marrying a black girl. That night after the reception she took off as soon as we all came to the lounge, and no one even acknowledged him. Besides Gretchen, we were the only ones that talked to him the whole time, and almost all of Gretchen's family was there."

"So."

"So the only thing weird is his fuckin' family. Think about it."

I did, and Neil made me feel sorry for him. I decided I would call and explain that I didn't want to be his best man. That would be after I called Ilo. I had to prioritize these new people, and at the time, I thought Ilo was most important.

At home I decided that watching *The Black Stallion* and *The Fish Who Stole Pittsburg* would inspire me to think of what I needed to say. The problem was that I found myself alone with Mandy after work because Charlie joined Neil at the shop. This wasn't so bad at first because she agreed to watch these silly movies and make dinner if I cleaned up and made margaritas. However, about one hour into *The Fish Who Stole Pittsburg*, she interrupted the precious silence in the house and one of the best fast-break scenes in the movie to tell me she thinks I made a girlfriend at the wedding.

I shook my head no and rewound the tape back to the rebound that began the break. As it played again, she told me she knew because there was a napkin with red lipstick hanging on the corkboard in my room, and I would rather go to Rikki Tikki's and wait for Charlie and Neil than spend an evening with her if I weren't planning to call later.

I looked at her, stopped the tape with emphasis, rewound, stopped again emphatically and slowly lifted my thumb up and back down again on the play button, hoping she would comprehend.

"Besides that," she said. "You saved *The Black Stallion* for last because you want to watch the mushy movie before you call your girlfriend." She looked at me with her mouth open to see if she had hit a nerve.

"There's nothin' mushy about horse racin', honey."

"You better call her. It's been two days; she'll forget about you tomorrow."

I didn't bother to rewind this time because I was afraid the stopping and starting of the movie was encouraging her.

She went into my room and came back with the napkin. "I'm gonna call her."

She held it up and flapped it in the air.

"Go ahead. I don't know whose number it is."

"I'm gonna throw it away then." She walked to the sink and turned on the faucet and the disposal.

"Don't!" I ran to the closet-sized kitchen where she somehow dodged me and escaped into the hallway. I caught her by the arm before she could slam the bathroom door, but she spun out of my grasp and crushed my stocking foot in the door.

"Ow, dammit. Gimmie that," I began to laugh.

She retreated to the shower and pulled down her running shorts as I stumbled into the bathroom. By the time I could get to her, she had put the napkin down the front of her underwear and replaced her shorts.

"Now what are you gonna do?" she asked looking up at me with mock expectance on her face.

"I'm gonna go watch the rest of my movie. The number's not that important."

"Okay," she said. "If you want it it'll be right here." She patted herself.

I watched the rest of the movie and began *The Black Stallion*, satisfied with the fact that I at least knew the location of the number. Mandy seemed to calm down after a while, and she lay on the opposite end of the couch from me, her legs on top of mine. In the middle of the scene where the little boy and the horse were being rescued from the island, Neil threw the door open, and its crash against the wall sent us sprawling to opposite ends of the living room.

"What the hell's goin' on here?" he asked with an enormous grin on his face. He walked over to me and dumped the remainder of his can of beer on my head and said, "That oughta put the flames out, you son of a dick."

Charlie shook a can, threw it to me, and I sprayed most on Neil's face and chugged the remainder. I noticed that they had invited the whole crew home, including Drew's fiancée Jenn, Keely, Kim, Kenny, and Craig.

They brought home a lot of food, and everyone sat around the coffee table in the living room scarfing pizza and finger subs. (Charlie tried to eat with his newly acquired cheese pincers.) There was a lot of noisy talk, and Charlie got up every few minutes and walked to the fridge and screamed, "Who needs one?" Neil would follow to make screwdrivers and fuzzy navels, and sometime during our feast someone turned up the TV's volume. We looked as the Black Stallion led all of the other horses by at least two lengths. Keely commented that it was her favorite movie, but everyone turned their attention back to the food, as the hyperbolized talk about the week's events and memories of the past once again drowned out the dialog and musical score.

Long after the stallion had run his last race, long after Charlie had taken a swim in the Kalamazoo River, long after Mandy had done a striptease for us all, long after the rookies had gone to Taco Bell and returned with even more food, and just about the time that Neil had topped off our glasses with the remnants of the last bottle of vodka, the phone rang.

"Yessir, he's ritcheah!" I heard Neil bellow into the phone. "Mitch! Phone's for you, guy, guy, guy, guy, guy, guy."

Everyone looked at me as if it were the last trick of the night.

"Hello there," I said, winking at my audience.

"Hi, Mitch." A girl's voice came lilting to my drunken right ear. "This is Ilo."

"Ilo?" I tried to ask this quietly, sensing that someone in the room was playing a trick on me.

"Did you call earlier? Your number's on my parents' caller ID."

"Yes," I lied, grinning accusingly at our guests.

"Well, I didn't wake you did I?"

"No."

There was a long pause.

"I'm glad you called."

An even longer pause.

"Did you wanna talk or somethin'?" she asked.

"Yes." I looked around the room, trying to determine the joker.

"I woke you up didn't I?"

"Yes."

"Did you know we live in the same town? Isn't that insane?"

"Yes."

"Are you drunk?"

PIZZA PIE AND POLITICS
HOW MITCHELL MOON LOST HIS CHILDHOOD

"No."

"Umm…okay. You can call me tomorrow, if you want."

"Who is this, really?"

"This is Ilo. I said…"

I hung up the phone and looked around the room. I was furious, but I didn't want them to know they had jilted me.

"Who wass dat?" Neil asked.

"You know who she said she was, asshole."

He thought for a moment and threw his index finger out in front of himself. "No, I don't."

"She said her name's Ilo."

He threw out his hands. "It mus' be fate, my man. Thass the girl from the wedding." He looked at Mandy. "Of all things, it mus' be fate."

"You guys are assholes." I finally erupted. "That was not funny." And I went to bed.

When I awakened later the next morning, I rolled over and saw Keely and Charlie lying on opposite sides of his bed. Charlie was reading to her out of my collected poems of Gaspara Stampa, as she was propped up on pillows applying make-up from a compact to her already perfect face. I looked at her for a long time, because I hadn't seen women putting on make-up very often and because I enjoyed the fact that there was a beautiful one in my room. She looked over at me and said hello and, "Are you gonna ask this Ilo girl to Brice's wedding? I think it'd be fun if three couples went."

Charlie looked up at me from my book and grinned. I shook my head at both of them.

"Ya know; that wasn't funny last night. What if that were really Ilo?"

Charlie became serious and looked at Keely for a moment. She looked down at her hands while he told me that it really was Ilo. After I went to bed, Mandy admitted that she called the number out of curiosity. She didn't realize that it was so important to me until I reacted the way I did. I felt slightly embarrassed for that, and I still didn't want anyone to know how I felt about Ilo, so I bottled my anger toward Mandy and tried to occupy myself before I began to sulk.

During a dizzying half an hour, which aggravated my hangover to the point of nausea, of bending over and standing up to dispose of the trash and empty cans and glasses in the living room, I realized that the phone call from Ilo was the very first time any girl I wanted to date had ever called me. The pressure to contact the people I had met was always on me, and I almost always happily avoided it by never talking to them again. I thought that if a relationship were to be, then I would not have to spend an hour staring at the phone, as if I were a nervous playwright trying to mentally script questions and responses to an inane conversation. If it were to be, then the damn phone would ring, and it would be for me. That finally happened, but I choked. And that brings me to a second point: I also used to think that there would be a girl who would make it so comfortable to communicate with her that I would pick up the phone and dial without hesitation. The thought of Ilo did not make me comfortable, but that morning I called her, on my way to the sink with the last two empties in my hand, without thinking.

Chapter 6

"Hello." The voice of an elderly man came through.
"Hello. I'm wondering if Ilo is in please."
"No. She's at work."
"Okay. Is there a number there that might get me through to her?"
"Course there is."
"May I have that number, sir?"
"If she wanted you to call her at work, you'd have the number already, wouldn't ya?"
"Well, actually just because I don't have the number doesn't mean…"
I was cut off by a couple of thuds on the opposite receiver and the man whispering something like "…and I'm not gonna let it happen again."
"Hello," a more soothing voice came through. "This is Ilo's mother. You can call her at Birch Creek. Goodbye!"
Birch Creek is a golf course on the west part of town near I-94. I called there immediately. A man answered and said she was most likely on the back nine. There was no chance of getting a hold of her unless I called her cell, but he would not release the number for personal calls unless there was an emergency. Then I asked him if he would page her and let her know that I was

coming to see her, but he informed me of the shortcomings of that idea because they were swamped, and she would be out there all day. Normally, I would have said fair enough and ended the conversation; instead, I asked him if I could make a tee time.

"It's first come first serve," he said as though he were talking to a completely different person.

I went back into my bedroom to ask Charlie if he wanted to go golfing.

He and Keely were in exactly the same position as they were when I left, except Keely looked as though she were dozing off. I was kind of jealous, and I thought about taking a short nap, but I shook this feeling off and asked Charlie if he wanted to go golfing. He looked around, as if I had just asked the most ridiculous question in the world and said absolutely not; he was perfectly settled for the morning. He was in the middle of reminding me that we don't have clubs when I explained why I was going golfing.

I pleaded with Neil to come with me, but he couldn't even lift his head out of his pillows. Then I got into my car and cursed their names for five miles because I had never set foot on a golf course, and I had no idea what to expect, except for valets, Mercedes Benzes, grey-haired men in expensive clothes making business deals and hundred-dollar fees. Even though I knew that I had gained all of this inaccurate information from the movie *Caddy Shack*, it still intimidated me.

When I arrived at the course, I pulled up to the bag-drop area, equating it with some kind of valet service, and looked for any tip money I might have had to pay the person to park my car. After a minute or two, I realized that no one was going to show up, and I looked ahead of me to see signs for golf parking.

After parking I followed others who had golf bags over their shoulders from the lot to a cedar-sided building. I could smell fried food blowing out of a vent somewhere. The golfers led me to a window at the pro shop in back where I was so relieved to see that nine holes and a cart would cost much less than one hundred dollars. I watched them pay and listened to how they made their arrangements, and when it was my turn, I said the same thing as the man in front of me.

"I noticed that you didn't drop any clubs," the cashier said. "Did you want to rent some?" he looked at me suspiciously.

"Of course."

He gave me a set in a narrow red and black plaid bag that looked like something I had seen in a Warner Brothers cartoon.

I found my cart and pulled up behind the group who I had followed from the parking lot. There were about twelve of them, and it didn't look like they were even planning on playing any golf. Some had cigars lit, and some were cracking beers right out of their golf bags. I waited for a while until I began to wonder what I was waiting for, and then I waited some more, occasionally looking out onto the deep green vista for any sign of Ilo "on the back nine." A few of the men ahead of me stepped up and teed off, but none of them were in any real hurry, so I decided to ask a man, who was kidding around with the golfers and looked like an official with his headset on, where the back nine was.

"Well, you've gotta play the front nine first today. We've got a few groups out there right now."

"Let the kid go ahead of us if he wants ta play," someone said.

"Tee up, Sparky," another said.

"Go ahead," the official suggested. "Have you played here before?" he asked glancing at my shabby clubs.

Upon my negative answer, he gave a few tips about the first hole and set me up.

I took out a club that looked similar to the club used by one of the men who had teed off before me. It felt awkward in my hands, but I held it as I had seen them do on TV. I stuck a tee into the ground, put my ball on it and made as if I were going to knock it out of sight.

"Wait!" the starter said. "Wait 'til those guys are down the fairway a ways." I leaned on my club and watched them hit some balls and drive across my view in their carts a few times. "Okay. Go ahead."

The men at the tee became very silent. This was out of etiquette, but I believed that they were all watching me, so I became very self-conscious, to the point where I considered throwing down my club and running for the car. I just had to knock it around a few times until the starter lost track of me, so I squared up and told myself that I held a field hockey stick and that there was a little net that I couldn't see up in the heavens. I swung the club and made contact that felt like the initiation of sex. My ball elevated into the sun until I couldn't see it for a few seconds, and then it came floating down. I heard the starter scream, "Oh Jesus, Fore!" The ball sailed over the heads of the men chipping toward the flag and landed about five yards from the green. A few of the men clapped and yelled to the starter, "What in the hell did you *tell* him?" I jumped into my cart, squashed the pedal to the floor, drove down the fairway with my clubs leaping half out of the bag upon every bump, past the players whom my ball had strafed, past the ball itself (for a second I thought of stopping to take another swat at the little fucker) and onto a trail that might lead me to Ilo.

Basically, I just drove around the trail reading the flags to see if I was heading toward the back nine and scanning the course for any very tan females in golf carts. Then I realized that it was going to be difficult to act cool when I finally found her, so I started thinking of alternate reasons for tooling around Birch Creek with rented clubs in my bag on a Wednesday afternoon. None of them made any sense. She would have to know that I came to find her; when I found her she would know that I was interested in her, and I thought there would be no turning back after that. I assumed she would have to love me right away or reject me on the spot. With the idea in my mind that all of the possibilities she held for me could be ended on this stupid escapade, I wandered the cart path for about fifteen minutes.

It was when I reached the top of a knoll looking down on two fairways that I saw four men that I watched tee off before me. Some were playing, and some were ordering beer from Ilo, who drove the refreshment cart. I stopped my cart and, like a general overlooking a battlefield, I assessed the situation.

I remember thinking that I shouldn't have done anything rash like this until I was completely sober. But for some reason I thought of something I had seen on TV at college late one night. It was a channel that had no sound, just a camera from space zooming in on different metropolitan areas in the U.S. However, it also showed that from fifteen miles up, the naked eye cannot see any trace of human life. Everything we think is so grandiose and so important and such a testament to human superiority cannot even be detected from fifteen miles away. With all of our myopia and vanity in mind, I figured I had the freedom to make a big mistake, so I wound my way down the trail and onto the fairway to order a Coca Cola from the girl who was most in my thoughts.

After she served the four men, she looked up to see what I wanted.

"What are you doin' here," she beamed.

"I came to see you." I thought I saw a flush appear on her cheeks.

"This is a surprise." She smiled for a minute. "So you're a golfer?"

"No. I just took a shot on the first tee because I kinda got roped into..." I trailed off. "Did you know you have some people who are pretty protective of your privacy?"

"You talked to my step-dad huh?" She held up her cell phone and said that he had bought it for her but will give no man the number. She scribbled the number down on a scorecard.

"Yeah, I would have been better off dealing with King Eurystheus." At that point I wished that words were bubbles that I could pop before they reached the ear of the listener, panicking about how geeky I might appear to her if I had to go into an explanation.

"Well, I hope I'm worth all of your labors," she replied.

Elated that she understood, I said, "We may never know the answer to that."

"No, but I'm glad that you came here instead of calling me. You guys made quite an impression on everyone Saturday night, and after all of the talk on Sunday, especially Brad's mom bragging about you, I'm glad to see that you're for real."

A voice crackled in on her walkie-talkie. She answered and told him that she'd be there soon.

"Well, I hafta get back to work. I hope you expected that when you paid your greens fees."

"I didn't expect anything. I didn't even expect to see you again…but here you are."

"Here I am, but I have to go." She looked at me as if she were sorry and gassed the cart to leave.

"What are you doing on the twenty-third?" I asked before she broke eye contact.

She shifted her eyes around pretending to think. "I'm probably working here."

"Well, I heard that it's gonna rain on that particular day and that people who work outdoors would be better off attending weddings with people like me."

"Oh, God, another one?"

"It's only the beginning. I'm at that age, you know. Everyone's getting married."

"Well, you'll have to tell my boss and my boyfriend that it's gonna rain, but I don't think they'll believe you."

I wanted to drag all of my clubs out and throw them at trees.

"You have a boyfriend, huh?" (It turned out that he was a fellow pre-law student at the U of M.) I wanted to ask her why in the hell she called me then, but I remembered that Mandy had helped me out with that one. Then I wanted to ask why in the hell did she give Charlie a number to give to me, but I didn't know the whole story about that either. All I could do is turn the color of a rickets victim and ask, "Is it anything serious?" as if her doctor had just discovered a tumor.

"We may never know the answer to that either," she said, as she pulled away toward men who thought they needed her more than I.

"She's got a boyfriend," I told Charlie as soon as I entered the pizza shop.
"So what? Keely's got boyfriends and she's goin' with us."
"When the fuck you gonna call Dreisbach, ya tool," Neil chimed in.
I had forgotten about that thorn in my side.
"I'm not worried about Dreisbach. He can find his own groomsmen."
"He's gonna win that election, and he'll be workin' in the Hart Senate Office Building next year while you'll be still wonderin' what you're gonna do with your poly sci degree."
"What does that have to do with a wedding?"
"Connections, connections for both of us."
I shook my head no and said, "He's not gonna win shit."
"That's not what you told him, man, and that's what really pisses me off about the whole thing. You're actin' like everyone else in this world who'll blow smoke up someone's ass just because they happen to be in front of you. Don't think people don't know when you've lied just because they don't say anything. He'll remember. Mark my fuckin' words he'll remember." He paused. "Be an original in this world and do what you said you were gonna do."
Before this I really thought that he only wanted a free trip to Chicago, but his points could not be ignored. I had to follow through on my words, even if they happened to be intoxicated. I called Dreisbach when the dinner orders subsided.
"E-party club house," a young girl answered very salaciously. I thought I had finally called one of those 900 numbers I have seen on TV late at night.
"Hello, is Theodore Dreisbach there please?" I asked.
She laughed and said, as if asking over her shoulder, "Is there a Theodore Dreisbach here, Mr. Theodore Dreisbach?" mocking the tone of a subservient secretary in an old black and white movie.
I heard a man's laughter on the other end.
"This is Ted."
"Hello. This is Mitchell Moon. I talked to you over the weekend about your upcoming wedding, and…"
"Mitch!" he paused. "What, were you outta town or somethin'? I left you a message, man."
"Ah, yeah, I have been doing some traveling."

"Do ya still think you could do this? I know it's a little sudden, but I'll pay ya for your trouble."

"No, I'm in. I, I think all three of us are in. I just…"

"Hey, ya know, Teresa suggested eloping, but I can't steal the dream from her just because my family won't cooperate, ya know what I mean?"

I had no idea what he meant. "Sure, sure," I said.

"Well, are you guys gonna do this then?"

"Yeah, we wanna do it, but you and I were a little tipsy Saturday night, and I just wanted to have a little recitation on the situation here."

Like a campaigning politician, he spent no time on the facts; instead he gave me the agenda for the weekend and mentioned frequently that it would be of no expense to us. Though he talked for only a few minutes, the specifics that stood out most were July 1, Palmer House Hilton, Chicago Athletic Club and a limo for the weekend. The fact that he was going to treat us so well made me suspicious, as if he were planning to "fatten" us for another purpose. However, he said that he would do his best to prevent the stress of his personal relationships and campaign from affecting us.

"Are you there?" he said. "It's okay if you wanna think about it. I just have to know for certain by Saturday, man."

I had a very hard time trusting anyone but Neil and Charlie, and I hoped that Ted didn't think this meant that I was his friend. I had a hunch that he was the type of person who had charmed all of his friends in life with a façade and had bought them with trifles. That was okay with me; I had been friends with people for worse reasons. However, I didn't want to become a fool.

"Yeah, we've thought about it. We're gonna do it; I just wanted to make sure that you're sure."

"I'm sure, man."

"We're on it then. I'll talk to you later."

"I'll keep in touch… Hey, Mitch," he said just before I hung up.

"Yeah."

"I wanna thank you for your advice at Leopold's."

"Umm…which piece of advice would…"

"…About creating my own persona before the media does it for me. I like it. It actually makes a lot of sense, being the black sheep of the family and all."

I told him that he was welcome, hung up and went back to work, trying all night to figure out why Ilo gave me her number if she had a boyfriend. I asked Charlie how she went about doing it, and he told me that before she left she wrote it down and gave it to him to give to me.

"Did she say anything else?"

"No."

In my obsessive state of mind, I thought that was a good thing. For example, she didn't leave the number because she wanted me to wash her car and mow her lawn. Also, her honesty at the golf course about having a boyfriend could mean two things: either she wanted to set it up as a hurdle to see how much I wanted her, or she realized that I was too interested in her due to the nature of my visit, and she didn't want me to go too much further. But then she gave me her cell phone number. My mind unraveled and raveled the problem so that I might unravel it again in a different way over and over until I couldn't wait until the next day when I would call her. The quickest route through time is sleep, and for the first time that summer, I went directly home after work and crawled into bed, even though Charlie and Neil were going to Rikki Tikki's.

Chapter 7

    I called her on Thursday afternoon and once later that week but came no closer to finding out where I stood. That didn't bother me as much as the fact that I had so many things I wanted to say to her, but the only thing I could talk about was Drew's, Charlie and Neil, college, pop music, and movies. From her I learned a lot of things I didn't want to know about her boyfriend and almost nothing about her. The consequence is that, even though we talked for hours both times, I hung up feeling disillusioned, and I never asked her for a date. I didn't try to call her at all the following week until about 4:00 a.m. on Wednesday. We hit Rikki Tikki's hard after work on Tuesday, and I tried to call her, insisting that my name was Randall McNally, with directions from her house to Ann Arbor where she could break up with her "candy ass" boyfriend.
    I didn't talk to her again after this for well over a week when she came into the pizza shop on a Thursday at about 9:30. It had been over two weeks since I saw her at the golf course, and she looked so good that I viewed all of those days as wasted time. She wore tight white slacks and a tiny silver blouse that showed her belly button. Before I could ask her what possessed her to come there, she said that the shop had a lot of character but that we should knock

out the wall between the front room and the prep area because it would be a gesture of confidence toward the customers, and it would also keep Drew's employees honest. Drew was pulling a pizza out of the oven when she said this, and he nodded ardently at the suggestion. Then she said that she and a couple of the girls she works with, who were out in the car, were going dancing. One lived close by, so they decided to stop and see what the pizza boys were doing. I looked out toward her car and recognized the girl in the front seat as someone I had met the previous summer. A feeling of guilt struck me, but I didn't recall any specific reason for it.

"Well, Charlie went home already, and Neil didn't work tonight. Maybe some other time."

"Okay."

I watched her strut to her car, her body put together like a Mozart sonata that people can touch.

"You're not a smart man, are ya?" Drew asked me while handing over a meal that needed delivery.

I didn't think about her again until that Sunday night when Keely and Mandy came over for a late dinner. Brice's wedding was only six days away, and the four of them were going over the weekend's schedule, trying to work in everything everyone wanted to do in East Lansing in three days and two nights. I felt banished from this conversation, though I was to be one of the five groomsmen, and this upset me because it was really supposed to be me, Neil and Charlie heading back to campus to party with all of our drinking buddies one last time. Neil and Charlie were acting married, appeasing to every whim that these two girls who had never met any of these people could contrive. I think Keely sensed my dejection because she suggested that I try Ilo one more time as soon as possible. At first I absolutely rejected this idea, but she explained that Ilo, based on what Charlie had told her, liked me.

"I can't believe she stopped at Drew's and asked you to go out with her. I would never do that," she said.

"But it's a good sign."

"It's a good sign, but she's not gonna say what you want her to say if you keep playing it cool. If she's going to admit that she's interested in you, she has to make sure that you're really worth it. She doesn't want to make the mistake of dumping her boyfriend for someone who…"

"…You're on the bubble, man," Neil said. "Make a move already."

Mandy grabbed the phone and brought it to me. I blushed at all of the attention, but I wouldn't key the numbers. Mandy didn't hesitate to pick it up herself, and I tried to call her bluff, suggesting that she didn't know the number. She scoffed at me and proceeded. After a moment, I decided that after all of the grudges we had held against one another that I shouldn't underestimate her memory, so I grabbed the phone from her and sat down.

"Hello," the voice of Ilo's mother came through.

"Hello, is Ilo there please?"

"Is this Randall McNally?" she asked.

"No, ma'am. This is Mitchell."

"It sounds like Randall McNally to me."

"No ma'am; I'm without direction this evening."

"That's too bad. I'll get her."

Ilo answered, and we went through the usual mundane ritual of pretending that we were doing nothing and that everything was stellar. All crap. So I went ahead and asked her if she remembered that I was supposed to be a groomsman at a wedding on the twenty-fourth and that rain was still predicted, and she said that I would still have to tell her boyfriend that.

"I want you to go with us," I said. "Just for fun."

"If I didn't feel like someone is putting you up to this, I would probably say yes," she said. "And both times I've seen you since the wedding it feels like I'm speaking to you through a bulletproof window. Mitch, I'm sure you're a good guy, and I really wanted to hang out with you this summer, but I don't think that you mean what you're saying; every time you say something to me, it's like you're taking away a piece of a completed jigsaw puzzle."

"I'm not trying to be complicated," I said.

"Maybe you should."

I knew that she wanted to hang up on me, but she was too polite to do so. I thought about saving her the effort, but instead I said, "I'm sorry."

Charlie, Neil and Mandy picked their heads up from the table and stared at me in confusion because I'm sure they had never heard me say this before. It didn't mean as much to Ilo.

"Goodbye," she said, deciding that was a more appropriate time to end the connection.

I was humiliated in front of my friends, but this was not a first. I actually felt a sense of relief: I tried my best, and it wasn't going to work out the way I wanted to, so it wasn't worth more effort. After seeing me rejected at their insistence, I didn't think they would feel inclined to bother me about her anymore. However, I was not able to forget what she said to me.

Chapter 8

On June 23 Neil woke me up at 8:30 by shaking my walls with the Michigan State fight song, and Charlie was outside pounding on the bedroom window. He was naked and drenched, and I couldn't determine whether this was from a swim in the Kalamazoo River or the rainfall that morning. Either way he looked like Mitchum or Deniro in Cape Fear.

"Get up, get up, Guy Guy Guy Guy Guy," his muffled voice carried through the window. "It's not every day that Brice gets married."

We each had two fingers of Bushmills in our coffee, had a toast, and drove to pick up Mandy and Keely. When they were aboard, I felt like we were in *The Great Gatsby* heading to the city, except I was crammed in the back seat between the girls, their hands grasping my knees through every turn. In pouring rain we were headed north on Capital Avenue, out of town and toward I-69 when, on a whim, I told Neil to make a left on Garrison.

"No, I wanna get up there by eleven," he looked at me in his rearview. "And you know what that means? We're gonna get there by…"

I lunged forward and turned his wheel to the left before we missed the street. He had no choice but to let go and continue accelerating because a car was coming toward us from about forty yards.

PIZZA PIE AND POLITICS
HOW MITCHELL MOON LOST HIS CHILDHOOD

"Okay now, it's just six houses down on the left," I said without taking my right hand off the wheel in order to discourage any further interference.

In the middle of the road, he slowed to a stop at the right place.

"Get out!" I yelled at him and climbed over Mandy to get through his door.

I ran up the stairs of a large veranda supported by tall Doric columns on the front of a white Greek-revival house and rapped on the door.

"We don't have time for this shit," Neil, sopping wet, screamed from the car.

A portly grey-haired gentleman who looked like a city councilman opened the door wearing black silk pajamas and red backless slippers.

"Can I help you, young man," he said, looking at me as if I was the paperboy coming to collect.

"Yes, sir. I am wondering if Ilo is home this morning."

"Well, she's in bed. Let me go and see if she would like any visitors." He didn't let me in but closed the door, and from what I could see from pressing my face to the glass, it looked like he went up a set of stairs to the left of the front door.

After a minute or two of Neil's honking and my stepping out onto the steps and ripping my hand across my throat for him to quit and Mandy's squeals of "Whoohoo," Ilo's stepfather let me inside and wandered into another room with the newspaper in hand. She came down the stairs.

She wore pink boxer shorts and a large white concert T-shirt. I smiled at her face from which her dark hair was pulled, and I watched her long legs and then her high-arched feet pad down the steps. She smiled back at me and asked what I was doing there.

"Well, we're headed to East Lansing for Brice's wedding. It's gonna be a blowout."

"Yeah," she said flatly.

"Do you want to come with us?"

"Oh, like I'm really gonna go with you right now." She looked at herself.

"Could I come back and pick you up tomorrow morning?"

"Well, I'm supposed to work," she said reluctantly.

"The Weather Channel says it's gonna rain all weekend."

Neil honked two more times, Mandy was yelling "Stop it, asshole," and Charlie, on the front bumper, was dancing to "Who Let the Dogs Out."

"Why don't you call me tomorrow morning, and we'll see."

"Okay."

"Okay."

I walked down the steps into the rain and turned around. She was still in the doorway looking at me, so I waved and walked slowly to the car.

"Is she coming?" Mandy asked.

"Let's go," Neil said.

"No, of course she's not coming," I answered, sliding through the driver's door, past Neil and into the back seat.

"You have to be assertive once in a while, Mitch!" Mandy said.

I was going to reply to this, but she had exited the car, pulling Keely with her. Before I knew what was happening, they were running toward the front door. Ilo's step-dad answered again. They rushed past him and, I assume, up the stairs to the left.

"I'm givin' 'em fifteen minutes," Neil reported. "If they're not down by then, we're outta here."

Forty minutes later the three of them came flying out of the house, laughing and holding bags and pillows above their waists. Neil told them that he wasn't about to repack the trunk for all of that shit and they would just have to ride with it on their laps. The girls fit into the back seat, we crammed ourselves in front, and Neil squealed out of Ilo's neighborhood, toward the second wedding.

The rain stopped by the time we merged onto 69, and we rolled the windows down and turned up the volume for a Dave Matthews Band disc. The girls danced the best they could in the back seat, swaying in unison and doing the body wave. Charlie and I laughed and began to bounce up and down in our seats until Neil said, "Stop it, fuckers." Then Mandy, who sat in the middle of the back seat, began flashing her store-bought boobs at him via the rear-view mirror. He lightened up and let us do our thing all the way into the hotel's parking garage.

We checked into our rooms, boys in room 332 and girls in room 334, and walked onto the street toward our old house, where Brice, Thom and Kirk were waiting for us. It drizzled a little, though the sun shined between rain clouds as we walked east. I walked with Ilo, telling her the significance of certain streets that we passed in terms of which of my professors lived down this one or that one and which party occurred where. It seemed like babble, but she asked questions that made me feel as though she understood that I was telling her about myself in an obtuse way. We turned left down one of these streets and immediately saw our three friends. They had the living room furniture on the lawn and lounged away watching a television, which was connected to a long, orange extension cord. When we got closer, we discovered that they were watching a Tigers game. Thom, in the easy chair, held a bowl of cereal on his lap. Brice, sprawled on the couch sipping from a blue bottle of ginseng tea, and Kirk relaxed in a foam chair with a thirty-two-ounce mug of beer. They wore their typical summer uniforms of faded and torn T-shirts, baggy cargo shorts, baseball caps and no shoes or socks.

When they saw us coming, they got up and held their fists out for us to knock, and we introduced them to Ilo and Keely. They asked us where our bags were, and we told them that we were staying in the hotel.

"You coulda stayed here," Brice said. "We got plenty a room."

Ilo looked at the dilapidated house and back to me. Her left eye read "N," and her right eye read "O."

"We already checked in," I said.

They took us inside anyway and showed us the only change to the house since we moved out in May, a silver half-barrel of Busch Light covered with ice in the bathtub.

"So you actually lived here," Ilo said aside to me in a tone of sincere concern.

"For a year."

"It's terrible. I mean this place should have been condemned a long time ago. It's terrible the way they exploit student renters."

I nodded my agreement, and hoped Neil didn't overhear because he was always eager to explain that Charlie and I had done most of the damage.

We all had a couple of beers and sat outside talking while the game played. A few strangers would walk past and stop to check the score, and some would stay for a beer if we asked them.

"Big party tonight," Thom would say to any girls who walked past. "Stop by around nine o' clock." (I knew that all of the things Mandy and Charlie and Neil had planned to do that night would be thrown out as soon as we sat down at the old house.) We got hungry at around 2:30 and decided to move the furniture inside and to walk down to The Casablanca where we ate lunch and played pool. Then we split up, the three of them back to the old dump and the six of us back to the hotel to get ready for the rehearsal.

The girls all wore high heels, so we crammed ourselves into the car instead of hiking a mile to the chapel. Everyone was outside waiting for the rehearsal before us to conclude when we arrived. We met everyone and talked to the bridesmaids and Sherry, Brice's fiancée, for a while until it was time for us to go through a routine similar to Leopold's wedding. I stood between Thom and Kirk at the front of the church, and they made sure to ask me if they could date Ilo when she figures out what kind of a lunatic she's dealing with.

"After a lifetime of involuntary celibacy, you show up with Miss America," Kirk joked.

Neil and Charlie stood to the right of Thom, and after the bridesmaids came down the aisle, the organist played the wedding march, and Sherry entered with her father. She walked about halfway down the aisle before completely falling apart. The tears came first (I could see the lights glazing them in her eyes before they even fell) and then her sobs, sniffles and whimpers echoed throughout the chapel.

"That's the same reaction she had when you met, isn't it?" Charlie said very loudly to Brice.

After the rehearsal everyone went back to the house for a barbecue. Neil cooked; Sherry's mom set up the buffet on a table in the front yard; Charlie poured the beer; Thom got drunk and began yelling at everyone who passed to come back at nine o' clock; Kirk kept the music going, and I played horseshoes in the side yard—Ilo and me versus Brice's mom and dad.

Sure enough, at nine o' clock strangers began to come into the house, forcing the elders back to their hotel rooms and forcing Charlie to take money from them at the top of the porch steps. Sherry and her bridesmaids left soon after, and the house filled with people quickly until it became nothing but a blur of faces and a thunder of voices. There was no room to dance, so a few couples just decided to cut to the chase and make out in any corner they could find. Every time I went to get another beer, Ilo had moved from where I left her, and I felt as though I were constantly trying to find her. She talked to everyone she could and met people she knew from U of M, and she Mandy and Keely cleared out the kitchen at one point and did a goofy dance to "Every Little Thing She Does Is Magic." Everyone was clapping and laughing, but in my maudlin state, a surge of emotion came over me upon seeing her have so much fun.

When the song ended, the party closed around them again, and I lost sight of her, so I mingled and went outside for fresh air and got into a conversation with a boy about Camus, and then I think I argued with someone else that one cannot be a Christian and also believe in Machiavellian principles. I remember saying something like, "It was Jesus set the example for all rulers to come. It was Jesus, dude."

Neil, who was just coming down the porch steps as I said this, grabbed me by the shoulder and said, "Come on. We gotta go get another keg." I hoped this was the last time in my life that I would do this because the barrels were heavy, and it meant thirty to forty minutes to sober up, which can cause a vicious "pre-hangover." Besides that, I really did not want to leave Ilo even though she was far from being alone. Regardless, I went with him, or rather I was dragged to his car so he didn't have to go alone.

We returned forty-five minutes later to tap the new one before an influx of people at around 11:30 caused the crowd to spill out of the house and into the front yard. Neil and I took Charlie's place in the bathtub filling cups. As it turned out, I didn't have time to think about being sick from a premature hangover because I was working my tail off trying to keep up with the drinkers. Standing in a small pool of icy water, we quickly realized that the keg was in a terrible place, so we moved it into the kitchen behind a card table.

At about one o' clock, we sent Keely and Mandy to get another barrel. Things got out of hand shortly after they returned. The leftover ice bags on top of the barrels along with the condensation from the barrel itself turned the kitchen floor into a lake, which apparently looked deep enough to swim in, as several of the drinkers took off their shirts and proceeded to dash from the front door to the doorway of the kitchen, whereupon they would dive into the puddle and hydroplane through the kitchen into the bathroom. We thought this was hilarious for about fifteen minutes, but suddenly Brice looked at me and said, "I've gotta get married in the morning. We gotta get these people outta here. It's two o' clock."

Neil heard this and stood in the middle of the kitchen. He held up his hands and screamed, "I hope everyone had a great time, but the party's over. I have to ask you all to go." A diver plowed into him, undercut his legs and sent him sprawling. I thought Neil would pick him up by his hair and send him back the way came, but he stood up, brushed himself off and escorted the man out of the house. "It's not your fault, buddy, but the party's gotta end sometime ya know," I heard him say. "The party's over, people. Go home, please!" he yelled as he walked the man out the yard. "Party's over, guy. Get the hell outta here," Neil said to the diver who had knocked him down. The man just looked at him coldly for a very tense moment. When the man left, Ilo, who was sitting on the porch, said she was going to call the police.

"No, you don't have to do that. It's all good," I said.

"No, it's not. Get those people inside and lock the doors. I've seen that look before."

I did what she said, and some of them responded quickly. I don't know what happened to the others, but I locked the door and went to the side door and locked it just as I saw the puddle diver leveling a pistol at me through the glass above the same door. I hit the ground and yelled, "Turn off the lights. Turn off all the lights, now." The house went dark, except for the light in the hallway in which I lay. Everyone was silent, and I waited until I thought I heard his footsteps trod away from the side door. Then I got up, lunged for the hallway light switch and rolled into the living room in complete darkness.

I heard someone crying and someone else said, "What the hell are we doing?" just as one of the bedroom windows broke.

"Everyone stay down. Get away from that doorway," I heard Brice say. "Is he comin' in here?" Thom asked. I wondered what Ilo told the 911 operator. It had only been a moment since she called, but it seemed like a half an hour, and I wondered where the hell the police were. As it turns out she was still on the line with the operator. I waited to hear gunfire.

"He's running around the house," Neil said. We heard another window break. This time it was in the back bedroom.

I saw Neil stumbling over people to get to the stairway next to where I lay. "Where you goin'?" I asked.

"I'm goin' to get Thom's rifle. I'm gonna take his ass out from the roof," he said mounting the steps. I reached up and tripped him in mid stride. "Asshole," he said. "What are you thinkin'?" Then we heard a gunshot, and some people shrieked.

"Is everyone okay?" I heard a girl's voice ask.

"It came from the back yard," Brice announced from the bathroom. "He shot your fuckin' car, Kirk. I can see him. He's running down the alley."

"Toward what street?" Ilo yelled.

"Division. He's gone."

We waited silently in the dark until the red and blue lights from the police cars spun around and around on the walls of the house. An officer came to the door bringing garbled voices from his radio, and that is how the party ended.

We woke up at one in the afternoon on the day of Brice's wedding because we weren't able to return to our hotel rooms until close to five that morning, and that was with the police driving us and escorting us to our rooms because they didn't catch the gunslinger until close to seven o' clock, after more than a four-hour game of hide-and-seek. We didn't hear this until we arrived at the chapel late that afternoon.

The worst part was that I was afraid to walk through the parking garage to our car when we were going to the wedding. In my mind someone in the shadows had a bead drawn on me and was ready to pull the trigger. He was just waiting for me to get closer to the car. I would have turned and made an excuse not to go to the wedding had Ilo not been squeezing my hand. Her death grip made me wonder if the same thoughts were going through everyone's minds, and I made it to the car and to the wedding, but I'm not sure if I'll ever know if I was the only one who almost had a panic attack in that parking garage.

Most of the people who were at the chapel early were at the barbecue, and putting together the details of the party that followed controlled the discussions everywhere I turned. I was often called over to little circles of men and women so that they could ask me the same questions the police asked me for an hour that morning. So when the wedding before Brice and Sherry's concluded and the guests could begin to be seated, we were all relieved and less subdued than when we arrived. None of us were in any condition to be the center of attention, so we groomsmen sat underneath a tree on the bank of the Red Cedar River before more guests arrived.

It wasn't long before we began hyperbolizing the night's events, talking about the girls that were there and laughing about things we heard each other say.

"It's Jesus, dude, it's Jesus," Neil mocked me with his hands in the air.

"He shot your fuckin' car, Kirk," Thom said.

"Is he comin' in here?" Kirk mocked Thom in a little boy's voice.

"It's a good thing that was our last party in the old shithole 'cause no one's gonna wanna come there again," Thom said.

"Man, I'll tell you what," Brice said. "I had cold feet about this before last night, but all I could do when I was in the bathroom last night was pray that I would be alive today."

Before long it was our turn to take our places in front of the congregation. I felt relaxed again, and I waved at Ilo and shot her a goofy smile. She got out of her seat, looking like candy with her red lipstick and mint and cream sundress cut to show off her brown arms and legs. She strutted up front to take a picture of us before the bridesmaids walked. Then the music played, and the flower girl came down the aisle with Sherry following. When she was close, before the wedding march ended, Brice stepped up and hugged her out of turn and didn't let go until the music stopped. Although he had encroached, I don't think anyone who knew what happened held it against him under the circumstances, and a lot of people cried. In fact it made the ceremony seem more tense and poignant, because when Brice kissed his bride, I heard sighs of relief, and even stone-faced men laughed uncomfortably. After all had exited the chapel, Brice and Sherry were taken to our first picture location in the botanical gardens in a carriage driven by a white horse. Ilo came up behind me while we watched them go and grabbed my hand.

"Thank you for trusting me last night," she whispered in my ear.

The reception was the last time that the six of us college friends were together as kids. We ate dinner like ten-year-olds in a hurry to return to the game they were playing. We danced with the energy of twelve-year-old gymnasts. We drank with a resilience that might have fooled many guests into thinking that it was one time of the year in which we let loose. And we partied as though we knew what kind of turmoil the next chapter of our lives held for us.

Chapter 9

We rode home in silence on Sunday. It was not a negative silence, but one between friends who were comfortable with the idea that we may or may not be thinking the same thoughts. By the time we arrived at Ilo's house, she had fallen asleep, in the front seat between Neil and me, with her head on my shoulder. I squeezed her arm a little, and she woke up with a deep sigh. Everyone got out of the car with her and gave her a hug, and I helped her carry her bags to the door. Her mom came out.

"Thank you for bringing my baby home safely, 'Randall McNally,'" she said.

I sort of half bowed to her. She took my share of Ilo's bags, gave her daughter a suspicious look and went inside.

"Will you call me," she said.

"Yes."

I turned and walked down the steps and turned again to see her still looking at me. She gave a short wave, as if she were wiping away a spider's filament that stretched from her to me.

When Neil came in to relieve us from working lunch on Sunday, he showed us a short article from the *Chicago Sun Times* about Ted Dreisbach and a rally he put on that Friday night in Grant Park. There was an art fair and a hand's-on kids art and science exhibit and an all-day concert that featured some local bands. There was a poet's corner, and street performers came in droves. There were organized political protests spanning the spectrum of current issues from abortion to stem cell research to legalizing marijuana, to the War in Iraq. Spokeswomen from MADD held a forum. A professor from the University of Chicago spoke about overpopulation. A homeless woman spoke about the need for more safe homes in the city. A representative from the Nation of Islam spoke. Factory workers spoke against NAFTA and the WTO. A church leader spoke about the way in which many of society's problems have been produced by a neglect to satisfactorily explain the seven virtues to the world. Dreisbach scheduled no appearances for the media and no speeches, and only wandered around the festival to seek answers from the people, "as if he were Socrates in the Agora," the paper read.

When Neil finished, he said, "I told ya this guy was a phenom didn't I?"

"They're setting him up to knock him down," I said.

"Quit being so negative," Neil said. "He's no scarecrow, dude."

"It's not gonna be all fun and games in Chicago; we don't even know the guy."

"You're the one that talked his ears off for over two hours. Hypocrite!"

"You're just hoping he'll be your 'in' in Washington."

"Hypocrite!"

"Sycophant!"

"Go home; your shift's over, asshole."

"Fuck you."

"Fuck *you*."

This set the tone for the rest of the week. I tried to call Ilo on Monday, but she acted very solemn and said that she had someone else on the other line. I immediately assumed it was her boyfriend and went on a tirade to Charlie, my only audience. I elaborately linked call waiting to the root of all that was illing modern society, much to his amusement. (He was the only one with whom I ever shared my rage.) I didn't call Ilo again until Thursday, and in that week Dreisbach left several messages for me, which I did not answer. I was utterly afraid of him and who he thought I was.

Regardless, he cornered me with a call at work that Friday. We went over the itinerary, and he wanted to know how many of us were coming. I told him five for sure: Charlie, Neil, Mandy, Keely, and I.

"No date, huh?"

"It doesn't really look like it."

"That's okay. I'll hook you up at the rehearsal."

I was sure that Ilo wasn't coming, because when I called her on Thursday she was very curt with me, and when I asked her what she thought about coming to Chicago with us, she told me that she wanted to meet me on Saturday so that we could talk. I immediately began preparing to defend myself and all of my intentions. For two days I tried to script the conversation in my mind based on other break-ups in real life, in books, in movies and on television. I tried to plan for the variables that would catch me off guard and make me too angry or emotional to get through to her. It was all vain, and I lost two days of summer worrying about how to control the outcome of a future event.

After a field hockey game in tempestuous rain and wind on Saturday morning, I finally talked to Charlie about meeting her that afternoon.

"I thought Mandy and Keely already asked her to come with us, and she said yes," Charlie mentioned.

"Maybe that's what she wants to talk to me about."

"She might be mad that you didn't ask her first."

I would have driven right to Mandy's work to rip her a new one for meddling, but I didn't have time. I had to get a shower and meet Ilo at her parents' in an hour.

When I arrived we sat down facing each other in a three-seasons room toward the back of the house. I sat on a wicker love seat, and she sat in a mauve director's chair and turned on the floor lamp next to her because it was gloomy outside. Before she could speak, I blurted, "Did Mandy ask you to go to Chicago? That really pisses me off 'cause I wanted to ask you; I didn't think the time was right on Sunday after everything we went through."

"Yeah, she and Keely want me to go, and I want to, but you have to understand something."

"God that makes me mad," I interrupted.

"Well, that's the thing; maybe you're wrong to be mad. Mandy and Keely are my friends, and you're my friend, but I have the feeling that you're getting a little too serious. If that's true, then I can't come to Chicago with you. I have a boyfriend; I told you that in the first place. And Brian's not just someone I go with until I find someone better. We've seriously talked about getting married next summer, and you don't think I can throw our relationship away for someone I just met, do you? That doesn't mean I don't care about you; it means that I can't lead you on, and I hope you can understand what I mean. Do you know what I mean?"

I nodded yes catatonically.

"I really wanna go to Chicago with you guys, but only if you understand that we can't take this any farther."

There was a long pause, while we looked at each other.

"I can handle that," I whispered.

"Are you sure? If I'm breaking your heart, tell me."

"No, not at all. I'm lookin' forward to it. I want you to have fun." I told her what she wanted me to say and forced an enormous smile.

I went into the house, like a deft D.A., planning to express my feelings for her and support them with concrete and undeniable evidence. Instead, I left feeling like a little boy who had just been scolded. It never occurred to me that maybe she was afraid of me for the same reason I feared Ted Dreisbach; I didn't want him to complicate my life.

Chapter 10

We ran late for our train on Friday morning, June 30. The night before we figured that, since the train wasn't scheduled to leave until eleven in the morning, and all we had to do was ride for most of the afternoon, we could close Rikki Tikki's and knock ourselves out for a couple of hours at home. Not one of the five of us went to sleep before six o' clock in the morning, and most of us didn't awaken until after ten. The early bird was Charlie, and he found time to make Keely an omelet, read to her a few things out of my copy of Zimmer's *Crossing to Sunlight*, while she ate in bed, take a shower with her, and pack all of his things before he bothered to wake anyone up at 10:15. Neil and Mandy didn't know this, but it wasn't hard to trace the evidence of his wakefulness, as I flew through the house only half conscious of what I was stuffing into my backpack while he and Keely sat on the couch fully prepared to leave.

We were out the door and in the car at around 10:45. Neil tore through the streets to get to Ilo's house first. I sprinted to the front door of her house and pounded frantically on the door. A moment passed, and her stepfather answered with no more recognition of me than the time before.

"May I help you?" he said.

"Yes, sir. I'm here to pick up Ilo this morning."

"Ah, yes," he cleared his throat. "Let me just see about that."

When he turned to take a look up the steps to his right, Ilo almost ran him over. I held the front door for her and took one of her bags.

"You guys are *so* late. I didn't think you were coming."

We ran to the car, flipped her bags into the trunk, and Neil squealed out of her driveway onto Garrison, turned right and tore down NE Capital toward the train station. During our white-knuckle tour, Ilo said something like, "No offense, but this car smells just like an empty bottle of Black Velvet."

In the circle drive of the station, the dashboard clock read 11:03. Neil told us to get out, grab the luggage, haul ass through the station and get into the first car we see if a train is still there. So we climbed into the Amtrak car that was parked most directly in front of the double doors for departure. Our manic boarding had no effect on the other passengers. No one but small children looked up from their own business when Mandy shrieked with relieved laughter or when Charlie screamed "All Aboard!" until his face turned red. I made sure, as they were stowing the bags and sitting down, that the conductor walking the sidewalk next to the train knew that we had one more coming. He looked at his watch and nodded and proceeded to pace the sidewalk. I came in and sat down next to Charlie, who had his feet propped up on his guitar. Keely, Mandy and Ilo sat across from us in identical red, vinyl seats. The whistle blew three times, and Neil came bumbling up the steps. At the top he squinted inside to see us, spotted me on the outside seat, sixth row and sat down across the aisle from me with three very polite ladies who moved their bags to make room for him.

As we moved out of the station, after struggling for momentum through maybe three hundred yards, it seemed as though the huge Purina factory slowly moved away from us. Then warehouses and the tiny residential houses shuffled after the cumbersome factory; then trees, like a flanking army regiment, sprinted behind the tiny houses, away from the former tip of the Great Midwestern Prairie and down the valley toward the Kalamazoo River. Battle Creek was gone. I watched Keely's wonderful legs move from Charlie's direction toward Ilo, who sat between her and Mandy, and the three of them made conversation about things only very new friends can discuss. I looked at Mandy with anger and love, and I felt good with Charlie beside me, playing a song to match the rhythm of the tracks and the melody of their conversation.

We made a quick stop in Kalamazoo, then Decatur, Benton Harbor, Niles, and Michigan City, and we began to realize that we were on the outskirts of

PIZZA PIE AND POLITICS
HOW MITCHELL MOON LOST HIS CHILDHOOD

Chicago. We bulleted between two sections of freeway traffic; level with us lay a street and the tenements of South Chicago so close together and similar, with their grey limestone and white trim to be a vast patch of mushrooms. On every block stood a brightly colored liquor store and a church spire pointing out of its surroundings, which were colored like the earth and stone from which the freeway had been cut.

Then, to my right, I saw the towers of Cabrini Green with every third window on every floor boarded and scorch marks on the building's exterior from constant, and possibly self-contained, fires. Men tried to keep cool on the screened porches that ran directly up the middle of every tower. The White Sox played in the stadium, also to my right, and I wondered if the men and women to my far right could see America's pastime from their points of view.

The train rumbled on for a few moments, then escaped underground where there was a moment that the brightness of the day, like an expired light bulb in a closet, popped and turned to black. Lights flickered on, and the conductor mumbled that we were headed toward gate twenty-eight. After a few more minutes, we were slowing and sliding into a space between two other trains. Then we happily exited the train and immersed ourselves into the smell of oil and soil and dank spaces and the colors of the crowd that led us down the landing between tracks twenty-seven and twenty-eight and into the chaos of Union Station.

After we negotiated our way through the terminal and up the stairs into the great hall, I immediately knew what was going to happen. Still I wandered on, leading the group to an exit that was to be determined. I had confidence that I would see a sign that would certainly bring back some sort of memory that would trigger something that Dreisbach had told me about a pick-up area. We wandered, like bats lost in a gymnasium, from wall to wall, back and forth through the crowds of the great hall, until Neil shouted, "Mitch, dammit! Where did Ted say his driver was gonna pick us up?"

"I'm not sure. I think it has to be this street here," I pointed to the nearest exit.

"Where we goin' after this?"

"To a tux shop at Water Tower."

Neil stopped at a kiosk and bought a Chicago map for $7.50. He perused it while the five of us stood looking around nervously.

As we stepped onto the street that Neil determined to be the most logical according to our next destination, an overwhelming gust of exhaust fumes and gasoline just about knocked me back into the hall. As we gathered our bearings, Mandy spotted a limo driver, standing outside of his car about thirty yards down the street, who held a white sign with red letters that read Dreisbach Wedding. It didn't take long for the girls to begin giggling again and for Charlie to take running high steps to the car, as if he were a halfback stretching for the end zone. He got the best seat next to the liquor; Neil, Ilo and I sat on a long seat perpendicular to the back seat where Mandy and Keely lounged.

The driver closed the door behind us. The engine roared to life and propelled us into the flow of the street. He was not a patient driver. He weaved in and out of lanes, as though he were by himself on a motorcycle. Sometimes cabs had to slow to make room for him, and they used their horns as safety devices, instead of as scathing insults the way drivers do in Michigan. In between the honking, the screeching of hundreds of brakes, and the surge and refrain of the limo's engine between lights, I heard many human voices yelling across the street in greeting, farewell, humility, anger, lust, and curiosity. The bottles of liquor remained untouched as our eyes remained fixed on the scenes of Chicago while we made our way to the Water Tower Plaza.

The chauffeur let us out and escorted us into the mall and up the escalator and into a glass elevator and up and out and into the tuxedo store without saying a word. There I met Dreisbach for the second time. He wore black jeans and cowboy boots and a white T-shirt with the cuffs tapered to the size of his biceps. Beside him stood his fiancée, looking bright in a white cocktail dress and high heels that showed off calves that looked so perfect they might have been produced by a lathe. He said "Hey, Mitch" and shook my hand and shook Neil and Charlie's hands and reminded Teresa of their names, and we introduced Ilo, Mandy, and Keely. Then we got to work trying on the style of tuxedos he had chosen. The boy working the store hurried around gathering our uniforms and "yes sirring" Dreisbach while several other customers waited. After we were finished in the dressing rooms, he looked at us very carefully, pulled a little and tugged a little at our garments, suggested some alterations, and Dreisbach tipped him and told him to do what he needed to do and send them along to Teresa's house when he was finished. We headed out the way we had come. Ted was ebullient about the wedding and the honeymoon and how he was glad that we came so he didn't have to elope, which his family would see as a victory. He didn't mention anything about why his family was against this wedding. (Maybe Neil was right.) He never mentioned the campaign either, and I didn't want to raise that subject because I was afraid to ask about something we might have covered thoroughly at Brad's wedding.

Once on the street, we found our limo, and Ted let us all enjoy it while he and Teresa hopped onto his motorcycle, which looked like an amalgamation of several old Japanese motorcycles thrown together by a penniless mechanic and which was parked illegally by the front entrance of the plaza. They led the way to the church for rehearsal.

The priest was a drill sergeant. We arrived at the church five minutes early, but he met us at the front door looking at us as though we had all taken turns peeing in the holy water. Apparently he was angry because we didn't seem to understand that we only had forty-five minutes to rehearse before the next party would arrive to go through the motions. Also, Teresa's bridesmaids, parents and grandparents had been waiting in the lobby for all of fifteen minutes. The three bridesmaids, to whom we would have been introduced had the clergyman not been so pushy, seemed very nonchalant and thoughtful. One wore a pant suit as though she had just come from work, and the other two wore clothes that I had only seen in dance clubs: short flashy skirts, heels with straps around the ankles and silk blouses tight enough to fit the average toddler. Regardless, all three of them looked very nice to me, but open-mindedness would not be the theme of the weekend.

The minister brushed past all of us and stood in the doorway of the cathedral to tell Teresa's family and our friends that they could sit down. He paused for a moment to look at Ted as if wondering how to ask him where his family was. He walked us to our places in front. I thought it would be more of the same type of rehearsal to which we had been conditioned that summer, but the minister condescendingly ordered all of us around for about five minutes, as if he were blocking kindergartners for a nativity play. He then went over the lines with Ted and Teresa, told us we were done and returned to his office without saying a word to anyone.

As we walked out of the cathedral and into the verve of the city again, I wondered how to approach Ilo. I wasn't sure if I even needed to because she seemed to be perfectly content palling around with Keely and Mandy. While she walked to the limo ahead of me, I thought that I wanted to hold her hand; I wanted to touch her shoulders, and I wanted to have her attention, but I couldn't think of anything to say to her that wasn't serious or weird. She looked over her shoulder and gave me a smile. I gave her a huge toothy smile and a little wave, but I still didn't know exactly why she was with us. In fact,

I still wasn't sure exactly why I was there, even though the intimidating minister sort of forced the groomsmen to become comrades with Dreisbach. It didn't feel right to be a friend to someone I hadn't known.

The rehearsal dinner had a completely different vibe than Brad's and Brice's. Everyone was cordial to each other, and we had a nice champagne toast, but Teresa's family seemed very subdued. I immediately jumped to the conclusion that they had picked us out as, not only imposters, but charlatans as well. Regardless, Ted an Teresa were in good spirits and tried their best to make the situation less awkward by introducing everyone. Teresa told little stories about all of her family members and bridesmaids, and Ted tried his best to explain where we came from. All of us sat around a very long rectangular table in the banquet room of a restaurant known for its buffet. It turned out that the establishment was a favorite of Teresa's grandmother. We ate a little of everything as if we didn't know from where our last meal would come. Teresa's father laughed at how Charlie gobbled his food without ever picking up his head, but he stopped laughing when he saw that I had noticed. I couldn't help feeling that he could see right through me and felt that our presence was a blight on the wedding. However, I had no business trying to read his mind, because I realize now that Dreisbach's family had insulted Teresa's father and her whole family.

Ted decided that he wanted to go somewhere in the limo with Teresa and her folks, so he caught a cab for us and sent us to a place called the Gin Mill. He thought we might like it because its walls were covered by Michigan State and Detroit Red Wings memorabilia. However, the ride there was the best part, because the city thrived on Friday night. People were everywhere as they had been earlier in the afternoon, but now they were in no hurry, and the whole world seemed at peace as I watched all of these wanderers of the night transcending the constraints of time.

Young people filled the Gin Mill, so much so that we had to squeeze our way up to the bar to order some drinks. I bought the first round, and Charlie waited with me as the bartender gathered our provisions. He carried a wine cooler, a White Russian and an Irish coffee, and I carried a Guinness, a Bushmills and a White Zinfandel to our friends who had found a niche in which to stand near the wall in the back room. A Cubs game played on a screen attached to the far wall of this room, but no one was watching. Next to us, a boy in a black turtleneck sweater and overalls stood at the head of his table telling a story that had his companions rolling, and many people around us were giggling at his antics. There was a couple behind us fortunate enough to have a table, and they were in the throes of passion, which made me believe that it wouldn't be long until they left us with a perfectly good place to sit.

The stereo played a song by Chumbawumba. It was supposed to be a tribute to the British working class, but one can never make a point with a pop song, and the misplaced middle-class Michiganders who populated the bar took the song as their own. A hundred drinkers jumped up and down to the tenacious lyrics.

At around three o' clock things began to wrap up at the bar, so we walked out onto the sidewalk and became engulfed by people who also wanted to go home. Getting a cab at that hour was next to impossible. We walked south for four blocks and finally found a vacant cab. Neil sat in the front seat, and Charlie, Ilo and I sat in the back seat with Mandy and Keely on our laps. I remember that the driver played Tejano music very loudly, and the windows were down. The breeze made my head feel numb.

I checked us into The Palmer House Hilton, which turned out to be the most expensive hotel in which I had ever stayed. Once inside the grandiose and ornate Great Hall that served as a lobby, I told the receptionist that we had reservations for the Dreisbach party. He smiled a little at his computer screen. The girl beside him disappeared into a room behind the counter, appearing a moment later with another girl, both of whom took long looks at us, especially the girls, as if they were sizing them up. They looked at each other, rolled their eyes and returned to the back room. Our clerk looked at me with a courteous smile and handed me two card keys. He mentioned that our luggage had been delivered to our rooms.

We walked slowly to the elevators through the Great Hall, almost wandering apart from each other to take in its magnificence. Our rooms were on the sixth floor. I was so tired that I must have seemed to lumber down the hall after everyone. Neil actually suggested that Mandy sleep with Ilo and Keely in the room across from ours. I unlocked our door. The rigid smell of cool met us as we entered the air-conditioned room, and Charlie turned on the light to reveal a cozy room, containing two double beds, a desk and a window that faced the street. I slumped into the bed near the window, kicked off my shoes, and lay back into a crisp cool pillow. Charlie got into the wet bar for a tiny bottle of some kind of wine and persuaded me to take a bottle of Rhine, which was spilled on the carpet because I passed out with it maybe two minutes later.

An insistent knock at the door woke us at around 9:00 a.m.. I opened my eyes and closed them again, taking a deep breath between my teeth to relieve the pain in my head, as the day was cloudless and brilliant and we did not close the drapes before sleep. I rolled away from the windows and gathered the courage to look at the door, which slowly opened. I wasn't cogent enough to wonder who it was, and I hadn't seen Charlie or Neil yet, so I just watched. Ted poked his head in the door, as if being careful to avoid seeing something that he would later regret, and said, "Good morning, fellas! I brought your tuxes." Behind me I heard the escaping air of a bottle being opened and the clank of a bottle cap falling onto the desk near the window letting in all the headache sunshine. It turned out to be Charlie having his third of the morning while playing solitaire.

Neil mumbled, "Who is it?" obviously not in the realm of reality yet.

"Don't seem so enthused," Ted said entering the room with his bodyguard behind him toting three suits. "It's my big day. Get up; get up!"

Charlie grabbed five beers out of the bar and coaxed Neil and me awake with two of them. Out of his breast pocket, Ted pulled a flask full of the most refreshing and silky brandy that I have ever had the pleasure to swill. We had a toast with the beers, and Ted gave us a last-minute apology about his family and a warning about the media:

"They're not allowed anywhere near the chapel, and they sure as hell aren't allowed in the CAC. What I'm worried about is some sneaky asshole, so be on your best behavior tonight, okay?"

We nodded our heads fervently.

Chapter 11

The priest was magnificent that afternoon. Not that a religious man should be connected to popular culture, but his transformation from a pedantic bastard to Bob Hope was downright perplexing. He even had a spring in his step that wasn't there the day before as he took the pulpit. After the bridesmaids and bride had come down the aisle, he made a joke about the lack of guests on the groom's side of the aisle: "I guess the ushers must be southpaws," he said as the congregation waited for him to begin the service. His homily told of a man named Ted who secretly fell in love with a girl named Teresa at the church's soup kitchen. My memory cannot do his story justice here, but basically, after a few weeks of timid questions and awkward gestures of interest, the two fell in love over a vat of tapioca pudding. Everyone laughed, and Charlie frequently looked at me with raised eyebrows and a red smirk as we stood in place in our black tuxedos with royal blue vests and ties that matched the bridesmaids' dresses.

One of Teresa's relatives or friends interrupted the service with a rendition of U2's "One," which she sang with so much vibrato that I yearned for an MP3 player. I thought we would get on with the ceremony after that, but three more of Teresa's friends took the mic to sing an off-key version of Roberta

Flack's "Night and Day," which might have made the most faithful Christian wonder what hell was like that time of year.

Finally, we finished the service, Teresa and Ted kissed, and we exited to form a receiving line in the sunlight near the street outside the church. We shook hands with all of the guests, and Charlie gave hugs to several of the ladies, much to their dismay. When the line subsided, we hailed a cab for Ilo, Mandy and Keely, making sure to tell the driver to take them to the Chicago Athletic Club. Then we sat on a bench under a large oak tree and waited for our next orders. Charlie went down the block to a bar to fetch some take-out, and we sipped on some cold ones until the photographer's assistant told us to come into the church for some shots.

At the CAC a bellhop met us at the revolving door and walked us through the lobby. On the floor were antiseptic and pure tiles, and the ceilings held polished oak panels preserved from the 1920s. A chandelier above our heads shed light upon all of the intricacies that made the building a special place. As we walked the stairs to the ballroom, I noticed the stairway was lined with an original and beautifully wrought banister, and the ceiling was covered in soundproof copper. The ballroom displayed more wooden paneling, rails, and moldings, along with red carpet, paintings and more chandeliers. The bellhop led us past the dinner room, where servers set the tables, and the clanking of glassware and silver accompanied us to the lounge where we ate strawberries and chocolate and ordered champagne from the open bar.

The champagne seemed to float into my system, so I went to the bar to get something with more density. I ordered a Bushmills straight, two Tom Collins and three margaritas. I wished I could get a drink carrier like they have at fast-food restaurants, but Neil saw my predicament out the corner of his conversation and came up to give me a hand. We walked past Charlie and the girls and staked a claim on the couches that surrounded a television playing a Cubs game. They followed and stayed there and chatted until we noticed that the crowd in the lounge began to break up and enter the dinner room.

There wasn't a grandiose introduction of the groomsmen as there was at our prior two weddings. Ted just came out and looked at us as if he wondered what the hell we were waiting for. People were ready to eat dinner, and they were waiting for the other half of the wedding party.

The girls were content to separate from us for a while as we sat at an elevated table on the back wall of the room. Ted seated them at a table with his bodyguard and three of Teresa's friends. I wanted to be next to Ilo. I didn't want to be a groomsman, sitting at a table covered with white paper. I wanted to be a suit out there in the dark sitting next to her. I just couldn't place myself there when she always looked so happy with Mandy and Keely and rarely cracked a smile when I was around.

I don't remember exactly what we ate. I only remember being bitter that Ted's bodyguard held a conversation with Ilo the whole time, whereas we couldn't seem to find a moment to talk to each other at all. I guess I got drunk at that table, mostly because of this and partially because the servers were so eager to keep my palate lubricated for my second speech of the summer.

The mood of the room seemed to match my attitude, as almost one hundred people ate their dinners in near silence. The DJ had programmed Frank Sinatra's box set into his machine long before we sat down, and no one had seen him since. Once in a while I could hear Mandy's obnoxious voice blurt out something like, "God, this thong fit so much better in the dressing room." And no one clanked on their glasses as usual until Charlie started to get bored and played a Calypso beat on his empty water and wine decanters. Apparently, this was cue enough for Ted, as he kissed Teresa briefly during one of Charlie's riffs. This got a cheer and some clapping, and some of the younger guests got out of their chairs and danced to Charlie's fifteen-minute funk, but it was a sudden barrage of enthusiasm that was quickly subdued by something that I couldn't understand.

In the wake of the momentary surfacing of our collective anxiety, one of the bridesmaids handed me the microphone for the speech. I felt as though someone had asked me to dance when I didn't want to dance, and I sat trying to contrive an excuse. I knew that Neil had agonized over his speech for Brice and had even gone to Charlie for advice. This was my second time as best man, and again I forgot my obligation to compose a speech. I decided to make it a short toast to the bride and groom, but when I stood up my eyes found Ilo's, I thought of something my dad told me one time when I was very young, only old enough to remember until it was time for it to make sense: "It's okay if you tell your mom and I what makes ya scared, but when ya start actin' like a wuss around the neighbors, that's how they'll always know ya."

Some people say that the trick to public speaking is to imagine the audience in their underwear. I just focused on Ilo, and though my knees were shaking and my right hand couldn't keep the mic still, I said all I could to two people I didn't know:

"I've been looking now for over three years, and I'm tired of watching people pass by. I see people coming and going through my life, and I wish I could just catch hold of one of their sleeves and have them take me to where they really are. Well, this morning, I went for a walk to the lakeshore. [I had to stretch truth.] I watched all of the sailboats coming and going; some seemed to sail toward the sun, some returned to their moorings. I wanted to be out there with them, just out of boredom with my own limitations. And I watched hundreds of people pass each other by on the walkway there because that's what we do; humans seem to spend a lot of time passing each other.

"But if the only thing I do in life is catch onto one person's sleeve, to find out who she really is, and if she gives me a lifetime to show me the answer (which is what it takes) then knowing where everyone else is coming from and going to is less of a mystery, because I'll have a destination of my own. Teresa and Ted didn't pass each other by. That takes courage and a lot of faith. Here's to their destiny."

The DJ was still MIA. Charlie guessed that he was in the natatorium enjoying some medicinal marijuana, but Teresa and Ted took the dance floor anyway and shared a song, and when the disc changer scrambled to another song on the box set, the groomsmen and the bridesmaids joined them on the floor. By the end of that song, someone had found the DJ, and he cued the cake cutting and played more Frank Sinatra while a few guests and the photographer took pictures of them. We thought the party would get started after this, but Teresa's parents left after dessert, and at least half of the party followed soon after. We sat with Ilo, Mandy and Keely and watched the reception fizzle. By 8:00, the only people remaining were a group of about ten friends of Teresa, the bridesmaids, Ted, his bodyguard, and the six of us. We pulled three tables together, and though the busboys cleaned up around us, we were having a good time. We ordered free drinks, danced a little (I did get to dance with Ilo quite a few times), and took pictures with the disposable cameras that sat on the tables. We finished those rolls and took more pictures with other disposable cameras that had been placed on adjacent tables. By 9:00 I took to scotch, and by 10:00, while Ilo was into her third dance with Ted's bodyguard, I decided to take a self-guided tour of the building, feeling that Ilo teased me one too many times. Basically, this consisted of sneaking down a back stairway, getting lost in several corridors, trying every door I saw (all locked), and auspiciously finding the lobby we had entered after the wedding. There was no one here but a receptionist and a young man in black slacks and a grey trench coat outside of the revolving door. I could see him facing me through the window, and the red bulb on the end of his cigarette glowed as he inhaled.

I remembered there was a bathroom there, and I wondered if that wasn't why I had walked all over the building in the first place. I nestled up to a stall and began relieving myself when the man in the trench coat came in and walked to a stall three down from me, to my left. He turned to me and nodded. He finished before me and stepped to the sink, took off his coat, rolled up his sleeves and pushed down the soap dispenser about five times. Then he turned on both hot and cold water and began to wash. He looked at me, and I turned back to the wall, as though I had not been studying him.

"So you're the best man, huh?"

"Yes, sir," I said to the wall.

"How much did he pay you to put on this act?"

"Excuse me?" I looked over my shoulder.

"I know you don't know Ted any better than I do."

I shrugged my shoulders.

"Look, I know you're Mitchell Moon, and I know you've only met Ted once before tonight. I'll save you all some embarrassment if you just give me a few words for the article I'm writing."

I shook my head.

"I'm with the *Chicago Daily*."

"No you're not," I called his bluff.

He finished washing, and I finished pissing. He turned around and leaned on the vanity while I washed my hands, lit a cigarette and said, "You know why there was a wedding today, Mitchell?"

"Course, two people who love each other usually…"

"I didn't think you did. This thing was thrown together seven months ago, just after Ted entered the Senate race for his E-party."

"I don't see what that has to do with anything."

"You don't know anything. That's what I want to tell you before you go back up there carrying on like an asshole."

"I really don't feel comfortable talkin' to you behind someone's back in a toilet, man. If you wanna talk to me, call me tomorrow if ya know so damn well." I threw my paper towels in the trash, and he cut off my line to the door.

"Let me put it to you this way. Your boy up there got all of his money to finance this campaign from investments in an Internet porn operation. I discovered that two weeks after he turned in his petition and entered the race and three days before he proposed to that girl up there."

"So? That's not illegal."

"So! You just stood up in front of a church as witness to a wedding that is totally bogus, and then you signed the papers making the lie legal."

"See, now you're changin' the subject." I looked down into his face. "Do you have a problem with the way he raised his money, or do you have a problem with a twenty-six-year-old knocking off that third-term what's-his-name who probably kisses your special-interest ass?"

His face turned red, and he opened his mouth to speak. I brushed past him and made toward the door.

He grabbed my sleeve, pointed his finger in my face, and said, "You don't know...."

I shrugged hard. I believe I inadvertently hit him with an elbow, and I screamed, "Get the fuck off my balls," as I walked to the door. I didn't know that I knocked him down until the next day, and I think I might have forgotten about the incident altogether for several hours.

Upon taking my last step up the back stairs to the ballroom, I heard our little party still carrying on. I saw Charlie do a little dance to illustrate some point to Teresa's girls, and they all laughed. I paused for a moment at the doorway. It seemed that the chandelier over their table shined on only them, and my memory took a photograph of that scene with four of them, Ilo, Mandy, Keely, and Neil sitting with eyes brightened in joy and Charlie's actions suspended. I could see the golden highlights in Ilo's hair shimmer, and the light bounced off from her burgundy nail polish at the end of her slender fingers. At that moment I began to warm up to the idea that this was the conclusion to our days together. In my mind I always pictured Charlie, Neil, and me together, but at that moment I began to prepare for the day when we would stand alone.

Ilo and I danced for a long time after I came back, until around eleven when the DJ began to pack up. We helped him take his equipment down to his van, saw Ted and Teresa off and hailed a cab for ourselves. Ilo claimed that the cab was too full after the four other had piled in, so we waited for another. We walked for a while, and she grabbed my hand, and we walked for a block like that until I decided to catch a cab for us. The windows were down, and while we were driven away, she said that she was cold. I leaned over her to shut one of them, but she grabbed my arm and said no and put her arms around me. I wrapped her in mine, and we held each other through the subtle luminescence of city streets.

I asked her to come to my room, as we paused in the hall between her door and mine, but she said that she wanted me alone and that I could wait until later.

"Tomorrow!" slipped out of my mouth.

PIZZA PIE AND POLITICS
HOW MITCHELL MOON LOST HIS CHILDHOOD

"No. Tomorrow's in five minutes, but maybe the day after that."

She gave me a kiss, and I told her she was beautiful, and she said, "You're beautiful too," and we unlocked our doors. Once inside the room, I didn't know what to do. I paced for a few minutes, looked out the window. She was just across the hall. I could knock on the door and beg. I went to the bathroom and splashed water on my face and lay on the bed, feeling as if we were foolishly putting off something that should happen when it was meant to happen. I lay on my side looking into a clear crisp sky, determined to go knock on that door. I just had to take a moment to think of what I would say to get inside. I fell into a deep drunken slumber.

I awoke to a female television reporter's voice funneled with excessive volume through a television speaker. Charlie frantically poked at me to wake up. I rolled away from the window and put my pillow over my head. Charlie wrenched it away from me. The reporter's voice stopped; then I heard my own voice, as if played on a small cassette recorder. This was striking, as I have never loved the sound of my voice played back to me. Regardless, the sound was unmistakable. At first, I thought it was a hoax that Charlie rigged to get me out of bed and down to brunch with the girls. But upon lying there for a few seconds, I realized that it was definitely my voice on a Chicago cable news broadcast.

"Get the [bleep] off my balls!" I droned.

I virtually leaped to my feet and scrambled to the television as if I could stop what I was seeing, which was a snapshot of Ted and me in our tuxedos in front of the CAC; a fade into the silhouette of my back; me turning toward some sort of camera that the "reporter" in the bathroom had evidently hidden; the man grabbing my sleeve; me swinging what looked like, from that perspective, a very clear and intentional elbow to his head, the man falling to the floor, and me like a criminal, walking past the camera.

"What the fuck was that?" Neil asked, laughing with uncertainty.

"Get the fuck off my balls?" Charlie asked, questioning my choice in confrontational diction.

They both laughed out loud until I hit both of them on their biceps as hard as I could so that they would quiet long enough for me to hear the reporter's commentary:

"The assailant, whose name has not been released, is a close friend of Ted Dreisbach, which does not help his already-controversial run for Senate. This assault occurred during Dreisbach's wedding reception."

The picture moved from the reporter to another distorted video of Ted and Charlie doing shots at the bar and Teresa's guests dancing to Charlie's drum solo. Then she segued into a story to accompany a mug shot of a young African-American holdup suspect.

"We hafta get outta here," I said throwing everything I could see into my overnight bag. "Ted's gonna have us killed."

I expected Neil to tell me that I was being a sissy, but he picked up the phone and ordered two cabs, not long after I had finished this sentence. Five minutes after we had seen the broadcast, we sat in the girls' room, completely prepared to leave, feigning nonchalance together on one of the beds. Mandy and Keely looked at us sleepily from beneath the covers.

"You guys seem like you're in a hurry today," Ilo, the first out of the bathroom, said as she began to carefully fold her clothes and meticulously pack her suitcase.

"It's just that Charlie forgot he has to open the shop today," Neil lied. "Sorry."

Around that time we heard pounding on our door, and I looked out the peephole to see Ted and his bodyguard across the hall. When I turned I must have forgotten to hide my fright because Ilo wanted me to explain immediately. I told her that I would tell everyone everything when we were safely on the train.

"I'm not getting on the train with any of you if you can't tell me the truth now."

I looked at the hem of my T-shirt in response.

"I'm calling my step-dad."

"Okay, I knocked down a journalist in the bathroom last night. Someone caught it on tape, and a cable station played it back this morning."

"You beat someone up last night? You can't go to the bathroom without fighting someone."

"It was an accident, Ilo. He made all these insinuations about Ted, and when I shouted him down he grabbed me, and I shook him off. My elbow hit him, and it just looked bad on tape."

The pounding on the door across the hall began again, and shards of the shady picture that the man in the bathroom had drawn of Ted swirled in my mind as if they were confetti in a vacuum. An uncertain feeling of doom began to develop.

"Your elbow hit him? It wasn't attached to you in any way at the time? It just detached itself and pounced at him? Is that what I'm supposed to believe? Neil lies and you condescend."

PIZZA PIE AND POLITICS
HOW MITCHELL MOON LOST HIS CHILDHOOD

She was going to make a good lawyer someday.

"Now wait a minute, Ilo," Neil yelled loud enough for our benefactors outside to hear. "You don't know the whole story."

"If you weren't there, then neither do you."

"That's why I'm not drawing any damn conclusions."

"Well, maybe you should. Here's one for ya: You guys are nothing but weak-willed infants whenever you have a moment to yourselves. I'm leaving."

She finished packing and jerked the door open. From my seat on the edge of the bed, I could see Ted's bodyguard shrug and turn in surprise.

"What do you two want?" she said, walking away.

Ted looked at her and then inside. "I just came by to get the tuxes," he said to Neil, who was standing in the middle of the room.

Charlie got into his duffle bag, pulled out five or six wads of clothing, and handed them to Ted at the door. He made a motion to his bodyguard, who took them.

Ted looked at me in a concerned manner. "She's not mad about last night?"

"Did you see the news?" I asked.

"Yeah, I told you to be on your best behavior."

Charlie and Neil looked at the door nervously.

"But that guy had it comin'. You don't grab someone in the john the way he grabbed you. He must be an asshole. I'm sorry she took it the wrong way," Ted said.

Charlie and Neil looked at him with wide eyes.

"I'm gonna need your honesty on something that just came up, so keep those phone lines open okay, bud?" he said. "I'll call ya soon."

"Sure, sure. Anytime," I said.

"I'll see you guys. Thanks a bunch."

On the way to the station and on the train ride home, Neil tried to explain Ilo's absence as overreaction; I tried to explain Ilo's absence as an effect of my panic, and Charlie played blues on his guitar, all in vain. Besides that no one spoke a word on the train home, and I quietly absorbed all of the tension between the five of us until I felt as though my body had turned to stone and nothing would ever be the same again.

Chapter 12

On Monday morning, after our weekend in Chicago, I expected (in guilt) to explain everything again. But Neil merely said hey at me with his mouth full, while he stood at the kitchen sink devouring a plum. I grabbed a Gatorade from the fridge, and Charlie challenged me to a game of John Madden. All he said was "Get the fuck off my balls," as he placed the CD into the Playstation. Besides that nothing was mentioned about my television appearance for quite a while.

Consequently, days went by without any word from Ilo. Neil convinced me quickly that no one really wanted her around anyway; she didn't understand us. "If she doesn't get ya, she'll try ta change ya. She wants a fantasy, dude. That's the only reason she came to Chi town in the first place." I thought that I had told him something very similar about Mandy before, but it sounded so good at the time that I believed it.

About five days later, after I had become comfortable with myself again, Charlie and I came home from work to find Neil and Mandy lying on the beanbag in the middle of the living room. They looked at me with smirks on their faces and turned back to a recording of the program they were watching—a satirical news program on the Comedy Channel. When Neil was sure that I had sat down he lifted the remote, rewound and played back a nightmare. I heard the anchor say, "Well here it is; I'm glad it's not me," a phrase that always concluded the show, and I saw myself and heard my voice scream the phrase that would become a mantra.

Charlie folded himself laughing, and Neil looked at me as if to say, "What are you gonna do about that?" I'm sure my face turned red, as I sat on the couch trying to think of a way to express my anger. Charlie threw his head back and howled, "Yes!" and Neil said, "Dreisbach's a genius. Here, let me show you the credits." He paused on a bundle of quick-moving lines at the end of the production.

"That's bullshit!" I finally emitted upon seeing that he was given credit for serving up the tape. "He had no right. He's gonna finish me before I even get started. That motherfucker. I'm gonna…"

I bounded to my room and retrieved his card from above my desk, picked up the cordless phone in the hallway and had it stripped from me by Neil. I really thought he was being cruel, and I took a swing at him. Forgetting to tuck my thumb into my loose fist, I jammed it against his forehead in a wild swing. I gashed his skin with a neglected fingernail and jumped around the apartment in agony.

"Give me the phone, damn you," I managed.

"No, listen, Mitch," Neil said with a middle finger covering his laceration. "Doncha see? He bought the tape." He looked at me as though enough were said. "He bought the tape from whoever had it, and he turned the tables. It's a comedy now."

I pretended to think about this for a minute, waiting for him to relax enough for me to snatch the phone. As soon as I felt the weight of it in my hands, I slammed it back into the receiver.

For the next three days, I went through the motions of a young man who has just realized that, no matter what anyone has told him, other people control his fate. On Monday morning, I looked upon the landscapers mowing the grounds of our apartment complex with envy. They had a purpose and a renewable source of income, and I regretted ever going to college to learn about something as obsolete as political science. I might as well have studied Latin. At work I let the phone ring six or seven times before answering to take another order from someone who would tell me exactly what I was going to do for the next thirty minutes. On Tuesday night I went on a tirade about the local news coverage. "It's a formula for stupidity," I said. "They're just putting images with the headlines I read while I was waiting for the cashier at the Shell station this morning." On Wednesday morning I got into an argument with Drew about the cleaning habits of the closer the night before, and I ended up calling this employee out of his fourth-hour class at high school to come and clean up his mess before I had him fired. By the time 3:30 came around, I was drunk and had smoked ten of fifteen cigarettes from a pack someone had left in a cupboard.

Ilo called.

"Hey, Mitch!" she said.

"Hey."

"I just wanted you to know that you're a jerk for letting me go home alone that day. And you haven't called me, you jerk."

"Well, I'm glad you didn't let me go all day without letting me know that. I would've felt like such a fool."

"You know, you're not perfect. If you didn't act like you're so perfect, you'd be perfect."

"Thank you."

"It's not a compliment."

For some reason, through the bulk of my afternoon's buzz, I realized that this was an important phone call. Inherently, I knew that if I let the line fall dead so was any control I had over my own silly life.

So in the impending seconds when the conversation fell silent, and when Ilo had just begun to inhale the air that would become the hopeless breath expelled to seal my fate, I became articulate. I knew it was time to try myself on someone who hadn't known me since I was five.

"I never wanted you to be my drinking buddy," I said.

"Mission accomplished."

"You make me remember the things I hoped for when I was eighteen, when I still believed that everything was possible. After I met you at Leopold's, I stayed awake some nights imagining that the life I wanted would be a life with someone like you."

"Oh, now you want to marry me?"

"I can't imagine holding you to any one thing: not me, not marriage, not your boyfriend in Ann Arbor, not any sort of decision on any given day."

"You don't know me very well," she said.

"No. But I feel proud whenever you're near me."

"You're full of it," she retorted.

There was silence, but I didn't feel that she was going to hang up the phone this time. Neil came into the shop to relieve me and grabbed the remote from beside me to flip through the channels in order to reestablish control in his second home.

"Except for Saturday night in the hotel, you can really be cold sometimes," she said. "I thought you were coming out of your shell, and I stayed awake thinking that you would turn out to be someone that I could trust. Before I found out what happened in the bathroom, I thought we might be more than friends, but after Sunday morning and after I heard about your little show, I realized how drunk you were. We were having a good time, but when I heard what you did, it all seemed like a lie. I can't tell who you really are, because every time we seem to be making progress, it turns out you were fucked up at the time."

I didn't know what to say. I looked at the floor and hoped that Neil wouldn't notice that I was two feet tall.

"Mitch, are you there? Aren't you even going to say anything? Why did you hit that man and say those things?"

"That's the thing." I came alive. "It doesn't feel like anything I did. It freaks me out because it's like something that someone else did or something that I did in a dream, and the thing that upsets me most is that you saw it and that you associate it with me right now. I don't wanna have anything to do with it. I don't care if anyone in the world thinks I'm a lunatic. I mean, I think it's pretty much a joke now, and I'm sorry if I scared you Sunday morning. But if I can change anyone's mind I wanna change yours.

"That's not the way I handle myself. I was out of my element the whole weekend—I can't be pampered like that. I can't stand it. And that guy in the bathroom knew something about all of us, I'm sure of it, and he was just waiting for one of us to make a mistake. I really believe he had his sights on one of us three groomsmen the whole day, and I'm the one he finally got.

"I know that you feel confused about me, but I feel confused about you too. And I'll be honest, I feel tense when you're around, only because I don't want to make any big mistakes. Now that I made one, maybe I won't be so afraid."

"Afraid of what?" she asked.

"Afraid to be myself."

There was an unimpressed sigh and a pause.

"I don't understand you, Mitch," she finally said.

"I feel sick about lettin' you go on Sunday morning. I'm sorry."

She didn't answer for a long time. (I guessed that if you've done something to be truly sorry for, you can't expect anyone to forgive you right away.) Still, the silence made me want to beg for acceptance or death.

"If you just say something, anything, I won't ever bother you again, if you don't want me too," I said.

"I want you to," she whispered.

Chapter 13

The next morning Charlie woke me up with the telephone in his hand. I thought that it was Ilo, so I took it immediately. However, the voice that answered my enthusiastic hello turned out to be a reporter from the *Chicago News*, a supporter of Dreisbach, he said. He sounded young and very empathetic, clearing the air with his version of the confrontation, claiming to have understood my reaction to the "reporter's" baiting. It was a telephone interview, he said, to go along with his story about Dreisbach.

"I don't want anything to do with Dreisbach," I said. "I don't even know who he is."

"I know you were one of the groomsmen at his wedding, and he's the one who gave me your number," the reporter, Rick, said. "You have to panic, man. I'm really trying to help Driesbach. I think he's gonna change everyone's views on young people in politics. He's gonna be a celebrity, and I wanna be the first to acknowledge it. I also want him to win this race. I'm working on a book and..."

I hung up.

I thought that was all I had to do: hang up. I could keep outside problems away by hanging up, and the three of us—Charlie, Mitch, and I—drove to the park to play a game of field hockey. After that Charlie and I hurried to spell Kenny from his lunch duties at Drew's. I wanted to call Ilo and tell her about the game, but we got busy and made almost thirty pizzas and deliveries from three-thirty to five o' clock. A few kids came in to help us around the dinner hour, and I had a few moments to call Ilo, but the game seemed to be a far-off victory then, only in my head instead of something to be really proud of, so I just did my work and imagined that she was sleeping anyway.

That night, at around 10:30, a young man wearing a white long-sleeved shirt, brown slacks and a brown tie, walked into Drew's. Neil stepped to the counter to serve him, and I peeked through the doorway to get a look at this stranger; it was too late for well-dressed salesmen to hit us up for their new taste in Buffalo wings and because his cologne invaded the pizza-shop smells of garlic and baking bread. Neil looked at me, grinned sardonically, and said that the young man would like to speak to me. Before I could say hello, wiping my hands on the dirty apron I had tied around my waist, he said, "*Now* I know why you wouldn't talk to me this morning. You weren't shitting me; you really don't know who Dreisbach is. I apologize, man; I didn't mean to seem pushy."

"Look, I don't wanna be a part of this. That thing at the CAC was just a mistake, and I would like to put it behind me. Haven't you ever made a mistake?"

"The biggest mistakes I have ever made are the times I believed what I saw on the news. Did I tell you who the jackass is who is going to have his reputation destroyed for crashing a wedding?"

I shook my head.

"He's a writer for the *Chicago News*. Those idiots made a front-page story out of Dreisbach's wedding." He paused, looking for some sort of reaction. "That kind of bad press always backfires on them, don't you see? They hate the idea of a kid Senator from an upper-class background, and they're too egotistical to keep their mouths shut and let things run their natural course. Instead, they did him a huge favor. He's front-page news now. He was on TV all over Chicago. You did Dreisbach a favor."

I shrugged.

"Well, it doesn't matter now, just as long as you know that he's the one who made the mistake, not you, and I'm going to take advantage of it whether or not you talk to me. But I'll tell you what; I think it would be better for both of us if you explain what really led to what I saw on television."

I couldn't believe this stranger had such tenacity, but I told him that I was busy and that he could wait until we closed. Neil made him a sandwich and brought him a beer, and he went to his car, nibbled on the grinder, sipped on the twenty-two-ounce bottle of Bud Ice, wrote some notes, made a few phone calls and waited until we finished our last few orders and turned off the outside lights.

He took that as a cue. Charlie, Neil and I stood in front of the oven, armed with cynical stares when he entered.

"Dreisbach's in the mafia isn't he," I blurted.

Rick laughed and told me that Dreisbach was not in the mafia. Our demeanor didn't change, so he started again.

"Okay, let's start from the beginning," he said in the tone of one of my old professors. "Ted Dreisbach is twenty-six years old. He is a resident of Chicago. His father comes from a long line of shipping magnates. He's been in some kind of office since he was eighteen. He started out as a city councilman, only because his high-school government teacher wouldn't give an A to anyone who did not run for public office. He wanted to go to school at Northwestern, and he wanted the A because he wanted the scholarship. (His father refused to pay for his college tuition.) He held that seat for two terms, while he went to school and grad school on a full academic scholarship, and now he wants to give up that seat for a seat in the U.S. Senate. While he was in college, he made a decent amount of money investing in the Internet during the boom. He made most of it on his friend Kevin Carlisle's old business. The controversy is that Carlisle used to make his money by producing porn sites. Now this isn't something that his opponents want to mention much because Carlisle will destroy them online, but they are trying to dig up anything else suspicious about him. He played right into their hands with that wedding, considering the fact that his family basically disowned him for marrying that girl, and the inevitability of an open bar at the reception. Now, Mitch, I know you want to put this whole thing to bed, but the world needs to know that those circumstances at the CAC were contrived by someone who doesn't like Ted."

"Let me see some fuckin' credentials, ya hack," Neil said, sticking out his right hand and wiggling his fingers in Rick's direction.

I expected a business card, but he handed me his driver's license, went to his car, and brought back a Sunday issue of the *Chicago News*. He showed us the front page, folded it to section D, pointed to the front page, left column, and showed us his name, Rick Degiglia, and picture at the top of the article. Neil took it from his and then grabbed the ID from my hand. He cross referenced the pictures and names, rubbed the paper between his thumb and forefinger, looked at the ink stains, rolled his tongue around in his mouth for a moment, and nodded approval at me.

We took him back to Drew's office, sat him in Drew's chair, and I told him the whole story, with Neil adding unnecessary support here and there and Charlie stepping back to play air guitar to the music playing softly in his head.

The next morning I bought a *Chicago News* at the Shell station. I turned to section D and read Rick's story, which offered me some vindication. In fact, the article read, "When questioned about the language one of his supporters recently used to defend himself, Dreisbach replied, 'Get off my balls is a mantra really for those of us who are sick and tired of a good-old-boy system which does nothing but recycle hypocrisy, a system that keeps those of us who really care about America on the outside looking in. I'm not going to Washington with the only goal of getting inside and doing whatever it takes to stay there. I'm going to do exactly what it takes to stir things up for four years, and if the voters want me there for another term that's their decision, but they'll be voting for or against me based on who I really am. I'm not holding back.'"

In the two weeks that followed our interesting meeting with Rick, I began to read his columns in the *Chicago News*. Almost every issue contained a story about Dreisbach, his philosophy, or his speaking engagements. He spoke at Loyola, the University of Chicago, Northwestern University, at the U of I in Champagne and Urbana, every coffee shop and microbrewery that would have him, and the Excaliber Nightclub, among many others. He also chatted daily, at a scheduled time, on one of Kevin's websites. I think I was sort of proud of him and of having known him, but in those two weeks enough had happened between Ilo and me that I hadn't thought of politics or that whole stupid incident at the CAC.

Chapter 14

I met Ilo for cocktails the night after Rick's story about the incident at the CAC came out, and I showed her the hackwork I purchased at the gas station. She thought it was a brilliant piece of PR and that I shouldn't worry about everything that everyone thinks, especially about me. "And isn't it convenient," she said, "that you freaked so much over a television clip that no one around here saw, and anyone important to you wouldn't have been swayed by it anyway, and now it's boosted Ted's campaign?"

I felt a lot of relief when she said that, because I think I had convinced myself that I was totally in the wrong that night, that I wouldn't have gotten myself into that position if I weren't a loser. I started to see myself in a different way instead of guessing at the way others saw me and believing that they judged me as harshly as I judged myself.

The next few weeks went by quickly. I worked hard to develop my friendship with Ilo in the month of July because she would go back to Ann Arbor in the middle of August, and inspired by the Dreisbach campaign, I began to look for work in the political realm, which meant that, after optimistically sending twenty-five resumes all over the country, I didn't know where I would be by the time she started school.

Ilo and I went to South Haven a couple of times and spent a few nights watching movies in the Crimson Rouge when Charlie, Neil, and Mandy had gone to Rikki Tikki's. (But she actually met us there after work once.) We talked about our childhoods, embarrassing moments, and little victories, and we tried to turn each other on to our differing musical tastes, constantly sharing CD's with each other. I tried to teach her the rules of field hockey, and she tried to teach me how to rollerblade. Although I bought my skates at a flea market, and they rolled as well as a pair of platform sandals. She still claimed that she saw her boyfriend and that she just wanted to be friends, but we did fall asleep in each other's arms, one extremely humid night, on the plastic patio recliner, which we had moved to the bank of the river.

Towards the very end of July, I picked her up at her house one evening, and we drove to all of the places that were significant in our childhoods. I took her to Kimball Pines where I remembered picnicking with my parents and their friends and playing hide-and-go-seek with their children among the trees until late at night. She showed me the landing on the river right in the middle of town where her real father used to take her fishing. I showed her my parents' first home and the railroad tracks I used to carry my bike across every day when I was five or six to visit my best friend, and she showed me the pizza place where she had her first kiss. She took me to the back of the building and showed me, on the brown wooden siding, in the middle of jackknifed etchings of different vulgarities, a big heart whose center read, "I LOVE ILO VE." She waited for me to look to her for explanation before she mentioned that the owner chased away the boy who gave her her first kiss before he could finish her last name, Velasquez. I laughed until my face was on fire, and she kissed me right there as if I were that boy.

Chapter 15

One afternoon, also in late July, Neil discovered that Dreisbach's platform now had a name, the E Party, and they had a website. On the main page was posted a story about an E Party rally on the street outside of the Excaliber nightclub. They built a stage for local rock bands and speeches by university students and veterans of e-commerce. The climax occurred toward nine o'clock as the sun was going down and before everyone began to enter the club or go off to wherever they were headed for the night. It was then that Dreisbach made his only appearance on stage. According to the story, he picked up a guitar and played a song with a band called Sad Paradise. While they played a video flickered into action on a giant monitor on the back of the stage. Sad Paradise's version of The Clash's "Should I Stay or Should I Go" blasted from the amps. I followed a link to this audio/video production. As the song played, it showed oil-burning buses and cars, huge strip-mining machines like the creatures from *Dune,* a satellite picture of Chicago's shoreline, which resembled diarrhea in contrast with the blue of the lake. After every one came the words "Consider"... "The"... "Alternatives." (Flash-Flash-Flash). Then models of new commuter trains transposed over the Kennedy, Eisenhower, Stevenson, and Dan Ryan Expressways followed.

After that it showed a field of wind turbines near the Mississippi Valley, models of gas stations used for fuel-cell and biodiesel-fueled cars only, and a retail warehouse that had a Discount Pharmaceuticals sign transposed over the actual business name. Then came an image of a strange machine that took trash out of a landfill and made building materials with it, inner-city high school buildings that appeared to be as modern as sports stadiums, popular politicians transposed in factories as if working, and a picture of the mountaintop where ancient Athenians assembled for democracy. The final shot, as the guitar and snare came down on the last seven beats of that song, was of me in the bathroom saying "Get the fuck off my balls," as if to the rhythm. The crowd erupted, as reported by the E Party's anonymous home page webmaster.

This was about the time when things at the Crimson Rouge began to change. One evening after finishing a lunch shift and helping Neil during the dinner hour, I came home, said hi to Mandy, and began to prepare for a date with Ilo. I immediately realized that one half of my closet sat bare. In fact, half of my bedroom was bare—bare bed, bare walls, and a lonely nightstand shivering under a bare window.

I rushed past Mandy, who lounged on the blue beanbag, threw open the sliding-glass door, and unlocked the storage closet outside. That's when I knew; that's when I knew I had been betrayed, because the one thing that Charlie would never leave behind, his Martin guitar, was not in the closet. That's when I knew my best friend was gone.

"Where did Charlie go?" I asked Mandy.

"I don't know. I haven't seen him."

"What do you mean you haven't seen him? You were here all day weren't you?"

"No, I wasn't. I haven't seen him at all. What's wrong?"

I snatched my keys from the stand by the door, and Mandy leaped from her nest and yelled, "Wait; there's a bunch of messages on the answering machine."

I stopped in my tracks. Upon pushing the play button, I heard, "Mitch, this is Ted Dreisbach. I think I have a sort of internship for you. Great opportunity, buddy—national ink. My number is … Please give me a call." Beep!

"Mitch, Dreisbach here. I think I have an opportunity for you." Beep! "Hey, Mitch, Ted again. Please call me. My number's the same as it ever was." Beep. "Mitch, I need to hear from you by the end of the day. Believe me; this is good stuff." Beep.

PIZZA PIE AND POLITICS
HOW MITCHELL MOON LOST HIS CHILDHOOD

I threw my hands up in the air and looked at Mandy. "What a fucking idiot!" I said as I left, hearing Mandy scream, "But what if..." as I slammed the door.

Of course I went to Drew's to see what Neil knew about Charlie. I had a feeling that my ignorance would all be my fault because I had spent too much time with Ilo, while Charlie informed Neil of every detail. Regardless, I didn't understand why my best friend since birth had left me with no warning. No "see ya, Mitch; I'll e-mail you when I get the chance," no "It's been a great time, but now I'm moving on," just me driving to Drew's to find out the inevitable—Neil didn't know where he went either, "but he's probably with Keely." He rolled a mound of pizza dough until it was flat and spun it in the air a few times to stretch it.

"I didn't know they were that serious."

"Well, you've been with Ilo a lot lately. No one blames you for that." He could sense that I felt guilty.

"I didn't see this coming. I never asked him about her at all. I thought they were just messing around."

"Maybe they are."

"It looks like he moved out."

"This summer wasn't gonna last forever, man. He was gonna leave in about four weeks anyway." He took the flattened dough to a prep table and looked me straight in the face. "So am I. You better start making some plans yourself."

It was all winding down, and the end did not fit the ideal. Neil was supposed to break up with Mandy, and Charlie was supposed to be, like a rabbit's foot, in my hip pocket forever. Instead truth presented itself, as I slipped off into an afternoon slumber: even though there are twenty-four hours in the day and billions of people in the world, I had to focus my time on one person, or I would lose her. Charlie was gone; Ilo wasn't yet. I had to believe that Charlie and Neil would always be my friends, even if we didn't talk to each other for months, even if we went our separate ways in silence instead of in an explosion of fireworks and celebration.

Mandy woke me at about 5:00 p.m. and sat on the edge of the bed the same way my mom used to when she had something serious to tell me.

"Mitch, I called Dreisbach for you," she said.

"*For* me?" I shot up. "*For* me?" I wanted to scream and shout at her, but for the first time I saw a goodness in her that I had never bothered to realize. "Why did you do that, Mandy? You've got no business. Dreisbach wants to get me to Chicago because he wants everyone to remember that it was I who said 'get the fuck off my balls,' on the news, not him. But he doesn't want anyone to forget the saying, oh no, even though it's just stupid."

"Mitch," she touched my leg. "Is that what you're worried about? You're the only one who thinks it's so terrible." She tried to pull me out of bed. "Are you gonna just hide and let that be the last anyone sees of you?"

"I think so."

"What if he does use you, and it turns out to be in your favor anyway."

"I just want some peace, so I can figure out where I'm going."

She pinched my butt underneath the covers. "Peace is for old widows. You figure out where you're going by going."

I rolled toward the wall and threw the comforter over my face. I expected her to go back to the couch and remote control. She held in there.

"He told me he wants you to speak at Grant Park on Saturday. He said that you didn't have to prepare anything; just come out and say a few words."

"See, Mandy; he wants me to be his jester."

"Okay, you just let things be the way you think they are. You're not a joker as long as you sleep through every morning and get drunk every night."

She slammed the door behind her.

Neil came home at around 7:00 that night. He looked at the answering machine, and I hoped that he wouldn't replay any of the messages from Dreisbach. I wasn't going to absorb Mandy's opinion on the subject, and I didn't want his. After merely glancing at the machine, he proceeded to the fridge, opened a beer on his way to the couch, and handed one to me. We decided to sit out on the porch, listening to a radio station's jazz hour and the crickets. Out of nowhere he asked me what I would say when Ted called again. (Mandy had obviously called him while I slept.) I shrugged. He looked out at the river and took a slug of his beer.

"I know you don't want me to say this, and I don't wanna fight, but I think you should do it."

"Do what?"

He sneered at me. "I know there's a lot of propaganda to get through, but if you read between the lines, you can see that he's got somethin' special goin' on here."

"Where is this comin' from? You've always believed in the two-party system. (The world's gonna end if we let Ross Perot run. The whole thing is in shambles if we let the Green Party on the ballot.) Blah, blah, blah, blah, blah."

PIZZA PIE AND POLITICS
HOW MITCHELL MOON LOST HIS CHILDHOOD

I made my hand resemble a chattering mouth.

He shook his head. "Yeah, I do believe in the two-party system. But I can't sit here and let you blow an opportunity." He took another swig of his beer. "I don't know what you said to Ted at Brad's wedding, but he trusts you. Everyone who knows you trusts you. You don't lie to us. That one season when you went ten games without a goal, you told everyone that you went ten games without a goal. When you went out with that neighbor girl and spent $150 and still didn't get laid, you told us you didn't get laid. Let me tell you, man; Not many woulda done that. You didn't hurt her reputation, and you didn't hurt yourself. You rolled with it. Somehow Ted picked up on that."

"I can't let my name be linked with porn and bar-room political rallies." I started smiling as soon as this left my mouth. I knew what Neil would say.

"It already is!"

We both laughed until the neighbor's dog started yipping.

"Look," Neil said. "This is your chance to tell thousands what you've been arguing with me about with a beer in your hands for years. You're good at it."

"No one's gonna listen to someone who doesn't even live in Illinois."

"That's the beauty of his campaign; he's got nothing to lose, and neither do the kids you're gonna speak to."

"I still don't feel comfortable about the porn thing."

"He's inviting *you*; you say what you want."

"Whatever."

"Whatever."

I chugged the rest of my beer and ran to the river and jumped in with all of my clothes on, the same thing Charlie would do when faced with a similar situation.

Ted called about an hour later. I guess it was about 9:00. When I told him I wasn't sure about it, he misunderstood the reasons and quickly said that he would pay for all expenses out of his own pocket, he would put me up in the Palmer House again. I didn't see why he would ever want me to do anything for him if he thought he had to buy me. While he babbled about the fringe benefits of "popping [my] head in to say hello to the crowd," I actually made a motion to hang up the phone, as I do when someone calls to sell me magazines or something. Instead, I put the receiver back to my ear and, without thinking, said, "I don't need to stay at the Palmer House, Ted," I interrupted him. "I know where Chicago is, and I know how to get to Grant Park. I can get there myself if I want."

"No, Mitch; it's not that; it's just…"

"...When I agree to do something for someone I don't do it because I expect to be coddled like some kitty cat in return. I do it because I agreed to do it."

"Okay, okay," he said defensively. "That's why I need you down here. I need your help. I need that perspective of yours."

"Okay, but if it's all the same to you, I'll just find my own way down there and my own place to stay."

"So you'll come?"

"Yeah."

"All right! I'll see you at Grant Park on Saturday then, 12:30, okay?"

When I got off the phone, Neil nodded yes and threw me a beer from the fridge. "It's about time you took a chance, chump."

I poured the beer down my throat, and we headed to Rikki Tikki's for some more.

Had I known that night would be our last together as kids, I would have savored every atom of the cayenne, salt, and garlic in the sauce that covered our Buffalo wings. I would have cherished the sweet hops and bitter barley in every sip of beer. I would have rejoiced at every triple twenty that we hit on the dartboard and every utterance and look and exchange of advice about cricket, field hockey, and life, but as it was, my mind was elsewhere, subdued; and instead of living that moment, I am forced to suspend it and knock it down.

Chapter 16

Neil put our names on the chalkboard to the left of the dartboards. A capacity crowd of seventy-five filled the little bar as always on Wednesday night for the ten-cent Buffalo wings. Most people weren't really there for the wings, but five or six whole families always showed out of necessity. Regardless, we sat second in line for cricket, so I squeezed into a spot at the bar to order us two drafts and two neat Bushmills. Journey played on the jukebox, and a toxic cloud of smoke hung just about at my eye level, a foot below the ceiling fans. As mentioned, no one really liked us here, but not once did I ever wonder out loud what we were doing there. Truly, I believe that I had a crush on one of the waitresses whom I met one week after turning twenty-one. Because of my infatuation with her, Neil, Charlie, and I went there every night during our first Spring Break as legal drinkers. I guess we never really thought of going elsewhere, unless forced to, even a year after she had quit.

I told Neil that I needed to call Ilo and tell her the news. He said, "Bad idea!"

"Did you tell her you were gonna call her?" he continued.

"Yeah."

"You dumb shit! Why didn't you call her from the apartment?"

"You practically dragged me out. Give me your cell phone."

"If I give you my cell phone, you're gonna go outside, and when the least bit of perturbance shows through her voice when she asks where you are, you're gonna lie to her. Things are going too well for you right now to lie to her, and they're going too well for her to know you're in this fucking dump on a Wednesday night. Her boyfriend's probably in the law library right now gettin' a head start on the bar exam." He took a slow sip of his whiskey. "You're not callin' anyone."

He didn't need to mention her boyfriend, but I certainly never mentioned his name while we were together, and I didn't want to think of how I compared. I thought of pursuing the issue further, mentioning that, logically, there were only three places I could be: at Drew's, at the apartment, or at the bar. There were no secrets there, and if those options bothered her, she never would have kissed me; she's not a capricious person. I stopped worrying about that when I suddenly realized that "Don't Stop Believin" had been playing since we arrived, over and over again. I looked at different faces in the room, as if I could tell, through telepathy or at least a snide smirk directed my way, which maniac put a dollar in the jukebox and chose that song four times. I was jolted out of my trance of deductive reasoning by Neil's elbow to my temple. It was time to play cricket.

We played well enough to stay at the board closest to the door for hours. The drinks we ordered only seemed to bestow upon us a Zen-like attitude, as we breezed through game after game until the first-shifters had to leave. The second-shifters began to arrive as quickly as the first-shifters left, and when we concluded that they were too tired to play, we played each other. Then, out of boredom, we changed the game from cricket to who can throw a dart closest to the other's foot. When that became boring, we began throwing darts at the metal beer advertisements on the wall. Not long after that, the bartender took our darts away and told us never to come back again after I punctured the front window of the Budweiser stock car with a tuning-fork ping that reverberated around the entire bar. We didn't mean him or the weary-eyed patrons any disrespect, but we couldn't stop laughing as he yelled at us. Though we tried our hardest, we never belonged there.

We left without acknowledging why we had been ejected, sat down a decent tip for the waitress, and wandered across the road to a bar, which was utterly foreign to us. Here we met two girls for whom we ordered several drinks and goofed off to the point where the bartender stopped serving us. Then they offered to drive us home.

PIZZA PIE AND POLITICS
HOW MITCHELL MOON LOST HIS CHILDHOOD

The catch was that they meant that they would drive us to their home, a fact that finally sunk in not less than one hour into several games of euchre. I don't think I would have realized the oversight if I hadn't noticed that the girl named Lynn was playing with Neil's package under the table. She had her hand right up the leg of his shorts. I raised my brows at him and darted my dilated eyes toward the door. The other girl, C.C., detected my expression, as any good euchre player would, and immediately went to the fridge. She asked us if we needed another beer. Apparently these particular beers had a certain amount of dirt inside the lip, so she brought them to the sink and washed them.

"Where did you put the dish towel that was on the oven?" she asked after shutting off the water.

Lynn shook her head.

At that point, C.C. took off her shorts and proceeded to dry one can off. Then she took off her tank top and dried the other with that, as if the shorts weren't absorbent enough to handle multiple uses. I could only peek out of the corner of my eyes, as I pretended to stare at the miserable cards I had been dealt. Neil gazed, as if watching the end of *Close Encounters of the Third Kind*. She was beautiful, but it was all wrong for us.

She noticed Neil's attention and said, "What? It's no different than a bathing suit," as she looked down at her sheer white bra and underwear.

"Yeah, but no one else is at the beach," I said under my breath.

"Now, why is that?" she asked.

I shrugged my shoulders innocently and looked at the cards again, as if the game were still on.

She stooped down and began to very gingerly remove my Rod Laver's. This took a long time, and she continuously looked into my eyes as if to make sure it was okay. While this happened, I vaguely remember Neil and Lynn going into the bathroom on the far end of the kitchen. After removing my tennis shoes, she ran her hands up my legs and up to my belt. She released it, tore it away, tossed it towards the bathroom, and unbuttoned my shorts. Obviously, I waited too long to avoid a catastrophe, but as she pulled my shorts to my knees, I jumped up and ran for the door, yelling for Neil. The only thing that I could manage to express was, "Come on, Neil; we gotta get to a phone!"

I ran halfway down the avenue before Neil finally shouted me down. He wore no shirt.

"What the hell was that?"

"I dunno," I slurred. "We gotta get outta this town."

"I gotta get outta this skin," he said, looking down at the blood bubbling in the fingernail gashes Lynn had left on his left peck. "I can't keep fucking up like this," he said as we walked. "I'd like to be a groom in one of those weddings someday."

I laughed at how serious he remained with his hair all disheveled, lipstick smeared on his lips, and his big, bright red ears. It looked as though he had been wrestling with a circus clown. Then he started laughing at me in my stocking feet, hiking up my beltless shorts with my right hand.

At the end of the block we saw a pay phone and decided to take a chance on Drew. He informed me that it was 3:30, and his bed was most comfortable at that hour. I told him that if I walked home, I wouldn't arrive until 6:00. He said, "Walk! Maybe you'll be sober by the time you get there." I mentioned that I didn't think Neil could be at work by 10:30 in that case. Drew said, "Good, that'll give me the chance to train the girl I just hired to take his place."

So we walked right down the middle of Main Street, until a police officer stopped us. He got tough with us for a while: Why are *you* bleedin'? You some kinda tough guy? Showin' off your red badge of courage are ya? Where the hell are your shoes, Pippi Longstockings? We didn't dare answer his questions with our story. We just told him that the bouncer at Rikki Tikki's wouldn't let us drive home after he found us wrestling for the keys in the parking lot.

"You guys been drinkin'?"

"Extremely," I blurted.

He ran our IDs through, told us he knew our older brothers, drove us home, and told us that if he ever saw us on the street in that condition again, he was taking us to the county jail.

I woke up in the morning with my head buried in Mandy's hair and my left arm wrapped around her waist. Thank goodness we weren't spooning because I had definitely split some morning wood. I looked at the far wall for a moment, wondering about the circumstances that brought her to my bed, and I quickly realized that I had no recollection of what happened after we entered the front door.

As if she heard my eyelids moving, she turned over to look at me.

"Morning," she rasped and closed her eyes again.

"Mandy, why are you in my bed, and why are you not wearing any clothes?"

"I asked you if I could sleep in here, and you said yes, and you saw me take off my clothes. It didn't seem to bother you then."

PIZZA PIE AND POLITICS
HOW MITCHELL MOON LOST HIS CHILDHOOD

"But why did you get into bed with…"

"…Charlie's bed doesn't have any covers, and…"

"…naked?"

She opened her eyes. "I always sleep naked. You know that."

"But you coulda slept naked on the couch."

She turned the covers down to her waist. After a moment of panic produced by the collision of fantasy and guilt, I realized she was trying to show me the welts around her biceps.

When she knew I noticed, she said, "I locked myself in." She pointed to the door.

"Oh, for cripe sakes!" I leaped out of bed and threw a shirt on. "I'm going to get some breakfast at my parents'. You two can settle this yourselves."

As I passed Neil's room, I saw that he sat up straight in his bed, as if he had no rest at all. I stopped and looked in, immediately noticing that he had three scratches covered with dark, coagulated blood down the center of his face.

"She uses cold cream for her own make-up, but she tried to tear these lipstick marks off my face with her fingernails," he said drowsily. (I could see that he had been crying.) "I think it's over this time, buddy."

I always wished he would say that, ever since high school; it should have been easy to take. Instead, I felt as though my parents were getting divorced. I felt nauseous. I needed to call Ilo; she was sane. I needed to immerse myself in water. I needed to leave. I left, without saying a word.

I wanted to call Ilo from my parents', but I couldn't tell her about Neil and Mandy without implicating myself, and I didn't feel right about inviting her to go to Chicago with me, just me, no Charlie, no Neil, no Keely, no Mandy. I wanted her to go to Chicago with me alone. I had fantasized about it. We'd stay at the Palmer House again, even if it made me broke; I would only leave to make a stupid appearance at Dreisbach's rally; then it would be back to a cozy bed, warm showers, room service, and a lot of wine—Greek wine.

I floated around my parents' pool for a long time, wondering what I would say to a crowd that consisted of around 1,000 more people than my last debate in Poly Sci 413. I couldn't even begin to imagine that much underwear. Since I would take the stage in just over twenty-four hours, I began hashing out a few wise words. I figured that I would take the Lapidary approach, sound bytes the media calls it, something simple, concise, and so obvious that the opponents would wish they had said what I said. All I could think of is "Get the fuck off my balls." Then I imagined the crowd being driven away by lightning and rain torrents that started over northeastern Iowa and gained momentum near O'Hare, fifteen minutes before I was about to go on. Only the dozen loyalists would stay, and I could get on with my simple life after Ted realized that it was all just a pipe dream. I could only conjure this image for a few minutes before spending a good twenty minutes trying to remember what, exactly, I said to Ted about politics at Leopold's wedding. I could think of nothing brilliant. I thought of Horace; I thought of Bunyan; I thought of John Silkin; I thought of Kid Rock. Then I thought of what Ilo would wear after we got to the hotel and after she showered. I smelled her, kissed her, took off her white, cotton towel, and fell asleep on an inflatable pool recliner until two in the afternoon.

I awoke to "Get outta the watah Jimmy Catah! I got work to do." My dad emerged from the garage with tubes over his shoulder and the pool vacuum attachment in his right hand.

"Just look at this shit in the pool. I'm gonna cut those fucking piss elms down someday," he pointed the vacuum toward the trees in the side yard. "And the birdshit!"

I got out, dried off, and headed to my dry clothes in the garage.

"Hey," he said as I walked away. "Tell them somethin' that needs to be said: somethin' that everyone's thinkin' of."

I turned and opened my hands and said, "Shit, Dad," incredulously.

"What?"

"I've got nothin'."

"Yeah ya do. You got nothin' to lose."

"Well that doesn't make me smart."

"Damn straight," he yelled as I walked into the garage.

When I walked into work, the first thing I heard after the screen door slamming behind me was Drew screaming, "Where the hell is Neil? If you guys don't wanna work, what in the hell did you come back to Battle Creek for?"

I walked into his office.

"Why are you still here?" he asked. "Everyone else is aborting the mission on me, bud."

"What are you talking about?"

"Charlie... Then three in the fucking morning; that's what I'm talking about. If you can't make it to work at 10:30 in the morning, you can't hang."

"Neil didn't show?"

"No. So just tell me if you can't work anymore, Mitch."

"I'm here."

PIZZA PIE AND POLITICS
HOW MITCHELL MOON LOST HIS CHILDHOOD

"Good." He left and shot gravel, presumably at me, from the tires of his car.

I realized three things as I tied the apron around my waist: Neil and Mandy broke up. This was clear, because Neil had never missed a day of school, a college class, or a day of work since I had known him. (I think that contributed to Drew's concern.) Secondly, Drew had no idea that I wasn't working on Saturday—I didn't tell him, and it wasn't the time to do so. I realized that we had finally made decisions that prevented us from turning back.

I wanted to call Ilo, but Drew left me with five orders to fill. It was only three o' clock anyway, and I never liked to bother her on the golf course. I finished those orders just as Kenny showed up to deliver them; then the phone rang incessantly for two hours straight. I called Neil for help at five, but he was drunk out of his gourd, singing a John Denver song at the top of his voice as soon as he answered the phone. I couldn't talk to him. At 5:30 there was a brief window in which I caught up with the orders, but the food I had made laid on the over waiting for Kenny to deliver. Again, I thought of calling Ilo, but I knew she was busy with the golf league on Friday. I didn't want to go to Chicago alone. I would pull a no-show. That's when a new wave of phone calls lit up the other lines, all complaints and inquiries about food ordered over an hour ago.

Finally, Kenny returned and picked up the deliveries, just as the six o' clock rush came. I filled the prep table's top with taped-on order sheets that swirled in the breeze of the fan as if they were leaves before a tornado. In a panic I called Charlie's parents' house and asked for Charlie. (I couldn't think of calling anyone else to help me with those orders.) This only worried his mom when she realized that he wasn't with Neil and me. To make her feel better, I told her that I thought he was with Keely, and I would surely find out where she could reach him. Then I called Keely's house. Believing that I was her employer, because that's what I told him, her father told me that she was in the Dells with a friend.

"Okay," I said. "Thank you very much, sir."

"You're welcome," he said.

"The Dells?" I yelled.

"Of Wisconsin," he returned.

"Oh."

"Goodbye," he said.

I had no idea where the Wisconsin Dells were, and I had no conclusive evidence that Charlie was vacationing there, but I called Charlie's mother back immediately and told her that's where he was, safe and sound with a beautiful girl. She was pleased. I tore at my hair. I couldn't believe I did that over a bunch of miserable pizza orders. I thought of quitting right there, walking out with a case of Busch Light under my arm. I actually stopped everything completely and seriously considered the consequences. As the phone rang, I pulled a case out of the walk-in cooler, sat it down on the counter by the door, took my apron off, and began to shut off the oven. In that time the same call must have rung twenty times. Thinking that it had to be Drew, I decided that it would be better to let it go. That way he would suspect that I had gone AWOL, and he would come to Kenny's rescue. But when I stopped to key in the alarm code for the last time, the last time my fingers would touch those numbers, I couldn't do it. The phone continued to ring. I sat my case down and answered it, trying not to listen to the rustling of the orders to my right. Something in my head said, "Those are easy; Things are gonna get tougher."

"Drew's Pizza," I said.

"Hey, Mitch," her voice soothed me like a shot of rye.

"Hey, I wanted to call you, but my management skills are for shit."

"Busy huh?"

"Yeah, I know you are too, so can I just call you around nine?"

"Yeah, well, I'm almost done. Do you need some help?"

"Nah."

"I'll come and help you. I can tell by the tone of your voice…"

"…It's okay."

"I'll be there." She hung up.

I worked so hard to finish those orders before Ilo came, but the pizza cheese ran dry, and since Neil didn't work lunch, no one had made enough pizza dough to get me through. In the twenty minutes it took for me to shred cheese and mix dough, the orders didn't stop, and none had been filled since I decided to quit. When Ilo came in, I claimed that I really had it under control; it could all wait; I had something important to tell her.

"You can tell me later. I'm not gonna leave you tonight. I promise."

She took a glance at the orders on the prep table and asked me where she could make the sandwiches.

"Look. It's nice to see you, but you don't have to do this."

"I don't see anyone else here."

I showed her where she could find everything. She memorized five orders at a time and, following the ingredients chart that Drew posted which no one had ever followed, she produced some of the most photogenic grinders I had

PIZZA PIE AND POLITICS
HOW MITCHELL MOON LOST HIS CHILDHOOD

ever seen. She did this in half the time it would have taken me, put them in the oven, came back to the prep table to dress the pizzas I rolled, pulled the subs from the oven, wrapped them in aluminum foil, and categorized them by address, from north to south.

By the time Kenny returned, no tickets remained on the prep table, and I stood frustrated and flabbergasted when I should have been relieved. After we helped Kenny load the Grey Ghost with pizzas, subs, pop, and beer, I actually wanted to lose my temper with Ilo. She made me feel like an incompetent asshole that needed help all the time at every turn. I swallowed all of the fragmented and crazed phrases that came to mind and said, "I guess I suck at this, huh?" as we walked back into the shop.

She walked to the rolling table, grabbed two hands full of flour, turned, slapped them into my face with a poof, and kissed me.

"You shoulda quit a long time ago," she said as she released me.

I told her that I was going to tidy up the shack, she could certainly help if she wished, and when Kenny returned, I would take her to someplace fancy.

"Rikki Tikki's Tavern?"

"No, not this time."

"Oh, that's *so* disappointing. I might have to wear shoes."

After some cleaning, as I began to sweep, I heard Drew's car pull up to the back door. The sound made my stomach constrict. His flippant requests for menial tasks would ruin one of my golden moments with Ilo. As he entered the room, I stood still, like a territorial dog, poised on the broom. He said "hey" to Ilo and walked past me toward the walk-in cooler. I relaxed and began to put the stupid broom away when he met me at the doorway to the front room. He grabbed the broom out of my hands and replaced it with perhaps the same case of Busch Light I had earlier.

"A retirement gift," he said.

"What?"

"You're done. Get outta here, and don't come back, ya filthy animal!"

I stared at him with a vacuous grin.

"I don't even wanna see ya until my wedding, either of ya! Out!"

He gave me a hug.

I looked at him. I looked at the case. "You don't mind if I trade this for four bottles of Chablis?"

He shook his head as he stood by the phone, flipping through the night's orders.

I made the trade, and Ilo and I walked out together.

Chapter 17

When I pulled to the curb outside of Ilo's house, she asked me what she should wear.

"Bug spray," I replied. "We're gonna have a picnic."

"Are you serious?"

"Yeah, get some bug spray."

"Do you take yours with DEET?"

"Decaf please."

She shook her head and mumbled, "I can't believe you took me all the way home for bug spray."

She returned wearing jeans, a long, white T-shirt and hiking boots and hopped in the car without showing the least bit of curiosity about where we were going.

"Why does my mom call you Randall McNally?"

"She never told you?"

She shook her head.

I smiled and took my eyes off the road to glance at her.

"I think she likes me."

"I doubt it. What did you do?"

I shook my head no.

"That's two questions I've asked now with no answers from you. That's not a good way to start an evening."

"I should really let her tell ya." I did not want to bring up the subject of her boyfriend.

After a brief drive just outside the city limits, I parked in a sand lot and shut off the lights.

"Oh, this is fancy." She snapped her fingers in the air as she exited the car. "Garcon!"

"You can't just see it as sand. You have to imagine what it could be: windows on the Pacific Ocean, decorative concrete; someday, a long time from now it'll be stone. Everybody likes sandstone. There's a lot you can do with sandstone."

"I thought you wanted to get into politics, not real estate."

"There's a thin line."

"You're walking on it," she returned as I dug through my trunk for a backpack, a flashlight, and a blanket.

"Every woman loves a man who keeps a blanket in his trunk," she said as I slammed it shut.

"It's left over from winter. You have to be prepared for the worst."

"*You* better be."

I stuffed some things into my backpack, took her hand, and we walked to a locked gate at the entrance of the biological preserve. We hopped it and walked through the dark parking lot to the trailhead. I turned on my flashlight, which revealed dense foliage and a hiking trail.

"Do you know how many unsolved mysteries begin this way?" she asked.

"You're a walking unsolved mystery," I said.

"And your forensics skills are nonexistent."

She suddenly released my hand and darted down the trail, out of the reach of my light.

"Ilo, stop it! There are bears in here. Ilo?" I shined my light into the woods on both sides of the trail.

"Ilo, there are gangs of teenage reefer addicts in these woods! Ilo?" I shined my light into the trees again.

"Ilo, there are mythological tricksters in these woods: Will o' the Wisp, Robin Goodfellow, Loki. They've got no respect for human loss. Ilo?"

I shined my light to the right of the trail. She jumped on my back from the left, just about brining me to my knees. I dropped my flashlight.

"If you can carry me to where we're going, I'll stay with you until the morning."

I left the flashlight in the middle of the trail and trudged on for about 200 yards, took a left when the trail forked and forged ahead for 100 more until we reached a sand dune. I stopped to make sure she saw where I was taking her, where the moonlight shone on the lake below. Although, I was not confident that we'd make it there in tandem, since I couldn't clearly see the trail ahead of me which I knew to be strewn with rocks and tree roots. Regardless, I hiked her higher on my back and stepped over the ridge. My arms ached; my quadriceps burned, and I thought I should put her down, but I knew I would never again hear an offer like the one she gave.

"Mandy called me this morning. She told me what happened last night."

"What?"

"Don't drop me. If you hurt me it's over."

"It's not how it looked when we came in the door. We were just…"

"Mandy told me Neil's excuses. I'm not gonna cross-examine you. Just don't drop me."

We reached the bottom of the trail where the trees completely shrouded the moonlight. I took my eyes off the trail to see where we were and immediately twisted my ankle on a rock. We began to fall headlong. I anticipated two faces full of dirt, but I felt my left leg plant strongly ahead of me. Then, like a drunken mule, I staggered to the lake, put her down on the bench, and collapsed next to her.

"It's not easy carrying someone on your back, is it?" she asked.

"It's a lot easier than having no one at all."

She looked at me surprised, then quickly looked at the ground smiling.

I dug into my backpack for the blanket, wine, and Swiss Army knife.

I opened one bottle of wine with one of the knife's tools and laid the blanket down. We sat peacefully for a long time, drinking from the bottle. The noises of hundreds of frogs echoed around the lake, and some night birds chirped. A couple of airplanes passed overhead.

"So why did you take me here?"

"Because I'm broke."

"It's nice. You can take me here again, even if you have some money. It's better than the bar."

"It is?"

She talked for a long time, enough time to finish almost three bottles of the wine.

PIZZA PIE AND POLITICS
HOW MITCHELL MOON LOST HIS CHILDHOOD

"I thought you'd be different when your friends aren't around," she finally said.

"I don't know what you mean."

She sat closer to me. "I dunno. I guess I thought you'd be more assertive." She put her hand on my thigh and rested her head against my shoulder. "I dunno. When they're around it's just hard to..."

In case she was confusing assertion with affection I kissed her. She kissed back, and we did that for a long time until she apparently got thirsty. We paused to share more wine.

"What's that?" She pointed toward the boat that sat on the bank.

"That's a skiff that the DNR uses."

"Let's take it out."

I shook my head no.

"Come on. It'll be romantic."

"It's chained to that tree."

She stepped closer to it and looked around.

"It's just a sapling." She brought a milk crate out of the bow of the skiff. "If you can stand on this and I can sit on your shoulders, we can get the chain over."

The tree stood at least twelve feet.

"Maybe we should put the wine away," I said.

"Come on. If Neil and Charlie were here you would have found a way. Why can't you have fun with me?"

I shook my head.

"If you haven't thought about taking this out before, why do you seem to know everything about it?"

"Why would I ever think of that?"

"We can do what we were just doing. We'll just do it in the lake."

I got up and stood on the milk crate. Ilo grabbed the chain, pulled the boat closer to the tree, and handed me the padlocked loop that encircled the sapling. I held it with my left hand and tried to help her onto my back with my right. As she threw her left leg over my shoulder, I almost lost my balance but steadied us by grasping the tree trunk. She threw her right leg over and sat for a moment. I handed her the chain, and she tried to bring it over the treetop.

"I don't think the chain's long enough," she stated.

"Hold the tree and keep us steady," I said.

I turned slightly and, balancing on the crate, I pulled awkwardly on the end of the chain until the boat's bow touched our plastic pedestal.

"Okay, let's give it a whirl," I said.

The tips of the branches were within her arms' reach.

"I still can't get it over."

She yanked on the chain until the tree shook.

"Don't yank it! Don't yank it!"

I heard branches pop, and we were slung toward the boat. I twisted and ducked as we fell, and I clutched at her, trying to break her fall, but I only managed to catch her shirt enough to turn myself toward her. Her head missed the metal seat in the aft by centimeters. My body fell into hers, and my forehead drove into the seat with a thud. I lay there for a long time. It wasn't that I was hurt too badly. I didn't feel any pain after the initial impact, so I immediately thought I was cut deeply, which meant I would bleed profusely, which meant the night was over. I lay there believing that, waiting for the blood.

"Mitch, are you okay?"

I stood up.

"Are you okay?" I asked.

She held the chain in her hands and nodded yes. I touched my forehead and felt a walnut-sized lump.

"Am I bleeding?"

"No."

"Then let's see if this bolt bucket floats."

I put the blanket and the backpack in the bottom, took off my shoes and socks, and pushed the skiff into the water. I used a pole for about twenty yards; then, after three wandering circles and a near spill, I figured out how to use the lone paddle to take us to the middle of the lake. We spread the blanket on the bottom of the boat and sat together, propped against the seat, finishing the wine. The skiff had no anchor, but we remained content with our aimlessness.

In between sips of wine from the bottle and some small talk that I instigated to avoid discussing what really troubled me: Dreisbach, Charlie, Neil and Mandy, Ilo's boyfriend, and the fear I harbored about my fate at the summer's end, and after a few long silences, she asked me if I felt all right. She touched my forehead and let her fingers rest on my cheek.

"You know, you need constant observation during the night when you have a head injury. I don't think I can let you sleep tonight."

After living with Neil and Charlie, I knew all about head injuries, but I didn't mention that. Instead I kissed her, and she kissed me back, and we slowly lay down side by side. I took off her pants and lay down again to cup the soft skin of her inner thighs as we kissed. I couldn't believe it was happening. It was such a dream since I met her at Leopold's wedding that I never even consciously fantasized about it, and now that it was happening, I experienced it from ten feet above, barely feeling anything physical.

She removed my shirt and kissed my chest. I moved one hand to the front and began to stroke her. She spread her legs and moaned into my mouth. I slid her underwear down as far as I could without leaving her mouth, which was in vain.

"We can't do this," she said.

"What?"

"I have to go to Ann Arbor tomorrow."

"Tomorrow? Why not Sunday? I wanted you to go to Chicago with me tomorrow. I finally agreed to show my face at one of his rallies."

"Oh, Mitch, why didn't you tell me?"

"Well, obviously it doesn't matter." I moved to the bow.

She was not moved by the self-pity.

"If it mattered you would have told me last night. You might have even called me for a ride, instead of going home with those tramps."

"It wasn't like that. It was…well, you're goin' to see your boyfriend aren't ya? Yeah! You're one to criticize."

She pulled up her underwear.

"I have to do something tomorrow." She searched my face for a gleam of understanding.

"What?"

"I can't tell you. Look at yourself; you'll take it the wrong way."

"I'll take it the wrong way because there's no right way."

"Just have some faith this one time, and I promise you won't regret it."

I wanted to leap from the skiff, swim back to the trail and go home alone, if it were not for the fact that I had no desire for the situation to which I would return.

"All right, I screwed up last night. You go do what you hafta do tomorrow. I can take it."

"I'm sorry I ruined the mood," she said.

"You didn't ruin the mood." I bit my angry tongue.

"We can go back. I'll stay at your place," she said, trying to keep her earlier promise.

"No. I don't wanna go home," I said.

"Me neither."

She picked up the wine, pulled the cork out and took a sip. She hadn't put her jeans on, and even though she basically rejected me, I thought there still might be a chance. I sat next to her again and put my arm around her. She slumped against me and closed her eyes. I decided that I didn't want her to go to sleep, so I took the bottle from her hand and offered it to her. She took a sip, closed her eyes again, and handed it back to me.

"Tastes like cork now," she said drowsily.

She was slipping away from me into herself. Now I would talk about what was really on my mind. I would bare my soul, and we would talk all night.

"So I think Charlie's in the Dells." I looked at her.

"Well, hi yo the derry-o," she returned without opening her eyes.

I covered her with my half of the blanket and fell asleep shortly thereafter.

In full daylight we woke to the sound of an object hitting the side of the boat. Another followed, but fell short with a "ker plunk." As I poked my head up to see who shelled us, a third whizzed by my left ear, and two children, a boy and a girl of about four and five, ran up the embankment giggling. The boy, wearing flip-flops, lost his footing and fell violently. As he cried the girl picked him up, and they continued. I took a groggy look around to see that we had landed in some reeds close to the apartment complex on the near end of the lake. The amount of traffic I heard on East Columbia told me that the day was in full swing. My tongue felt like wool, and the knot on my head throbbed piercingly, as if it were its own entity. On top of that, my body felt as if I had spent the night crammed in a car trunk.

I looked around me and realized the true condition of the skiff: slimy, greasy, muddy, and rusty. In fact, until I looked closely, I could not distinguish the mud from the rust. The rust had caused a hole in the bow that may have been the reason our bottoms were soaked. It was not a good place to make love, and until later that day when I got horny again, I remained satisfied that we avoided that.

I closed my eyes again to see if some sensory deprivation would provide relief, and I asked, "What time is it?" without opening them.

"I don't know."

"How do you feel?"

"I feel like I went camping with Hank Williams Jr."

"That's not bad." I looked at her, and she didn't want to open her eyes either. "Do you have anything to do today?"

"No," she said pensively. "When do you have to be in Chicago?"

PIZZA PIE AND POLITICS
HOW MITCHELL MOON LOST HIS CHILDHOOD

"Mother fu…" I swallowed the last syllable. (I didn't need to panic on top of the adventure I had put her through.)

I calmly grabbed the paddle and began to push us off from the reeds into the lake.

"You're not going to paddle all the way back?"

"I can't leave this here. Some little kid'll find it and take it out, and this thing is less than seaworthy."

"Mitch, it'll take us forty minutes to get back to the car that way."

"Shit!"

I threw down the paddle and poled us around the reeds to a clearing where we landed the boat. We left the wet blanket and the empty bottles, and on second thought, I used the pole to thrust the skiff back into the lake. After running up the embankment, we walked quickly through the backyard of the apartment complex and two blocks of the little neighborhood to my car. The clock inside read 8:30. I was supposed to be in Grant Park by 12:30.

My apartment was closer to the preserve than her house, so we stopped there. The door was unlocked, beer cans littered the living room, the TV showed Warner Brothers cartoons, and the stereo played so loudly that Ilo turned it off as soon as we entered. As I picked up the phone to call Ted's cell phone, I noticed three empty tequila bottles, an overturned blender, and a sticky trail of margarita that flowed down the cabinet into a coagulated pool on the floor. Ted didn't answer, so I left a message that I might be late.

I bolted to my room to change, instantly grabbing what I knew to be the easiest clothes to throw on instead of the most appropriate clothes for the occasion. When I walked into the bathroom to splash some water on my face and hair, I realized that Mandy had taken all of her beauty products. This meant that the vanity sat vacant, except for a green glass fish that held two toothbrushes and a snaky tube of toothpaste. When I came out of the bathroom, Ilo asked me if that was what I was going to wear, so I turned on my heels and sprinted back to my bedroom to change once again. For some reason, in addition to the new look, I grabbed the camelhair jacket that my dad gave me for graduation. Ilo said that's better, but leave the jacket. Instead, I grabbed a flask from the cupboard, filled it with a half pint of whiskey I hid in the bottom of an old box of Corn Flakes, put it in the interior jacket pocket, and we were off.

TROY PLACE

When we passed the park on the way to her house, I remember looking past her, down the hill at the field where my field hockey team would play in thirty minutes. They didn't know that Charlie, Neil, and I wouldn't be there, and I felt terrible. I knew that I had played my last game.

Chapter 18

When I dropped off Ilo, I felt as though I should say something to her. I was kind of embarrassed about the night, and rushing to get her home did not feel right to me, but she kissed me and made sure that I would call her on Sunday. I remember that she said "Sunday is ours." It seemed nice, but I didn't understand it, so it didn't stick with me as it should have.

Misunderstanding this comment I thought about her and replayed the night's events in my mind for about the first hour of the trip. I tried to think of what I could have done better, how I could have made her more comfortable, and how I could have tried harder to persuade her to come with me. When I came up with no conclusions besides the true one, that she wanted me to call her on Sunday, I began to taste the bitter fact that I was alone on I-94, heading into a situation without friends who could testify, at least in private, that I did exist, and who would give me the benefit of the doubt when I didn't appear to be perfect.

I realized that the second costume I chose, black work boots, destroyed blue jeans, and a black silk shirt, did not agree with the heat and humidity of the late morning. At the Indiana border, I rolled up the window and turned on the air conditioning. I lost my radio station shortly after this and scanned through my radio dial, only to fall upon a variety of country music stations. I thought of what Ilo said about Hank Williams Jr., and I started to laugh out loud. Then my chest shook impulsively, and I almost started crying. I had to focus. I needed food, but I also needed to make good time. I turned off my radio and began to think of what I would say to the crowd. Once I really shut everything out, experiencing something close to silence for the first time in weeks, I didn't find it difficult to dredge up some topics to cover. And I think what helped me most is that I finally disregarded the lost memory of what I said to Ted at Leopold's wedding. He saw something in it, but if I could think of nothing else, then I would know for sure that I had no business speaking to people. Looking back now, I know this is overly critical, considering the mundane nature of the political realm, but it made me feel better at the time.

As I sat in traffic on I-90 outside of Chicago, I mentally ordered the topics I might discuss by importance: what would I want to hear most if I were a spectator? I narrowed the answers of this question to three items, because time would be limited and I chanted them until I approached Chicago. After another forty minutes on 90/94 and the Stevenson Expressway, I merged onto Lakeshore Drive, and despite the panic I felt about the possibility of the traffic sweeping me away to Wisconsin before I could merge left, I made it to Michigan Avenue and spotted a sign for the parking area beneath Grant Park.

I pulled my Cavalier into a compact space in a garage that sat beneath two streets. Before I shut off my car, the clock read 12:40. I made sure that my pocket held my keys and slammed the door. After walking about one hundred yards, I realized that I left my jacket, so I ran back and pulled it out, which was ridiculous, because even the temperature of the parking garage, cloistered from the sun, felt like ninety degrees. Regardless, I retrieved the jacket, reached into the pocket for my flask, and took a long pull from the tiny spout. Burning in my chest rather than my stomach, it made me feel much worse than earlier that morning, so I stuffed it back and threw the coat over my shoulder. I walked out the way I had driven in. A large black stage sat in the northwest corner of an almost empty field. I gazed to my left and down the street to see the vast blue specter of the lake. I only wanted to leap into it and forget that I ever met Ted Dreisbach.

As I approached the structure, I could see Ted on the stage talking through a microphone to a sound man who stood behind some equipment about fifty yards away from the stage. A drum kit sat at the back of the stage, and three guitars stood around it. I walked in back and up a short staircase to the entrance of the stage. I had never been to the back of a stage, and I don't know what I expected, but I saw the bodyguard first. He nodded at me and patted me on the back; then I entered to a small group of people lounging in outdoor furniture.

"Hey, there's the Michigan kid," a voiced yelled from across the room.

I saw Rick walking toward me with a short, shock-headed, and bespectacled young man in tow.

"Mitch, I want you to meet Kevin Carlisle."

I shook his tiny hand. He barely squeezed mine and looked down at his brown oxfords. I thought I had finally met someone more shy than Brad Leopold.

"So you're in the dot com business I hear," I said.

"Yeah, yeah," he looked at me briefly, then looked around and back down at his shoes.

"I guess your company didn't crash like a lot of 'em did, huh?"

"Uh, well, a couple of them did, but my present company seems to be very popular, so I'm doing okay."

"Kev's gonna try to get Ted to debate with the big boys on Wednesday after the primaries," Rick blurted.

I was ready to ask him directly if he was a pornographer (He certainly didn't look like one), but Teresa came over. She gave me a hug and told me to stand back so she could take a look at me.

"You have to lose the jacket." She laughed, removed it and folded it over her arm. "Otherwise, not bad. Marcy, could we get some make-up on Mitch please," she yelled to a girl who sat in front of a mirror smoking a cigarette.

I could hear Rick yelling, "Ted, Michigan Kid's here!"

"Oh, wait," I said, retrieving the jacket from Teresa and digging into the pocket for my whiskey. I unscrewed the top and took a long drink, until the flask felt a little lighter in my hand.

The bodyguard took it away as soon as I removed my lips. He buried the flask in his copious front pocket and waved his index finger at me.

"No alcohol today, Mitch. This isn't a frat party."

Teresa pulled me toward Marcy. I noticed four shirtless young men walk to the stage.

"First rule for a politician. If you're gonna get drunk, don't leave the house," I heard Ted say.

I looked to my left to see his head poking through the curtain.

"That's my line," Rick said, following Teresa and me.

"Then you stole it from Kerouac," I said.

"I paraphrased." He shrugged.

Ted yelled that he would be over in a minute, and I plopped down in the make-up chair.

"Don't touch his hair," Teresa said with her hand on my shoulder.

The humidity and sweat matted it down in wild layers.

"In fact, spray it. I don't want it to move. That's the look we want."

"So what are you gonna tell 'em today?" Ted walked toward me as I submitted to the cosmetic treatment.

"I think I might tell 'em to vote for ya."

"Sounds good."

I heard a drummer hitting his snare, and the bass player played a couple of notes, then a short lick. Someone yelled something to the soundman.

"You know, if this goes well, and you like it, it doesn't have to be a one-time gig," Ted said. "If you want we can sit down tonight, and I'll explain how you could help me out later on this month. I've only got about five people I can trust right now. Teresa's got a helluva dinner planned. So if you want to come over…"

"They're aren't many people out there," I said.

"They're comin'. A lot of 'em will be here to see Sad Paradise; some of 'em will be students from U of C and Northwestern, and we've been advertising it for two weeks. We're gonna start when we get a crowd. The red line stops at Monroe in about fifteen minutes, and the green, orange and brown are comin' into Madison and Wabash. You'll see how it works. Anyway you're goin' on after S.P.'s third song, which will probably be at about two o' clock or so. We've got a band, the guys out there right now, to warm up until we get the crowd we want; then I'm gonna go out for a monologue; then Dr. Sims from Northwestern; then it's Sheila Dano from Philip Morris; then it's S.P.'s first set; then you come on." He paused. "Hey, Dr. Sims," he yelled. "I'll see you after the show, Mitch. We'll get crazy."

Marcy finished, and I got up and headed directly to the buffet table: I wanted to shove the cold cuts into my face by the handful. Teresa, out of nowhere, grabbed my arm.

"You have to wait until afterwards," she said. "Your makeup." She pointed to my lips; then she turned on her heels and walked to the stage entrance to greet a couple who had just entered.

I didn't know what to do with myself. The first thing I considered was rescuing my flask from the bodyguard. So I walked to the stage entrance but stopped at the circle of Ted and his entourage. I pretended to listen to their conversation while I looked at the bodyguard's pocket. He didn't seem to be paying attention, and I thought that I could ask him for it without making much of a scene. But as soon as I took one step toward him, he looked at me and mumbled, "You want it don't ya?"

I shook my head yes.

"I don't have it," he said out loud.

Ted looked up and said, "Oh, Mitch, I'd like you to meet Professor Sims and Sheila Dano."

I shook their hands.

"I'm Mitchell Moon," I said timidly.

"He's helping us today. He was involved with that catastrophe at the CAC this summer."

"Oh?" Professor Sims raised his eyebrows.

I shrugged and blushed.

"He's quiet now, but he gave me some good advice once. He's the one that gave me the idea to contact you, doctor. He's a wiley one—creative."

I said that it was nice to meet everyone and walked to the back stage exit.

"Where you goin'?" the bodyguard asked.

"I'll just be out here lookin' around," I said.

"If I smell it on your breath, I'm sendin' ya home," he replied.

I walked into the daylight, wished that I had remembered my sunglasses, and looked around. I walked across an empty street and sat down on a bench that faced a wall, which acted as a barrier from the city and made the small area a sanctuary. A fountain ran near the wall, and a sign said the property belonged to the Art Institute. I just sat, closed my eyes, and listened to the water run its infinite course to clear my mind. I don't know if I fell into a trance or, more likely, fell asleep, but the sound of Ted's voice on the P.A. brought me out of it. I thought that I should go back. Then I decided that I would wait until someone came to get me—being backstage made me want to puke.

The band began to play after Ted stopped talking. I took a long look at the Sears Tower behind me, wondering if the people who stood up there on the tower's observation deck could really see the Kalamazoo River on a clear day. I thought that if Ilo and I got married someday, we would come to this very spot, and we and our children would go up to that observation deck on a clear day when we could almost see where we live, a home they could find just over the curve of the earth's surface.

I thought of Charlie, who would have talked me into jumping into the lake with him, and I thought of Neil, who would have told me to get my ass up and go in there and meet some people.

The band stopped playing, Ted introduced his first speaker, and all of that peace of mind gave way to my heart, which shook my body uncontrollably. Initially, I put my head over the fountain and began to dry heave, sending four or five streams of yellow bile into the water. That eased my nerves for a minute until my heart, like a three-legged horse, fell back into stride. I wanted pure oxygen, but I compromised for a bucket full of water, which I believed that I could get backstage.

The bodyguard met me at the door and looked at me strangely.

"You just threw up didn't ya?"

I nodded.

"We got a hurler," he yelled. "Michigan Kid just tossed his Pop Tarts."

Teresa Came over with a bottle of water. Ted followed.

"Are you all right?" he asked. "You're not nervous are ya? Don't be nervous."

I sucked the water down and asked for more.

"Just go out and tell 'em to vote for me, just like you said. Next time bring a book or somethin'. Otherwise, you're gonna drive yourself nuts waiting. Try to listen to Dr. Sims. That'll take your mind off yourself. Come on. Sit over here with me."

This would have calmed me if I had not realized that quite a few hundred people had come to the park during my nap. Ted placed two chairs near the far wall, in front of the buffet table, and we sat. I listened to Dr. Sims finish his discussion about the connection between urban poverty, the drug problem, and prison overpopulation. His solution was that American businesses, especially the sporting goods, toy, and clothing industries, could solve the problem if they stopped sending jobs overseas. He cited a study that he did when he mentioned that American consumers would be willing to pay five to ten dollars more for a sweater, or a wiggly worm, or a tennis racket made in the U.S.A. if it meant that less of their tax dollars were spent on prisoners. If jobs were brought back to urban America, he believed that it would restore a sense of order and purpose to a culture that has been completely, and unnecessarily, alienated from the marketplace. I knew it was too simple, but when he finished, I heard applause, and Ted left his chair to support his hypothesis and to briefly discuss his plan for urban renewal. I knew of some cases in the past, but that was the first time I had ever heard a politician outline specific plans for such an idealistic goal before election day. All of the others only made generalizations until they were elected, and then they made more.

PIZZA PIE AND POLITICS
HOW MITCHELL MOON LOST HIS CHILDHOOD

Next Sheila Dano came out with a passionate speech about the millions of people in America whose livelihood depends on the tobacco industry, from the farmers to the convenience store owners and employees. "They cannot make a living on pop and bubble gum," she said. "Without cigarette sales many small businesses would not exist, and as far as the retail outlets go, you might as well plan to pay twice as much for gasoline and ten dollars for a gallon of milk and a loaf of bread, just as examples." She said that smoking is a part of human nature, people will always be drawn to smoking no matter what the hazards, and many economic opportunities for small businessmen in this country stem from the tobacco industry. The problem, she said, is that the cigarette lawsuit money that state governments garner is not being used to fund cancer research; therefore, state governors are as responsible for the cigarette problem as the industry that was forced to face the consequences for its dishonesty. The solution, she said, is that all of the taxes accumulated from cigarette sales should be used to create a Bureau of Cancer, not linked to the FDA, in order to speed the approval process of new drugs and treatments, and to more fully fund the work of scientists most capable of finding cures for cancer and emphysema. She basically implied that we would be a stronger country if we could cure the effects of cigarette smoking. The crowd booed her off the stage before she finished, but Ted hopped up and told them that the campaign is not about pointing fingers and taking sides; it's about gathering data and making the best decisions. The crowd roared.

They stood in silence until he introduced Sad Paradise. The rush of noise made me realize that I would be speaking in front of close to a thousand people.

The three songs that they were scheduled to play turned into an hour set, which pushed the crowd into a frenzy. They would not stop. After every song, my gut tightened, and I prepared to take the stage, but then another song would start. I became mad at the band. Then my insides turned to 220-degree goo, and I felt as vulnerable and confused as a fly in a four-door sedan. On top of that my head ached from its apex down to my eyes. I was not a public speaker, and I wanted out.

I developed a plan as the concert droned on: as soon as the set ended, Ted would get up to introduce me, and I would bolt. No one could catch me. I knew the bodyguard would try, so I decided that I could cross check him out of the way before I even looked for the door. In my mind, under those circumstances, I knew that I could do it. I looked at him frequently, trying to figure out which angle would most easily put him on his ass.

Finally, S.P. paused for a moment, and Ted jumped up to put an end to it for the time being. After a moment I heard him say, "That was above and beyond the call of duty, ya freaks. They'll be back shortly...S.P.!"

"S.P. S.P. S.P. S.P." the crowd chanted.

"Okay now. Okay!" Ted yelled.

The crowd slowly hushed.

I crouched and set my feet to run. I made sure that I had a clear path to the door. Then I decided that I would wait just a moment until I heard my name over the P.A.

"Now I've got a surprise for you. Some of you might remember him from the news. He had a little scuffle with someone who tried to dig up dirt at my wedding reception by hiding in the men's bathroom. He's a gentleman; he's a romantic; he sails on the winds of the American dream; he's Mitchell, Michigan Kid, Mooooon!"

The crowed roared. I left my chair with force, toppling it into the buffet table, and I ran...

onto the stage.

Ted waited for the crowd to quiet down and handed me the microphone. I can't remember precisely what I said, but I know the first words out of my mouth were, "Hi, I'm Mitchell Moon." I quickly realized that the decibels of the concert had muffled my sense of sound. I felt as though I were speaking from inside a bottle, and it was the most surreal experience I ever had.

After I said those first words, I felt as though I had just learned my name after decades of taking it for granted and forgetting what it meant. I opened my mouth again and said something like, "Ted will have a long career in politics, even if he doesn't win this election, because he makes people feel significant, because he was not controlled by special interests, which meant that his voters would not be controlled by special interests, and because he would move a culture that had been in self-denial since 1964 to wake up and take the initiative to vote for someone who would hang his balls under the guillotine for them, and he would do it for years and years."

I believe that's what came out of my mouth, but it didn't matter much to them. They already knew it, and when I stopped talking and turned the microphone over to Ted, instead of applauding half of the crowd chanted, "Get the fuck," and the other half yelled "off my balls."

As I slinked away, I felt a nervous and ecstatic energy that made me want to run in place and talk to everyone backstage at once. But in the back of my mind, I wished they would quit chanting, and I wished I hadn't said something as stupid as that sounded. It could mean "Don't manipulate us." Or "Stop trying to make us into something for which we are not biologically suited." However, I realized long after that day, that it was a mantra for a group that felt stifled, afraid and cornered, trying collectively and inarticulately express latent anger.

Teresa gave me another hug, and Rick shook my hand. Others came around to congratulate me, and I talked to a lot of people, including the lead singer of S.P. and the lead guitar player for the opening band Minors in Possession, but I don't remember a thing I said.

While this was going on, I remember everyone pausing to listen to Ted shortly after I left the stage. When they finished chanting my mantra, he said, "Who has balls? That's only about half of you. My campaign is for all of you. I just want everyone to remember that." Then he introduced the former researcher from Adelphia Electric Automotive.

I couldn't settle down, and with shaking hands, I finally made myself a plate of food that I could not eat. I just sat back in my chair bouncing my meal on my knees. I managed to guzzle another bottle of water, but my only solace was the thought of a tall, cold pint of Guinness, which would bring me back down to my comfort zone.

Even though I barely made it off stage without tripping over my own two feet, I began to wax egotistically. I thought of more speeches. I thought of my own political career. I thought of impressing Ilo with the way I could handle a crowd. I thought of becoming Ted.

He sat down next to me while the engineer spoke. "That was a hell of an entrance. You left like you just stole somethin' though. What was up with that?" He patted me on the back. I beamed and thought of conquering impossible things. Unfortunately, I put Ilo into this category. I began to fantasize about finding out where her boyfriend lived, driving to Ann Arbor, and rescuing her from having to spend another night with him. In that state of mind, it didn't take long for me to begin to act on this fantasy.

"Well, how do I get there?" I asked.

"We're takin' the El, buddy, same way we came in."

I couldn't imagine how time consuming that trip would be, considering the fact that he had rock-star status in Chicago. However, I knew it would be the most tedious and slow-moving trip across town since the invention of the horseless carriage. I couldn't take it.

"Well, I gotta go."

"What? I thought you were comin' over for dinner."
I said goodbye and thank you and left.
"I can call you a cab."
I kept moving toward the door. The bodyguard took out my flask and tried to hand it to me.
"I don't need it."
"You got that right," he said.

I felt as though I were baking inside aluminum foil as I trudged back to the parking garage, and by the time I started my car, the clock read 3:43. Sweat soaked my shirt and my jeans down to the hips, and any of the elation I felt an hour before was sapped by a sudden and harsh sense of fatigue. I turned up the air conditioning and merged onto Lakeshore, no longer dreaming of Ilo but scheming a way to get her away from that boy.

As soon as I cooled off and exited the city, two things happened: I began to doze off at the wheel so often that I was absolutely petrified to blink, and the reality of this obsession hit me. I couldn't just drive to Ann Arbor. I only knew my way around Battle Creek, Kalamazoo, and East Lansing. I was lost anywhere else in the world. Even if I knew how to navigate my way around Ann Arbor, I had no name and no address to go by. So unless Ilo's boyfriend lived in Michigan Stadium, I was screwed.

However, I knew that Ilo talked to Mandy on the phone quite often. I wished I had a cell phone, and I wished that I had Mandy's phone number. So despite my best judgment about the logic of this next decision, I pulled off from I-94 in Indiana and stopped at a gas station to call Neil for Mandy's number. I remember pulling very carefully up the pay phone so that I wouldn't have to get out of my car, and I remember rolling down the window. But I don't remember anything until about an hour later when the gas-station attendant rapped on the roof of my car.

"This isn't a hotel, sir. Other people might need to use the phone."

I opened my eyes to look at the source of this voice. My arms were wrapped around the telephone and metallic cord on my chest.

"I'm sorry. I was just waiting for a call."

He shook his head unbelievably. "I don't know what kinda business you're in, but this isn't your office. You gotta move or I'm callin' the police." He walked away.

I tried to start my car, but it wouldn't turn over. I tried it two more times before looking at the gas gauge. I couldn't believe I had fallen asleep with the car running, the air conditioning on high, and the window open, and then I, along with quite a few patrons, couldn't believe I was pushing my car from the telephone to the gas pump.

The embarrassment didn't change the pitiful fact that I could not wait until Sunday to see Ilo and that I could not bear the thought of her spending the night with anyone but me. I would endure ten times the mortification if it meant that she would love me. I would run naked through a church during a funeral if I could earn a more secure place in her life by doing it. Consequently, I decided to drive home, where I could call Mandy directly.

I wanted Neil to be there when I arrived, and I remember standing at the door with my key in the lock, hoping to see him on the couch or at the telephone. Of course, when I opened the door, the apartment was black, and I cringed at the sight that I would see when I turned the switch to my right. The first thing I saw was the couch with a broken back, slumping to the floor. Its dingy brown fabric sagged pitifully in the middle. The TV sat face down on the floor, and the same beer cans lay randomly around the living room and kitchen. I had a feeling in my gut that was comparable to seeing my mother sick in bed when I came home from school: guilt, emptiness, and abandonment. I called Mandy's house, but she wasn't there, and her mother kept me on the phone for at least fifteen minutes to discuss the situation between her daughter and my best friend. I did manage to get in a word in order to find out if she knew where Neil was, but she believed that I knew the answer to that and immediately wanted to hang up to call his parents. I let her do this after I found out where I could reach Mandy.

I called Mandy at the Texarkana Steakhouse. A jerk answered and got all defensive about who was calling Mandy and under what circumstances. I actually had to tell him that if he would not hand the phone over, I would go out there in person and embarrass everyone involved.

"Hello," Mandy answered.

"Hey, Mandy."

"Mitch! You survived. How did it go?"

"I have no idea."

"Well, you did it, didn't you?"

"Yeah."

"I am *soooo* proud of you. Can you call me back on my cell in fifteen minutes? I've got a twelve top and…"

"Yeah."

I kicked the beer cans that lay on the floor into a pile. I put the TV back onto its stand, and I used a damp rag to wipe up the margarita on the counter, cabinets and floor. I turned the blender onto its right side, and I put some of the cans into a black garbage bag. I looked at the clock on the microwave that read 8:58. Then the phone rang. Immediately, I hoped it would be Ilo, then Neil inviting me to come join him at Rikki's. It was Mandy.

"Hey, sexy," she said.

"Mandy, where's Neil?"

"I don't care."

"Yes you do."

"I haven't spoken to him."

"This place is trashed, you know? He didn't do anything."

"What's your definition of anything? I'm just wondering, because in your guys' little pocket dictionary it must include taking the one who loves you for granted."

"He never took you for granted. You should see this place. It looks like a party broke out in a halfway house."

"I wasn't just talking about me, Mitch. Ilo was not too happy about what you guys did."

"I know. Why did you have to tell Ilo? You can be such a meddling bitch."

"Now you know how I feel when Neil comes back to you guys with every little detail about what we do and where."

"Okay. Okay. I just wanted to know if you know what Ilo's boyfriend's name is."

"Why?"

"Because I'm going to find his apartment in Ann Arbor."

"Is she in Ann Arbor too?"

"Yeah."

"Are you sure?"

"Yes, dammit. Now do you or don't you know what his name is?"

"I wouldn't tell you if I did."

"Well, that's fanfuckingtastic, Mandy. Thanks for the help. It was nice knowing you for the past ten years. Goodbye."

I didn't hang up.

"Mitch?"

"Yeah."

"I know one thing about her boyfriend that will help you find him, but I need you to do something for me."

"Okay."

"Well, there's a mini disc in Neil's closet, under his sweaters on the left-hand side. I need that."

"You got it."

"And there's a bunch of pictures in his nightstand drawer under his underwear. I need those."

"Okay."

"Bring them here, and I'll tell you how to find Ilo's boyfriend. I don't care if you look at the pictures, but please bring me that disc in as many pieces as possible."

"I'll see you in about twenty minutes," I said.

I got the disc first, stomped on it twice and shattered it against the wall. Then I went to the kitchen to get a sandwich bag to store it. After I put it away, I went to Neil's nightstand and retrieved the pictures. I wanted to run out the door (It was past nine o' clock), but I couldn't resist the temptation to look. The first showed Mandy in a Santa Claus hat on a bed with her naked breasts framing her smiling face. She wore nothing but red lace underwear. I hastily flipped the picture to the back of the stack and looked at the next one. Same pose, but her underwear was missing, and I saw the one part of her that I had never seen. I sat on the bed and paused a moment, staring at the picture in my hands. My left hand wanted to go through the stack, but my right hand clutched it conscientiously. I looked at the clock to my left. Then I looked at the pictures. I looked at the clock again; it read 9:15, and I realized that I could not resist another peek. I turned the second picture over to see her on all fours, looking over her left shoulder, with her behind to the camera. The middle part of my body tightened in excitement, but my stomach turned with guilt. I stuffed the pictures into a brown bag that I found behind the dryer. Then I stuffed the bag of mini disc pieces into the same bag.

I drove to the steakhouse and walked into an empty lobby to see a sparsely filled dining room. The host greeted me and walked over to the table on which Mandy was waiting, where there were about a dozen drunken softball players huddled around vacant mugs. A haze of cigarette smoke hung over their heads, and they laughed in unison every few seconds as Mandy laid down a tray full of frosty ones and filled her tray with empties. While she turned, the group's eyes and heads followed, and I saw one slap the chest of another with the back of his hand and throw his head back as if he had been stuck with an arrow. The hostess stopped her, and she looked, nodded her head at me, and set the tray on the bar.

"So you're really going through with this?" she asked as we exited the front door.

"I've got the video and ahh…and those pictures." I'm sure I blushed.

"You looked at those pictures didn't you? Are you sure you love Ilo? Why would you look at those pictures if you love Ilo so much?"

"You told me I could."

"That's because I didn't want you to watch that video."

"What?" I opened my car door and snatched the paper bag.

"You said you were in a hurry, which meant that you'd only choose one. I know you better than anyone, you monster." She kissed me on the cheek as I handed her the bag.

"I looked at three of them."

She looked into the bag. "And you're still going to Ann Arbor instead of staying here with me? I guess you must *really* love her," she said sarcastically. "I should stop you, you know."

"I wish you could."

"What are you trying to do anyway?"

"She doesn't take me seriously, and I…"

"…How do you know? Have you asked her?"

"Have you?"

"How do you know what someone thinks about you? How do you ever know, Mitch? Have you asked Neil what he thinks of me? Because I'd like to know the answer to that one. Maybe you and I should just fuck all week and see if anyone cares."

"Ah shit, Mandy. Neil ran outta that place like his hair was on fire." I paused and changed the subject. "He doesn't know what to do without you, and he's guilty as hell. That's why nobody knows where he's at."

"It's his way to avoid admitting that he's wrong and he's gone too far. How can I stay with someone who can't admit that? He's the only one I ever wanted and he's an asshole. What does that say about me?"

I gave her a hug. "I have to go. Will you tell me where to find her?"

"I think it's a mistake, Mitch. As a friend I have to tell you that."

"Just think of it as me doing what Neil should do now, if he loves you."

"Does Neil love me, Mitch? I have no clue."

"You should see the apartment. The only two things that could do that are a family of hungry raccoons and a man who's crazy in love."

"I don't deserve this."

"Yeah, it's his turn to come to you, which is what I'm trying to do if you'll just tell me…"

"…His parents are looking for him."

PIZZA PIE AND POLITICS
HOW MITCHELL MOON LOST HIS CHILDHOOD

"I know; I talked to your mom. He was at the apartment earlier…" I would have checked my watch if I had one because it was getting late. Actually, it was too late, but I persisted. "I'm sorry but I really gotta go. Will you help me or not?"

"Have you been drinking?"

"No."

"If you want her to take you seriously, you can't show up drunk. She'll run you out of town and never speak to you again."

"No, I haven't been."

"But don't you think she's smart enough to make the right decision for both of you without a cavalier barging in on her life?"

"I don't think she can make the right decision unless she knows how much it hurts me to think that she's with another person right now."

"Oh God! Whenever you guys even sense that you're losing control, you hide and trash your apartment or you drive across the state to beat someone up, which only proves that you can't even control yourselves."

"Whoa! What about you? You don't trust Neil with the porn, so you have me take care of it, and I saw more than Neil would have ever shown."

She looked at the bag thoughtfully. "We never know."

"We never know. That's why I need to go."

"I know, but Mitch, isn't a part of getting older being able to stop yourself when you know what you're doing is a mistake?"

"Just tell me dammit." I looked at the sky. "Just tell me where that motherfucker lives."

"I won't."

"Oh, come on, Mandy. I just got up in front of a thousand people, and all I could think about is making Ilo proud of me."

"You can do this tomorrow. Why don't you just wait for me? I need a ride home. I'll help you clean the apartment. You can have a few beers at the bar while I tab out."

"I'm going whether you tell me or not."

She expelled a combination of laughter and tears. "You'll get lost. Oh my God, Mitch, you don't know west from east."

As she laughed I tore the bag out of her hands, threw it into my car, slid into the driver's seat and started the ignition.

"Oh my God, Mitch! Give that back."

I put it in drive and started to roll.

"Okay!" she ran in front of the car and spread her arms. "He lives above a bar called Victor's Valiant."

I reached into the bag and pulled out the third picture I had viewed. "I'm keeping this one, just in case you're not telling me the truth."

"I don't care." She ripped the bag away from me. "Go ahead. Go ahead and ruin everything."

Chapter 19

Traffic was sparse. I expected the Detroit traffic to slow my progress outside of Jackson, but no such friction occurred, which only made me doubt and fantasize. The simple passion of merely seeing Ilo and telling her everything that fermented in my mind had subsided, replaced with the cumbersome truth about my need for her to choose. Instead, I wished that I could stop at a motel, sleep the night away. Then I would have tomorrow to consider how I would connect with someone so far outside of myself. We almost made love the night before, but the only thing I could see is myself kissing her. I couldn't picture it as two people together, and I thought the whole problem lay in her relationship with her "boyfriend." Just as easily, it could have been that the three bottles of wine distorted reality enough for her to want to be with me. I couldn't wait to find out if someone, besides my parents, legitimately loved me.

It made me feel more confident when I realized what I was trying to achieve, but I still couldn't picture what I would do when I stood in the open apartment door, perhaps in front of her boyfriend with her in the background: stutter? Ask her if we could talk? (Could I honestly explain what I was worried about? I couldn't ask her if she loved me.) Ask her boyfriend if I could talk to her? (That would be completely chauvinist.) Then I imagined myself beating the possessive bastard so humiliatingly that Ilo couldn't think of him with the same respect that she had for him five minutes before I brought them out of his bedroom with my knock on the door.

"What am I, seven years old?" I thought. "I've got to be honest here or I'm going to blow it. I'm going to lose her forever if I'm not honest with her now."

My clock read 10:54 as I cruised northeast on Main Street in Ann Arbor, watching for a Victor's Valiant sign. This section of town turned out to be very busy: I became so preoccupied with my awareness of pedestrians, bikers, and double-parked cars that I had no clue as to the names of the bars and restaurants I passed. As an alternative I followed a blue parking sign to a side street and entered a garage next to an open but ramshackle Caribbean restaurant. I chose a space on the top floor next to a full-size van and a Ford F-150, even though there were plenty of spaces. I opened my door about eight inches until it made contact with the van, sucked in my stomach, and pulled myself through one leg at a time.

I smelled the food rising from the street, primarily garlic and grilled meat, and immediately remembered that I wanted something to eat. If I just stepped into one of these places for a quick bite, maybe I would think more clearly, but I was too afraid to stop. In less than a month, she would be moving back here and, inevitably, a new routine would begin, one of which I may or may not be a part. At that point I truly believed that a sandwich break could seal my fate. Insanely, I thought that if they had gone to dinner and a nine o'clock movie, then they would return at about the same time that I arrived, which would offer them little time to become intimate. I could interrupt them before they did it.

I took the stairs down to the street onto which I turned and made my way back to Main. I was thoroughly lost. Two teenagers on skateboards approached.

"Excuse me," I yelled and put myself in their path.

They both slowed to a stop with right feet still on the boards.

"Do you guys know where Victor's Valiant is?"

"Do you have cigarettes?" one asked.

"No."

"Can you buy us some beer, dude?"

"No."

"Come on. We'll give you some money. You just have to buy it."

I looked at them confusedly.

PIZZA PIE AND POLITICS
HOW MITCHELL MOON LOST HIS CHILDHOOD

"I know how it works; I'm just in kind of a hurry."

I left them staring at my back. It seemed like a complete minute before I heard their wheels resume clacking on the seams of cement.

At the corner, while I waited for the light to turn, I caught the eyes of a grey-haired couple waiting next to me.

"Excuse me; could you tell me where Victor's Valiant is?"

The man, closest to me, looked to the lady for guidance. She shook her head.

"Is it that new clothing store?"

"No. I think it's a bar."

"Never heard of it. Sorry," the man said.

As we crossed the street, I began to consider the possibility that Mandy lied to me. I asked the next person I saw, possibly a college student, attached to the hip of a slender girl who wore purple sunglasses. After one look at him, I could tell that he had some wine with dinner—about two liters I assumed.

"Excuse me; do you know where Victor's Valiant is?"

"Victor's what?" the girl asked.

"You know, like the fight song title. It's a bar."

She rolled her eyes and proceeded to pull her boyfriend down the street.

"Ha Hahhh! That's a good one," the boy, brushing past me, barely stabilized by his girlfriend who thought that he was hilarious. As he sang the U of M fight song, his voice wailed and heightened upon every "Hail!" as if he were desperately screaming for help, while he staggered down the street. People stopped to stare at him with honest concern. I gathered that his wasn't typical behavior in this part of Ann Arbor.

I approached a restaurant and decided to ask the host or hostess to see if this business really existed. If not I would call Mandy from the nearest pay phone. My first inclination was to scream at her for interfering with my life. I realize now how selfish I was. I had not begun to admit how much I had interfered with hers.

I walked into the waiting area of a restaurant, which looked like a saloon in an old western movie, except the tables had white cloths and candles. Although many of them were occupied, the hostess looked at me tentatively, as if she hoped I didn't want a meal at that hour.

"Hello. Can I help you?" She was a stout blonde girl with innocent blue eyes.

I asked her about the bar; she thought for a moment and wagged her head from side to side. She turned into the darkened dining room of tinking dishes, light jazz, and the scent of marinara, then returned with a large dark-haired man who wore a red tie against a black shirt.

"Lookin' for Victor's?" he asked in a loud and friendly manner.

"Yeah, thank you."

"Yah, we call it Victor's round here."

It was funny to hear him use the hard nasally Rs that the younger generation had abandoned for the more abstract and dreamy R sound. He probably didn't know that he had just served me a reality sorbet. His honest answer to my honest question made me realize that this wasn't a fantasy. My urge could develop into an action that might affect other people. I couldn't stop myself.

"Go down three blocks," he pointed north. "And take a right on Huron. Go down about three more blocks, and you'll see it on the right side of the street."

"Thank you very much, sir."

I walked to the Huron intersection, crossed Main, and followed the sidewalk until I thought I had walked three blocks. I began looking at doors and into windows until I saw a dark door with two small windows to the upper left and right. The neon beer advertisements provided enough evidence for me to enter, but I walked to the curb to see if there was a sign on the awning and if there were apartments above. All of the lights were off if there were apartments, so I decided to look for a way up. I assumed there would be a doorway leading to an apartment stairway just to the right of the bar's door, but there was no such thing.

My heart beat fast, and my head hurt from anxiety. I opened the door hastily enough to disturb the handful of patrons, all of which looked at me as though trying to remember if they knew me or not. The bar, which smelled of cigar smoke and bleach, was very dark, and separated in half by dark wainscoting and flat, two-inch-wide dividers. On one small half there was enough room for two pool tables. On one stood two older men, wearing black jeans, T-shirts, and leather biker vests. A younger group of three tattooed men sat at a table next to the divider. At the bar sat a thin man with a full grey beard and a brown tweed suit in front of a low ball of bourbon with an expensive pipe between his lips. I sat three stools down from him. I didn't see a bartender.

I decided to ask him.

"Excuse me, sir."

"Yes," he said without altering his distant gaze into the mirror behind the bar.

"Do you know if there is an apartment above?"

"I don't know, but there is a stairway in back. It must go somewhere. Why don't you go see where it leads, and then come back and tell me." He didn't look at me.

"I'll do that."

I rose from the stool and exited the back door. I saw a stairway that hung parallel the back wall of the building with a small porch and door at the top. My vision of Ilo's boyfriend had changed from that of a nerdy legal eagle to a whiskey-drinkin', gun-totin' biker who didn't mind rolling my ass down those stairs, but I climbed regardless. I knocked at the door…no answer. I knocked again, harder and more insistently, but there was no answer. I listened for noises inside, but there were none. I gave up and decided to wait at the bar, hoping Mandy told me the truth.

When I returned to my stool, I noticed that the bartender had returned and busily filled a cabinet-style cooler, under the liquor shelf, with a case of Bud Light. She wore a tiny black shirt with cut-off sleeves and low-rise jeans, so as she worked, I could see the top of her bottom and two white strings of her underwear. The man in brown watched intently. She noticed my presence and stood suddenly. She was tough looking with long black hair, dark eyes, and plum lipstick.

"Can I help you?"

"Do you know if there's an apartment upstairs?"

"It's not available right now. Check back in August."

"Oh, no. I'm supposed to meet someone up there, but no one's home."

"Well, if you're drinkin' you can wait here."

"I'll have a Bushmills neat."

I drank that and another until the clock read 12:13, which meant that I had been there for about a half an hour. I decided to try upstairs again, but there was no answer. All kinds of assumptions came to mind; the worst being that he decided to take her to a hotel room with a Jacuzzi, instead of spending one of their rare nights together in a dive above this hole in the wall. Although I was almost sure I wouldn't see Ilo at that point, I decided to wait anyway, probably because in the past, I had been sure about a lot of things that were not true.

I ordered another Bushmills and decided to play pool at the vacant table. I had just put my coins into the table for my second play when two extremely drunk and loud young men came through the front door. The taller one with blonde hair walked behind the bar as if he owned the place and poured drafts for himself and his buddy.

The bartender came through the service door and said, "What the fuck are you doing, Brian? Get on that side, you asshole. You guys are too drunk."

"Whadaya mean; we just started. We just came in," Brian said. He and his buddy giggled like seventh graders.

"It's last call for you. Drink these and you're both done."

"Then we'll have a twelve-pack of Miller High Life take out please, bartender," he said in one breath.

"Fuck you. If you want it so bad maybe your friend over there will buy it for you," she pointed to me. "But there's no way you guys are drinking another ounce in here." She took their mugs away from them and poured them in the sink.

"Rad! I've got a friend here." Both men decided to join me. Brian, Ilo's boyfriend, had blue eyes and a build like a Wolverine quarterback.

"What's up?"

I shook both of their hands.

"You look familiar. Where do I know you from?"

"I don't think you do actually," I replied.

"Well, why the fuck does she think you and I are friends?"

"I came here to see Ilo."

"Oh shit," his friend said.

"Ilo? Ilo? Oh, I know who you are, you motherfucker."

He picked up my glass from the edge of the table and dumped it over my head quicker than I had time to react. I stood dumb for a moment, but as soon as I realized what he had done, I belted him between the eyes with the fat end of my cue. As quickly as I had acted, his friend kicked me so squarely in the balls that I thought I would puke. I'm sure we looked like the three stooges, but the men at the other pool table rushed over very seriously. One took hold of Brian, and one took hold of me. Brian's friend punched me in the eye before the man could turn me away.

"You two can just take it outside," said the man holding Brian.

The bartender ran out from behind the bar.

"Don't you dare put them two outside together, Brutus," she said. "Get him the fuck outta here."

I guess she meant me, because a moment later I was being thrown to the sidewalk outside. On the way back to my car, I noticed that the streets had cleared considerably. The few people who walked on the sidewalks did so more slowly than before, and no one looked at me as I thought they would, since my hair and shirt were soaked, and my face throbbed as if swelling. I

PIZZA PIE AND POLITICS
HOW MITCHELL MOON LOST HIS CHILDHOOD

walked swiftly to my car, checking my back every forty yards or so.

Once inside my car, I turned the ignition and checked the clock: 1:14. I should have slept in my front seat, but the only thing I thought was that I could make it to Ilo's window by 3:00. The fight only raised my adrenaline enough so that I wasn't ready to call it a night yet. I was slightly aware of the fact that, since waking up in a skiff the morning before, I had been trying to put too much into too little time, but I could not let it go. I needed closure on that day, whether it be good or bad, so much that I was willing to take the chance.

On the interstate I set the cruise control at a safe sixty-five, five below the speed limit. As I drove further from Ann Arbor, I-94 became a desolate path, and in long periods of utter darkness, I became a stranger in my own state. I was lonely, and the fact that the few radio stations that would come in seemed to only play Bob Segar, the Eagles, and country music didn't help the situation at all.

I parked on the street outside of Ilo's at about a quarter to three. I found a few pebbles in the street and proceeded to throw them softly at her window. I went 0 for 3. I thought that I saw a whole pile of pebbles near my driver's side door, so I stepped away from the house to find them. I began to feel sick and dizzy.

I woke up in the middle of Ilo's yard, clutching the Sunday paper as if it were roses on my deathbed. I could only guess that the paperboy decided to have some fun at my expense. Embarrassed, I thought that I could get up and away before anyone noticed, but as soon as I processed that thought, I heard the front door open and close. I looked up but no one was there, so I jumped to my feet, laid the paper near the walkway, and began to jog toward my car, not to look back until I heard Ilo's voice behind me.

"Mitch, Mitch, what are you doing?" She was smiling and laughing. I felt like I was going to levitate; I was so relieved to see her smile. Her father came out. I picked up the paper and handed it to him.

"Morning," he said without looking at me, as he turned and reentered the house.

"Mitch, why were you just lying in my yard?" she asked in a coy tone.

I almost lied to her, but I didn't know how long her step-dad had been awake or if he talked to the neighbors.

"Well, I ah…well I meant to wake you up, but I guess I fell asleep."

"How long have you been here?" her smile faded.

"Since three… I think."

"You passed out." She pulled her head inside and came through the front door after a few seconds.

"I don't understand why you drink so much, and you drove." She pointed at my car. She was angry.

Upon realizing exactly how angry she was, I began to babble: "I'm sorry. I thought I could make it, but I hadn't eaten all day, and Friday night was weird, and I couldn't stop thinking about you and what you thought about it, and I spoke in front of a thousand people, and I came home to see you, but you weren't… uhm, uh, uh." I slapped the back of my right hand into the palm of my left.

All of my dreams meant nothing if I couldn't articulate them. All I wanted was for her to understand me. Instead, I must have sounded like a schizophrenic street person.

"Whoa!" She grabbed my hands. "You smell like you took a bath in whiskey; your shirt's stained, and you have a black eye." She touched my face, which stung. "How did you get a black eye?"

Again, I could have lied, but I was sure she would find out sooner or later.

"Your boyfriend's friend hit me."

"You went to Ann Arbor last night?"

"I was afraid that…"

"…You thought I was going to spend the night there?"

"Well, that's how it sounded this morning."

"No, Mitch. Do you think I would go and sleep with him after… Do you think I'm the type of person who would…" She shook her head and seemed to think for a moment. "I went there to break up with him. I broke up with him, and now you're fighting people and passing out on my lawn? I need to think about this, 'cause this isn't a good beginning." She looked at her front door and turned from me slightly. "I really need to think." She walked up the steps and went inside without looking at me.

I was sure that I didn't go to Ann Arbor to deliberately start trouble, but it didn't matter. I should have been more patient, and I should have had more faith, but I really could have used some from her too.

Chapter 20

I drove home to see the same mess that I had seen the night before. My first inclination was to clean it up so that it looked orderly and new, as if the apartment were my life, but I had to eat. I opened the fridge to see four peaches on the middle shelf instead of the fruit drawer, a kiwi fruit in the egg container, a stick of butter in the fruit drawer (along with a head of lettuce), a brick of cheese on the top shelf next to a package of bologna, eight bottles of Busch Light, a jar of Miracle Whip, and a quarter loaf of bread. I picked out a peach, bit into it and spit it out. It was long past ripe. I looked at the bologna, which was partially green, so I decided to try the lettuce. Its surface, beneath the plastic, was slimy and brown. I removed the plastic and the rotted leaves and crunched into the head as if it were an apple. When finished I made myself several sandwiches, consisting of Miracle Whip and toasted wheat bread, and ate them until my jaws grew tired. The clock read 10:03. I washed my meal down with two glasses of tap water and began to clean the house, wondering why I didn't save the lettuce for the sandwiches. That would have been much better.

While cleaning I played some music to keep me company. I had nowhere to go, very little money, no job, which put a damper on my social life (unless

I went back to live in East Lansing), no career prospects, my chances with Ilo were in grim jeopardy, and I didn't know the true locations of the two people who did as much to raise me as my parents. It took me three hours to clean the apartment, and then I wanted to sleep until my thirtieth birthday. My twenties were going to be hell.

I woke up to the sound of keys being dropped onto the breakfast bar. I heard someone throw himself down into the living room chair with a grunt, and I heard the TV come to life. A news anchor was on location at a voting place, talking about Tuesday's primaries. I rolled over and looked at the clock, which read 6:07. I threw back the covers and joined Neil in the living room, holding back my relief over having someone to talk to.

"What's up?" I lay down on the beanbag near the couch.

"What's up?"

"Nice job on the couch."

"Yeah, it was a piece a shit anyways."

We watched the election coverage on three or four different stations.

"Where you been?"

"On one helluva binge."

"I guess. What did you do?"

"Well, Mitch, if you have to know, I drank all day Friday righ' cheer." He pounded on the arms of the chair. A plume of dust rose and faded quickly. "Friday night I went to the comedy club. I drank shots with some bikers and went with them to a pig roast at a trailer park. I passed out in a tire swing. In the morning I drank whiskey with some guys who had also spent the night, and they took me canoeing on the Kalamazoo. I went to dinner with them at Tom Thumbs, and the next thing I remember is waking up this morning in a lawn chair on my parents' porch."

"Did they know you were there?"

"Well, yeah, I had to ask my dad for a ride to the comedy club so I could get my car."

"Oh shit, what did he say?"

"Do you remember that night, when we were about fifteen, when we snuck out…"

". . And went to Trina Jefferson's keg party."

He nodded yes.

"It was that bad?"

"Worse. They made me promise to leave town tomorrow."

"You're kidding me."

He shook his head no.

"You're leaving?"

He shook his head yes.

"Well, what in the hell am I supposed to do about rent? We're already two days late, and you fuckers..."

"...Hold on, hold on. My dad's gonna cover my share for the month."

"Well what does he expect you to do, sleep in a terminal at Dulles until you get your first paycheck?"

"No, man. I'm gonna stay at my Uncle Todd's in Arlington until my job starts."

"That's just embarrassing. I mean you're twenty-two, Neil."

"I know it. I know it. But I can't afford to move to D.C. on my own. I haven't saved any money, and I need that job."

I sat shaking my head in frustration.

"What about Mandy?"

"I don't know."

"You can't just leave her without saying anything."

"What in the hell do you care. What, you're a big fan of Mandy now?"

"Well, don't your parents care? She's like a daughter to 'em. She was worried about you. Her parents were worried. Shit, Neil, you know she's gonna be over here every day crying on my shoulder. I don't deserve to clean up your mess just because your parents say go. I'm gonna call her right now."

"Fine."

I walked to the phone and dialed her parents' number. I left a brief message, informing them that Neil was home.

"There's no answer."

"I'm sure there are phones in Arlington."

"It's not the same, and you know it, you irresponsible toddler."

"Whatever—I need to pack."

I wanted a fight, but he went to his room, and I went to the fridge for a beer. I was so angry and nervous that the beer I swallowed made my stomach convulse, sending the froth back up my throat and mouth and into the sink. I poured out the remains of the bottle and smashed it on the counter I had polished just hours before.

"Mitch," I heard Neil yell in one long melodious syllable, as people sometimes use when they are afraid of something.

"What?"

"Come here please."

"What?" I stood in the doorway of his bedroom. I didn't know it at the time, but my palm was cut.

"Has Mandy been here?"

"Not that I know of; why?"

"Well, there were some pictures in my nightstand, and now they're gone."

"She has 'em."

"Who? Mandy?"

"No, Queen Elizabeth. Yes, Mandy has 'em. I gave 'em to her, asshole."

"Well, what in the hell did you do that for?"

"I traded her for some information about Ilo's boyfriend."

"If that's why you have a black eye, you deserved it. He just saved me some time. And if you…" He shook his head deliriously and sat on the bed. I thought that he had finally realized what was happening. I let him stew in it for a while. That's when I realized I had cut my hand.

I washed off in the kitchen sink and wrapped a dirty towel around it.

"She wanted them back and the disc." I stood in his doorway again.

Still sitting on the bed, he shook his head. "So it's over? What do I need to call her for if it's over?"

"It's not over unless you want it to be. That's why you need to talk to her, instead of taking her for granted, instead of not calling her because you're afraid to say you're sorry. In fact, if she asks me why you left without talking to her, I'm going to say—Well, Mandy, Neil's afraid that people might think that he's slightly vulnerable, so when someone catches him out, he runs away in defeat."

"Since I'm in a hurry, I'll pretend that you didn't just say that. I just wanna know why you care about *her* all the sudden."

"Neil, you gotta understand that you and Mandy don't have any past relationships. You aren't pulling that baggage around with you. You've never had to wonder about the guys she used to fuck because there are none. At your age, you'll never find that again, ever. Mandy is the last girl you'll ever meet who only loved you."

He looked down at his hands with a smirk, which is the only indication he ever gives that he might have absorbed what someone said to him.

"She'll be crushed. Ya know; she was probably just trying to get you to take her seriously by taking back those pictures."

"Ah, shut up."

Within the hour he finished packing, and I helped to carry two duffel bags, a garment bag, a box of shoes, his stereo, and a box of compact discs to the car.

PIZZA PIE AND POLITICS
HOW MITCHELL MOON LOST HIS CHILDHOOD

I had been accustomed to listening to those for so long, I almost objected to his taking them. I thought some were mine, but there was no way to be sure.

"If I left anything, keep it until you move out."

"If I move out."

He looked at me with curiosity.

"Otherwise, you can just take it over to my parents."

"All right, man; I'll see you soon."

"See ya soon. You'll tell Drew I'm sorry about leaving on him?"

"He fired us."

Neil laughed. "Well, you tell him I'll see him on Labor Day weekend."

"I will, buddy."

"See ya, bud." He hit me on the left shoulder.

"Take it easy."

I shut his trunk. He shut his door and drove silently out of the complex.

It pissed me off to see him leave like that. All those years of listening to his sexual escapades with Mandy, and he gave me no time to share mine with him. I guarantee that he never almost did it in a DNR skiff. It wasn't fair.

I ate dinner at my parents', and this time I actually listened to my dad when he stressed the importance of finding a good job at that point in my life. Although I should have enjoyed the fact that I had the rest of the summer to myself, I just couldn't quite ride it out as well as I should have for the simple fact that I hadn't planned it that way. I didn't want to be alone, even though being without Charlie and Neil for a while is just what I needed.

The good thing is that he agreed, after I finally told him that I got my black eye in a field hockey game, to pay the last month of my rent, if I would prove to him that I was actually seeking gainful employment. He wanted me to take some time off to find a good position, instead of a dead-ender in Battle Creek, which would only prove to be a "distraction." I had the intention of getting extremely drunk when I returned to my lonely apartment, but it took me a full hour to finish one of the beers from the fridge, so I went to bed at 11:30.

In the morning, while I lay in bed dreading the job of finding a job, the phone rang. Ilo or Charlie? Ilo or Charlie? I asked as I raced to the phone. I picked it up eagerly and nervously, only to hear the voice of Kim, who wanted to know if we were going to play field hockey anymore and why not. Why not? She asked until I begrudgingly told her the whole story, beginning with the night at the lake when Charlie kissed Keely, with all the gritty details I could think of, until she finally hung up on me.

I went to the library and searched the employment web sites. As it turned out, there were dozens of positions across the United States for which I qualified, but I was sure that I wouldn't leave the state while Ilo remained, so I found three: all in the lower peninsula of Michigan. I revised my resume, cover letter and references, made three envelopes, and drove from the library to the post office. It was after two o'clock, and I couldn't bear the thought of going home to no one, so of all things, I went to hang out at Drew's.

My hanging out turned into working a seven-hour shift. Drew paid me in cash and told me not to come back; he had "fresh hands lined up." Again, I was in bed by 11:30.

In the late morning, I decided to go for a swim in the Kalamazoo. I thought about my future: I didn't want any of the jobs for which I had applied, but I would be living from my credit card until I started working. I could imagine eating a bowl of algae from the far end of the bend in the river before I could imagine signing a contract that obligated me to give my days to someone else. I didn't feel that I had myself figured out enough to concentrate on someone else's business for forty hours per week. I wondered when I should call Ilo and how I could make a new beginning for us. I wondered if the days of doing nothing would last long. I wondered how to go about making new friends. I wondered if my worries would be much more serious in the future. If so, I didn't think I could take it.

I took a shower and decided to go to my parents'. On the way out of the door, I almost called Ilo, but calling her without much to say wouldn't be a good way to begin. I latently wanted to call her before she talked to Brian. (Who knows what kind of a spin that asshole would put on the incident?) But I imagined being talked into excuses and apologies so I let it be. There was really nothing I could do.

I mowed my parents' lawn, weeded my mom's garden, washed the windows that faced the street, and floated around in the pool, sipping iced tea until my mom offered me dinner.

"Well, you must be bored to tears with the guys out of town," she said, passing me a tossed salad with yellow peppers, cucumbers, and tomatoes from the garden. I doused the fruit with Italian dressing and ate it from the serving bowl. I was so hungry.

"In your life how many days have you spent without seeing one of those boys? I remember taking Charlie on vacations with us because you couldn't stand leaving him here."

"I appreciate the work you did around here," my dad interrupted. "And

PIZZA PIE AND POLITICS
HOW MITCHELL MOON LOST HIS CHILDHOOD

I'm not even gonna ask you if you've even tried. I just really want you to look for jobs, Mitch."

"I sent three resumes out yesterday."

"When do you think you'll hear back?"

This was a very annoying response to me, as if my best attempt wasn't fast enough, as if they were going to give me the job as soon as they saw my name on the cover letter.

"I have no idea, Dad."

"Where are they? What are they for?"

"Two are in Lansing; one's in Detroit."

"City?"

"Yup."

"Well, I would go to Lansing tomorrow and introduce myself to whoever's doing the hiring."

"I can't do that."

"If you can't get a job, you should join the military. The army's good for someone your age. A military background's good in politics isn't it?"

"No, they'll just use your military record against you," I replied.

"That's not the way it works these days, Jim," my mom defended. "If he goes in like that, he'll have an unfair advantage in the hiring process, and they won't hire him because of liability issues if someone sues."

"Well, I'd say the fact that the kid a 3.99 G.P.A. at State would cover it."

My grades weren't nearly that impressive, but my dad tended to round up or down conveniently when he needed evidence to support his argument.

"Then what does he need to be pushy for? Everyone has to wait these days."

"It's not being pushy; it's proactive, as they say."

My mom and I laughed at his word choice until his face turned red. He began to chuckle too.

"When I graduated from college," my mom said, "I was offered a job at every place I interviewed. But things just aren't that way anymore. It takes a lot of time, and his field isn't in demand."

"Well, look around. You can move anywhere you want. You're young; you're unattached. Ya gotta go for it now, buddy," my dad added.

"I think I wanna stay in Michigan actually."

My dad looked at me, as if waiting for a sign that I was joking.

"But you've always hated Michigan. Just three months ago you said…"

"Jim, I think Mitchell has a girlfriend."

"Well I…" I began to explain a lie that began to form in my mind.

"Who? Who is she? Do I know her parents?"

"Her name is Ilo Velasquez, but she's really not my…"

"That sounds Hispanic. Is she a…" my dad began to say.

"She's beautiful, Dad. And charming. She could make an elephant do back flips."

My dad smiled shyly.

"Let's take you two out to dinner," my mom said. "Let's go out Friday night."

"We can't do that, Mom."

"Saturday?"

"No, Mom. It's not like that."

"What is it like?"

"It's like I love her, but she's not my girlfriend."

"You're not gonna stay in Michigan for a one-night stand?" my dad bellowed.

"But she might be my girlfriend, someday."

My mother and father looked at each other, proceeded to finish their dinner, and went outside for a walk around the neighborhood. I guess some problems have to be your own, especially if there is no logical way to explain them to anyone else.

When I returned to the Crimson Rouge, there were two messages on the machine. One was Dreisbach, telling me to give him a call, and the other was Charlie, who said, "Hey, fools; this is Charlie. Pick up the phone." About a second later he hung up. I guessed that his was the last call, so I used the star-69 option. The call went through to an answering machine, but I didn't recognize the voice on the other end. She only gave the number, which I remembered for long enough to grab a pen and scratch it on the wall above the phone.

I said, "Hey, Charlie, this is Mitch. Neil's gone. Call back."

I called Ted immediately after that, excited to have someone with whom to talk.

Teresa answered Ted's cell phone and handed it over to him.

"Hey, Mitch, you caught us at…" His voice faded, and I heard nothing but static. I waited for about a minute and hung up. I called again.

"Hello? Hey, Mitch. Sorry 'bout that—you caught us at the restaurant. Now that we know who I'm up against, we're sitting here trying to strategize."

PIZZA PIE AND POLITICS
HOW MITCHELL MOON LOST HIS CHILDHOOD

"That sounds fun."

"Well uh…the reason I called is that I need your help again." His voice became softer, and I wondered if he had stepped outside. "I've got to get out and press some skin. These rallies aren't gonna win it for me, not if the same people keep showin' up to hear Sad Paradise. I've gotta get the message out to people who weren't there."

"I don't think I'm ready to leave. And I don't know if I can do anything for ya."

"Well, look at it this way. You don't know who I am, and you don't care. You'll argue with me just like at Brad's wedding. I can talk politics with you. You're passionate. You care. All of those people sitting at that table tonight are putting all of this time and money into the E Party, and they act like the discussion's over when I start talkin'."

"Ah, either way Ted, I'm almost broke. I need to find a job. I can't travel around Illinois on my credit card."

"Oh, gimme a break. I'll pay you."

"This is all kinda sudden don't ya think? You're just gonna hire me?"

"I'm not saying that you have to do this. I thought you might like to. I'm giving you the chance to make a few decisions in the biggest campaign Illinois has seen in years. You're not gonna do that as an intern or a page." He waited for a response until he realized that there would be none. "You're right; this is sudden. This is now. Now's the time to decide if you're gonna be a bullshitter or a bullfighter. Think about it. Call me tomorrow."

"If you had so much going for you, you wouldn't be calling me."

"I never said that I had a whole lot going for me. I need help. I need you, and I need a lot of volunteers."

"I'll know for sure by tomorrow," I said, instead of being straight with him about not wanting to do it.

I thought about it, mainly because he did say that he would pay me. However, I was sure that he wanted me in Chicago immediately, which made me panic. If I left, my chances with Ilo that summer dwindled to the point where there was no hope that I could see. The problem was that I saw her as someone to be won, and I didn't think that I could compete from Chicago. (I was secretly willing to follow her to Ann Arbor for her senior year.) I might have been wrong to approach the possible relationship so dramatically, but in the first stages of love, jealousy, envy, possession, and even delusions of grandeur come naturally, and no one could tell me to curb those feelings or to approach the situation differently. I believed I could choose the one who seemed perfect, and from there I would fight to make love happen. I believed this even when the person with whom I would gladly spend the rest of my life may or may not have loved me in return. So in my state of confusion, which was not self-inflicted but a simple consequence of respecting possibilities more than reality, I decided not to go to Chicago. I would stay and make Ilo love me, or I would die in Battle Creek or Ann Arbor trying.

Chapter 21

I didn't realize that I had fallen asleep in the chair with the television on until around 3:00 a.m. When the phone rang, rousing me out of a strange dream with vivid red, yellow and green colors, sunshine warmth, and aromas more relaxing than vanilla. I lay in a white vinyl recliner waving to Ilo and Mandy, who sunbathed on an anchored raft in the middle of a secluded lake, surrounded by thick foliage from a forest of old oaks and dogwoods. It wasn't unlike the lake in which Ilo and I spent the night.

"Hello," I said with my voice subdued by sugary phlegm.

"Hi, this is Magic Johnson; me and my team, Magic Johnson's All Stars, are broke down on I-94 outside of Albion, and we're wondering if you could give us a lift to Branson, Missouri."

"Hey, Charlie, don't mess with Magic." I looked at the clock. "Just getting back from the bar, are we?"

"Yeah, I got a job playin' Buffet songs for the tourists in the lounge at Howard Johnson's."

"What? I thought you'd never play in front of a crowd. You said it's for people with low self-esteem. And you never liked Buffet."

"I do now. The crowd loves it." He paused. "Hey, Mitch?"

"Yeah."

"I don't think I'm goin' to grad school. I think I'm just gonna perform for a while."

I had the impulse to try to talk him out of that, but it wasn't the time. "I heard you're in the Wisconsin Dells."

"Yup."

"With Keely"

"Yup yup."

"Have you seen the Cliff House yet?"

"No." He seemed to think for a moment. "And I don't think we will. Keely's parents aren't too happy that I'm crashing here. They're comin' tomorrow."

"Oh shit, Charlie."

"Oh, don't worry. We got two tickets to Key Largo for tomorrow morning... We're not going though. We were going to, but then she's been feeling guilty all day, so I told her we should just stay and face it. The thing is," he lowered his tone to almost a whisper, "I think we're getting to like each other, a lot, you know what I mean? So I figure we should just stay and hold our ground on this one. I don't wanna look like a gigolo, ya know?"

"I don't think anyone's gonna mistake you for a gigolo, Charlie. I'm pretty sure you're safe from that nasty preconception. I mean, you don't own a comb or a brush, and you bathe in the Kalamazoo River, dude."

"Shut up. I'm serious."

"Then you were asking for it." I paused. "You know, Neil's gone."

"No shit?"

"Mandy dumped his sorry ass."

"That's a new one. How was he?"

"I dunno. Drunk. Hungover."

"Ah, that won't last more than three days. Where'd he go?"

"Arlington, to live with his uncle for a few weeks."

"Rough life. So your grand summer plan is pretty much shot to hell, huh? Of course, I guess I didn't help much."

"Ah, it was shot when I met Ilo at Brad's reception."

"I guess I noticed that, but it didn't seem to slow you down much. I mean, it seemed like you two had something going on, but she had that boyfriend, and I thought it was just a summer thing, ya know, part of the grand plan."

"I did too, but I got all serious Saturday, and you know what happens: you get in bar fights, and pass out underneath bedroom windows, and parents come to Wisconsin to beat your ass."

He laughed. "I thought you decided to go to that rally."

"I did. And I came back. Mandy gave me the name of a bar for Neil's stockpile of nudies."

He laughed out loud and changed the subject: "A bar fight, huh? Mitchell Moon in a bar fight. I'm sorry I missed that. So you must have found her boyfriend?"

"I was lookin' for her."

"She'll know your heart was in the right place."

"Well, people tend to think you're stupid when your heart's the only thing in the right place."

"So have ya heard from Dreisbach?" He changed the subject again.

"He asked me to come down there."

"Oh ya gotta go, Mitch. You've always wanted to be a part of that, ya know? Plus, maybe it could lead to a real job in Washington. You and Neil could be in Washington together, just like you guys always dreamed about."

"Yeah, I'm not goin'."

"What? Are you crazy?" He paused. "Oh yeah, bar fight, bedroom window. Well, shit, man; I got your back. Keely gets along with Ilo; I'll have her talk to her. We'll invite her everywhere we go. I'll keep you fresh in her mind. I promise."

"So you're comin' home?"

"I don't think there's any way around it. Even if her parents see that we're serious, we still have to show good faith, ya know?"

There was a long pause.

"I'll see ya soon then."

"See ya, Mitchie."

Chapter 22

Ted called much too early the next morning. His final pitch to me was that he wanted to hire me as assistant to the campaign manager, Julie McDermott, an MBA student at Northwestern and former poly sci major at DePaul. She worked on the Democratic gubernatorial campaign in 2002. Knowing that Charlie would return, I responded with a curt no thank you. He told me to call back if I changed my mind. "But if you do, it better be within twenty-four hours. We have to move, Mitch."

I spent the day doing nothing which, yet again, I did not enjoy. I obsessed about the future without allowing my mind to consider the possibilities beyond all of the barriers. I couldn't even imagine myself outside of Battle Creek. I never considered it a sin to stay in my hometown, contributing to the community that raised me, but now that I was sure that I didn't want to leave, that maybe Ilo was only an excuse to stay, that something inherent over which I had no control would keep me there forever, I began to wonder if there were something wrong with me.

Charlie returned late that night, just after I had fallen asleep. I had the wherewithal to utter a groggy "What's up?" but I don't remember getting an answer.

PIZZA PIE AND POLITICS
HOW MITCHELL MOON LOST HIS CHILDHOOD

Late the next morning we went out for breakfast. Over pre-cooked steaks, as thin as the leather on the toes of my Rod Laver's and flavored with nothing but MSG; eggs (two sunny side up for both of us); two cups of coffee; and two large glasses of orange juice so filled with preservatives that it tasted more like marmalade (It was all delicious), I told him that we no longer had jobs, as if it mattered to him.

He laughed to discover that I would worry about such a thing. "He's doin' us a favor, ya know? Remember the summer after our sophomore year when we went to Colorado for a week without telling him, and last summer when we had the keg party in the backyard after we closed? When he fired us those times, he didn't really mean it. He knew he could get another summer out of us, but he has to replace us now. It's over. We've become his crutch during the summer, and he's ours. He's not comfortable with it anymore, and neither are Neil and I. He's trying to tell us to move on. It's the end of an era, Mitch. It just happened sooner than you expected." He paused to feed himself a bite of steak. "I'm surprised to see you take it so seriously. I mean, you never seemed upset when he fired us before, ya know?"

"But he's firing us for good this time."

"Fuck an A right it's for good. I don't know about you, but I'm ready to take some chances. Neil's got a plan, but you an' I are gonna have to do some crazy shit before we find the right jobs. Goin' to Chi town might not make sense, but you'll learn more than how to make pizza, ya know what I mean?" He paused, smushing the yolks of his eggs with his fork. "And I don't mean to sound crass, but if Ilo's not reciprocating, maybe you can find someone who will."

"I haven't given her much to reciprocate. That's the thing. It's too soon to count her out. I don't wanna be one of those guys who's so worried about career status that he moves from woman to woman, only looking for the one who kisses his ass the best."

"Well, have you called her since Sunday?"

"No. I'm being patient, dammit! Plus, we need a new beginning."

"How do you know?"

"It was implied."

He laughed. "It's Thursday, Mitch. Maybe it's about time."

"It's about time all right. It's all about time. If I go to Chicago, it's the end, not the beginning."

"See, you wanna go to Chicago. I know you, Mitch. You're afraid to succeed. You're afraid you'll turn into another one of the world's assholes. I'm right, aren't I?" He paused to take a drink of coffee. "I mean you're a dick sometimes, but you'll never be an asshole."

"I just can't help feeling stuck."

"You can't be stuck. She's either gonna want to see you again or she's not. Don't you think you should find out about that?" He took another bite of steak. "And if she wants to see you again, maybe it won't matter that much if you spend the next few months in Illinois. If she doesn't wanna see you again, and you wait too long to ask, then you just passed up on your best job prospect for no reason."

I shook my head in understanding, but I didn't think it was that easy. I assumed that she didn't want to see me again *at the time*, and that I either had to do something extraordinary or wait until she was ready to see me again, even if it took a year: chivalric code.

Shortly after we returned to the apartment, Keely called, and Charlie was off to South Haven. I pulled a chair up to the phone and stared at it, wishing I had the courage to call Ilo, because Charlie was right after all. I couldn't be stuck. However, the thought of rejection prevented me from moving or thinking. I'm not sure how long I sat there, mentally blocked, until I heard the high-pitched trill of a bird outside my window. I started to wonder what kind of a bird made that noise. Then it occurred to me that I didn't know what noises any birds make, except for owls, and geese, and ducks, of course. I sat in my apartment, sweating, worried, and ignorant while the world lived. I reached out. I dialed the number.

"Hey, Mitch, change your mind?" Ted asked before I even said hello

"Yeah… I did." My response wasn't conscious. It was as if someone had asked me a flippant question as I read the newspaper. I knew he wouldn't reject me.

After that I couldn't think of anything else to do but pack my belongings into a suitcase, a duffel bag, and four plastic storage containers. I sat in the living room chair for a long time before deciding to stay at my parents' that night. Before I left, I wrote a note to Charlie and stuck it to his Gibson. It read, "Charlie, I'm moving on to something better but not quite as good. -Mitch"

I looked into the apartment one last time and closed the door. I imagined the sound to be that of a vault's lugubrious door. That perfectly planned summer and any pretense of childhood were laid to rest inside.

On my way to my parents', I decided to call Ilo as soon as I walked in the door. I had been so focused on a new beginning that it became much easier to say goodbye. After pulling into my parents' driveway, I saw my dad (who worked in the garage) out without saying hello, and I bounded silently over my mother's legs as she weeded her flower garden. I used the phone in the kitchen to call her cell phone, but I only received her voice mail message. I tried her parents' number.

"Hello," her mom answered.

"Hi, Mrs. Velasquez. This is Mitchell Moon. I'm wondering if Ilo is in."

"No, she's not, Randall. Can I take a message for her?"

"Well, I need to speak to her. Do you know where I could reach her?"

"She said she was going to the mall."

"Okay, thank you, Mrs. Velasquez."

I hung up and walked outside to tell my mom that I would be leaving for Chicago in the morning.

"Oh, things aren't working out with Ilo?" she asked intuitively.

"I don't know. I told Dreisbach that I would come and work on his campaign. I don't know why." I hoped for some insight.

"Don't let anyone talk you into doing anything." She spoke to me without looking up from her work. "Use your best judgment, not your instincts."

"What if my instincts are my best judgment?"

"Then you're in trouble." She finally stopped scraping at the dirt. "It's easy to be confused at your age; all decisions are hard when everything seems within reach. But if you can't learn to commit to the choices you make, all your dreams will stay the same as they are today: you'll have nothing to show for them."

"All right, Mom," I agreed. "I'll be back for dinner. I'm goin' to the mall."

She looked at me with confusion and opened her mouth as if forming a question. (I hadn't said such a thing since I was seventeen.) She must have concluded that my decision about Chicago was fickle and meaningless.

I searched through every pertinent store in the conservatively sized mall, Marshall Fields, The Gap, Victoria's Secret, etc. before imagining that, at that hour, she might have stopped for a bite to eat. First, I checked the open food café to no avail. Then I poked my head through the doors of the restaurant near the mall's entrance. People in the lobby stared at me for entertainment as I searched the dining room for her. Of course, I couldn't see the whole space from that vantage, so I walked inside, slowly stepping and rubbernecking until the hostess said, "May I help you, sir?"

"I'm looking for someone. Do you mind if I just…"

"Sure, go ahead."

I wandered around until I heard someone say, "Hey, Mitch, whatcha doin'?"

I looked toward the voice to discover that the bartender knew me, though I wasn't sure who he was: someone I had met while drinking, I assumed. I threw up my right hand in greeting and stepped closer to see if anything could be clarified. He extended his hand across the bar, and over his shoulder at the far end of the bar, my eyes met Ilo's.

"Mitch! What are you doing here?" She smiled.

I walked to her.

"This is my roommate, Katie."

"Hey," I smiled.

"Hey, Mitch." She scanned me from head to toe with her eyes, looked at Ilo, and smiled.

"Hey, can I talk to you real quick outside?" I asked.

"Sure." She put down her margarita and raised her eyebrows at Katie, who, mesmerized by the purple bruise on my face, didn't notice.

I followed her to the door. She wore a short jean skirt and hot-pink flip-flops, and I watched her legs until we reached the door. I opened the door for her, and when she reached the six-foot-tall mall directory, she turned to me quickly.

"So what's up?"

"I couldn't stop thinking about you on Saturday, and I think I got a little carried away. I didn't go to Ann Arbor looking for trouble. I was looking for you."

"But you thought I was with Brian. You can't deny that." She looked into my eyes. "I broke up with him because he's been a pompous ass ever since he came back from Europe. Now he thinks I broke up with him because I was cheating on him."

My heart was utterly broken.

I said, "So what happened Friday night was your excuse to break up with him, not the reason?" I think my voice began to quiver.

"It was neither, Mitch." She looked into my eyes to see if I understood. "I don't think I can jump into a relationship with you."

"Because you're afraid that everyone will think you were cheating on him?"

"No, because of what you did. I told you that Sunday was ours. You didn't trust me."

Unconsciously, I backed away from her and looked away.

"I'm going to Chicago tomorrow."

"Oh, you're gonna work on that campaign. That's awesome."

PIZZA PIE AND POLITICS
HOW MITCHELL MOON LOST HIS CHILDHOOD

My last chance was that she would beg me to stay.

"You're gonna do great things, Mitch," she squeezed my hand.

"Maybe I'll call you when I get there."

"You can call me anytime you want." (I'll never get a hold of you, my conscience replied.) "Or, next time you're around you might just come and find me, huh?"

I hugged her. She kissed me on the lips, turned, and walked back into the restaurant. I waited for a moment and followed, but I stopped and gave the hostess a crumpled wad of bills. It was all but the last fifty dollars I had.

"This is for their next round of drinks." I pointed to Ilo as she sat down.

Chapter 23

I woke up at 7:00 the next morning and ate pancakes covered with strawberries and maple syrup. My parents gave me hugs; I threw one duffel bag into my Cavalier, and drove across town to I-94. I had good directions, but once I reached Gary, I often wandered into the traveling lane so that I could drive slowly enough to review them. Fortunately, Ted told me how to find Teresa's place by following Lakeshore, the only road I knew, as far as possible. After three hours of driving, one half hour stuck in construction and one half hour stuck in traffic on I-90, I found Larabee without much confusion. I drove down the clean, tree-lined street, determining by the house number he gave me that his house must be on the left. I slowed to about ten miles per hour when I sensed, by watching the house numbers, that I missed his house. A small van behind me honked and, out of frustration, I turned around and showed the driver my face and my middle finger. He decelerated considerably, as if he tailgated and honked just to make sure that he was still an asshole. I stopped and let him pass, staring at him as he did. I looked at the house number to my left. (I couldn't have missed it by more than three buildings, but when I looked for a place to park, I realized that the street was lined with more cars than trees, parked bumper to bumper at 11:45 on a Friday afternoon.) So I backed up slowly until I found Teresa's two-story building, one of the largest on the street, adorned with at least six windows per floor on the front, and made of stucco or possibly cement that had been painted grey. I turned on my hazards, walked up the sidewalk, which split two patches of plush blue-green grass, and rang the doorbell.

About a minute later, Teresa opened the door. I smelled the aroma of garlic bread and some sort of cheese, and I hoped that I could eat whatever I sensed.

"Well hello, Mitch," she said. "Come on in."

"Thank you." I bowed slightly and looked around upon entering. The floors of the apartment's entry and foyer were of wood, as were the kitchen and living room, as I would learn later. The floors, made of modern tongue-in-groove planks, matched the original woodwork of the home. I noticed the doors mainly, baffled to learn that someone's apartment could have so much solid wood. I remember sensing a lot of light, as if there weren't a dark area in the home, and I noticed only a minimal amount of decoration, but the dark red and purple paint of one picture in the dining room glared in a three-dimensional manner, which interested me, probably because I had only seen original paintings in museums. There was another painting to my left in the entry way, and I remember two or three ebony sculptures, and also a vase that looked like a calla lily on an antique plant stand near the kitchen's doorway. Everything else I could see from that vantage—the light fixtures, the tables, and chairs—were of glass or silver.

Ted walked to the door quickly and shook my hand. "Mitch, make yourself at home."

"Michigan kid!" Rick the reporter yelled from the round glass table in the dining room, raising a glass of wine.

"Hey there." I couldn't remember his name at the time. "Hey, Kevin," I said.

Ted looked at me with a serious demeanor, and then looked at Kevin, who merely raised his eyebrows at me. There was a third man, who looked young, possibly fresh out of college by the way he dressed: a blue pocket T, old blue jeans, and flip-flops (no socks).

"Come on in," Ted reiterated.

"I'm double parked. I can't seem to find a space."

Teresa looked at Ted and ushered me out of the door. I gave her my keys, and we drove to the end of the block and down a side street to a parking lot. I saw the fee on the sign and began to argue.

"Don't worry about it. We'll come back and get this later. There'll be spaces on the street come nine or ten."

She parked and we began a brisk walk back. We were silent until I saw her building. I had something to get off my chest before we entered.

"Why am I here?"

She looked at me with surprise. "Don't you wanna be here?"

"I don't know. Why does Ted want me here?"

"We all want you here."

"But why?"

She shook her head for a moment as we closed in on the building. I needed an answer before I entered, so I stopped. "I think you connected with him. You made a friend of him in fifteen minutes." She laughed. "I thought you were so crazy. I mean, you came up to us like you knew us, like someone insane, but you talked to us like we were the only people in the world."

We had reached the sidewalk.

"What am I supposed to do? I don't know how to help."

"Just be patient; this is everyone's first time doin' this, except for Julie." She opened the door for me.

We walked in and I sat down to the left of the one wearing flip-flops. On the table's glass top, there were dinner plates, linen napkins, silverware, and water and wine glasses in front of every chair. Rick was the only one drinking wine until I poured myself a glass. Ted looked at me with a knowing smirk as I did so.

"Mitch, this is Reggie Connelly." Ted pointed to the one I sat beside.

We nodded at each other.

"This is a nice place, Ted," I said before taking a sip of wine.

"Tell Teresa that. I just moved in."

"Hey, Teresa, Mitch says you got a nice place," Rick yelled.

"Thanks, Mitch," she yelled in return.

"Julie and P.J. must be running late, but I'm too hungry to wait any longer." Ted got up and went into the kitchen, returning with a dish full of cheesy focaccia bread and a tall, lithe bottle of olive oil.

We ate and talked about the Republican incumbent and the Democratic primary winner. Ted and Rick briefed me quite thoroughly about both: their regional strongholds, their weaknesses, their strengths, their values, in addition to the trite Republican and Democratic policies, of which I was well aware.

Over a half an hour later, the doorbell rang, and two girls entered, taking the chairs next to me.

PIZZA PIE AND POLITICS
HOW MITCHELL MOON LOST HIS CHILDHOOD

"Introductions in a second. I'm gonna go get the food," Ted said.

He and Teresa returned with two serving bowls full of noodles, carrots, sugar snap peas, grilled peppers and onions in some sort of spicy peanut sauce. We all took turns filling our plates; Rick poured himself another full glass of wine and emptied the bottle into my glass. Ted looked at him with skepticism.

"Okay, people, this is Julie, my campaign manager." Ted pointed to the green-eyed redhead next to me. "And this is Patricia Johnson (Call her P.J.), my speechwriter." P.J. had black hair with a streak of grey on the side, which was curious because of her youth. I didn't know if it was a style statement or nature. And she wore black-rimmed librarian glasses.

"Julie and P.J., this is Mitchell Moon..."

"...Michigan kid..." Rick interrupted.

"...Julie's assistant." Ted raised his voice and glared at Rick. "And this is Kevin, our fundraising manager. You both know Rick." Rick winked at them, took a sip of wine, swallowed and let out a guttural, Ahh! "This is Teresa, my wife and lawyer. And that is Reggie, our accountant. Now, as we eat, I thought you could tell us a little more about yourselves. Or a lot, we're a team now; we have to know each other."

When it was my turn, I gave the basics about my education and interest in politics, but then I nervously trailed off into an explanation of how I received a bruise on my face, extending into a soliloquy about Ilo and my reservations about being so far away from her.

"Don't worry about it, Mitch. There plenty of fish in the sea," Rick responded. "We'll go out tonight, and I'll prove it to ya." He hit the table with a fist.

Ted shook his head at Rick. Julie and P.J. told their stories. P.J., who had just lost a press-release-writing job at Boeing, received her B.A. in English from DePaul about three years prior.

"Hey," Rick interjected as soon as P.J. finished. "We gotta get Mitch out in public with that shiner. That'd help our rebel image to no end."

"He looks like he got his ass kicked," Ted retorted.

"It's a distinguishing characteristic. It's something that'll stick in the voters' minds when they're in the booth trying to decide."

"I'm not sure if that's the direction I want to follow yet...which brings me to the first thing I want to discuss, yet again at Mitch's expense: What about the 'Get off my balls' mantra. I thought I could put it to rest on Saturday, but it didn't happen. Our supporters seem to like it. However I'm wondering how much you all like it."

"We should embrace it," Rick answered.

"I don't like it," I replied. "Doesn't it kind of exclude certain people? I mean, Ted can't win this on the votes of the 18- to 34-year-olds who've been at those rallies."

"What do your stats say, Julie?"

"It's negligibly possible."

"I don't like it either," Teresa stated. "It's gender exclusive."

"Julie?" Ted asked.

"Of course it isn't politically correct," she answered. "But it is a slogan that the people have made for us, and it embodies the campaign well."

"We need to test the public's opinion," Ted suggested. "So, as soon as we can get some more volunteers, I need some people out there asking questions about this."

"I don't know about that," I argued. Everyone looked at me and then at Ted, as if they wondered what method he would use to put me in my place. He listened. "It's time consuming for one. Plus, if you're out there asking, people are gonna realize that you're not confident in supporting their statement. That goes against your own theme."

Rick nodded his head vehemently. "That's what I was gonna say."

"I say, don't worry about it; if it becomes a real mantra for the campaign, so be it," I suggested.

"All right then, who's in favor of that?" Ted asked.

Julie laughed. "Well, it's not for a committee to decide on this. The fact is that 'Get the F off my... *balls*' is going to stick. We need to forget about it and move on."

I liked her.

"Okay, let's move on," Ted said with a mouth full of noodles. "We've got plenty of volunteers in Chicago; I hope; we'll find out tomorrow. But, as Julie and I have discussed, we need a network of volunteers in other parts of the state. Julie."

"One of us," she looked at me, "is going to have to travel. We need to get the volunteers we have here to venture into other parts of the state for two reasons: number one, to register new voters; number two, to recruit a few people at each location to do some work for us. Mitch will focus on college campuses, and we may need to post fliers to advertise our web site. Since we're on the ballot, students can use their experience with us to fulfill public service, lifelong learning, and honors credit obligations. We need to stress that, Mitch."

"What's gonna happen, Mitch," Ted interjected, "is that I'm going to speak at all of the schools you and your team visit. You'll send two people, before my speaking dates, to hand out literature and register voters, and they'll do the same thing the day after I leave. So you can see the need for a strict schedule."

I nodded eagerly, though I don't think I saw what he wanted me to see at that time.

"We should give them something for registering," Rick added.

"Like what?" Ted asked.

"Like a CD or a T-shirt, or shot glass," I offered foolishly.

"Which is cheapest and quickest, Kevin?" Ted asked.

"T-shirts aren't the cheapest, but they are the most effective if people wear them."

"All right, Mitch. That's job number two for you," Ted pointed at me. "Tomorrow morning I want a campaign T-shirt design that kids your age will wear," he paused. "A rough sketch will be fine."

Julie said, "We need to talk to some community groups in Chicago, Rockford, Peoria, Champagne, Bloomington, Marion, Joliet, Kankakee, De Kalb, East St. Louis, etcetera," she slowly looked up from her notes, "in order to set up more speaking engagements for Ted. This campaign can certainly appeal to older voters too."

"Do it," Ted said and looked around for a minute. "Okay, if you're bleary about your duties, we'll clear it up at the office. Other than that, any questions?"

Rick said, "My glass is empty, do you have any more…"

"…No time," Ted answered.

"Where am I gonna sleep?" I asked seriously.

Everyone laughed viscerally.

"Sleep's not on the agenda," Ted joked. "No, I've already checked you, Julie and P.J. into the Palmer House Hilton…until *Friday*," he stressed. "You'll be on the road after that, Mitch."

He helped Teresa clear the table, as the rest of us made small talk. We began to think of silly ideas for the T-shirts such as, "My deadbeat parents finally registered to vote, and all I got was this cheap T-shirt" and "4 out of 5 homeless people recommend Dreisbach for Congress."

"Okay," Ted reentered the room. "Let's meet in the office at," he looked at his watch, "three-thirty. Mitch, you can ride with us."

Ted, Teresa, and I rode in Teresa's Volvo, first to my car to move it closer to Teresa's house and to retrieve my bag, then to Monroe Street. It didn't seem like more than two or three stops and turns until we were flanked by concrete buildings and ambushed by mobs of pulsing traffic. And only minutes passed until we escaped into the cavernous parking garage. We parked, crossed the street, and entered the revolving door of an old office building that must have been more than half vacant, judging from the sparsely filled directory above the security desk. The lobby smelled of cigarette-smoke and ink, and it reminded me of a school building with its tile floors, and green fabric wallpaper from the '70s that covered the concrete walls halfway up to the twenty-foot ceiling. We rode the elevator to the seventh floor and entered the office at the third door on the right.

The office was filled with three long, grey metal tables (the tops of which were covered with a synthetic material painted with multi-colored whisks that resembled dog hair) and metal chairs padded with fake grey leather. Two of these tables were lined with four or five dingy and well-used computer monitors, which looked like old thirteen-inch televisions, and keyboards. In the four corners were four desks that resembled the tables. One of these, in the corner next to the door, was to be mine. The third table, lined with telephones, faced the window.

I walked around this table and looked onto the street. I saw the entrance of the Palmer House across the way. Porters wearing green shirts and caps hailed taxis and unloaded luggage from cars parked awkwardly parallel. Things looked chaotic on a Friday afternoon.

The office, however, was quite silent, so I opened one of the windows to let in the rhythms of the city. Ted showed me my desk. It contained a computer, a printer, and a sleek, black cordless phone. I sat in the metal chair with worn grey padding, and he told me that I wouldn't be spending too much time there in the ensuing weeks. Students would be returning to colleges soon, and he needed me to travel to them. He pulled a cell phone from his messenger bag and displayed it to me.

"This is yours," he said, handing it to me.

It sat in my hand as if it were a dog turd. I looked at it with much trepidation.

"Here, let me show you how to use it."

He went over the basics and told me to try it.

"Call Julie," he suggested and spoke the numbers to me slowly.

"Hello," she said.

"Hey, Julie, this is Mitch. Where are you?"

PIZZA PIE AND POLITICS
HOW MITCHELL MOON LOST HIS CHILDHOOD

"What?"

"I said where are you?"

"I can't hear you."

I hung up, shook my head, and pursed my lips in disgust.

Ted handed me his business card, along with Julie's.

"Don't lose these, and don't go anywhere without that phone, and answer it when it rings."

After a few minutes, Julie and P.J. came in, followed by Kevin, Rick, and Reggie.

"Okay, let's get to work," Ted said without warning.

He, Teresa, and Kevin sat down with Reggie, the accountant, at the desk in the corner. I watched P.J. sit down at her desk, against the same wall as mine. She pulled some papers from her briefcase, turned on her computer, and began to type frantically.

"Let's sit down over here," Julie suggested to me, as we walked to the long table in front of the windows. She explained to me that she didn't have any idea of how many volunteers would show up the next morning, how many would show up again on Tuesday, or what responsibilities each was capable of doing well. But she and Ted did have a plan for me. I would be in charge of a group who would travel first to some suburbs and local colleges, then to the more rural colleges, and maybe to some of the more industrial towns and cities. We went to my desk, and she typed in a URL on my keyboard, showing me a map to give me an example of how to accomplish this.

We went over these things for almost an hour and a half, until Julie said that we should check into our rooms across the street.

The porter knocked at my door, brought my bags inside, and waited until I gave him a tip. I moved them to the bedside and reached into my duffel bag in order to retrieve my fingernail clippers. I remembered the mini bar most fondly from our stay in July. I crouched at it and used them to sever the black zip tie that locked the cabinet. I withdrew a tiny bottle of Southern Comfort, thought again and reached for a Heineken. I opened it, drank most of it in one pull, and reached for another, along with some expensive-looking wafers. I munched and washed down the remains with my second beer. Then I located the remote control on the nightstand, lay back against the headboard, and began to scan the channels, squeezing the device as if only to relieve stress.

When my attention span began to broaden slightly, I decided to stop on a sports channel. I began to think of the T-shirt and the fact that Ted needed people to tone down my stupid comment. I wanted to accomplish this. Even though on the surface it's just a silly word, I was still embarrassed about it, because of the context of its origin. Every time I heard it, I was reminded of how out of control I could be. However, once I stopped thinking of myself, I began to realize how easily my comment was turned into positive publicity for Ted's campaign. I understood that many people, like bats, make conclusions based only on what they hear, abstractions that shift and turn depending on who is making the noise.

This led to my simple conclusion that the T-shirts should read "Get off my balls." I understood the risk of alienating female voters, which could have been a contradiction since Ted's policy exuded opportunity and respect for those who would give life to the next generation of Americans. But I figured that it was a good compromise: fuck is aggressive; balls are silly, and if a female voter wore the shirt, it would add an extra touch of irony to the campaign, which would suit the average American's attitude toward politics.

I immediately associated the new slogan with "Don't tread on me" and decided that the shirts should contain an image of a rattlesnake with a red, white, and blue tail.

I turned off the lights and the TV and commenced to shifting here and there over the surface of the bed, trying to get comfortable, trying to overcome a sense of excitement that I hadn't felt since the hours before my commencement ceremony, just three and a half months earlier.

In the morning I awoke to a triple knock on my door. I looked at the clock, which read 6:38, and regretted the fact that I had forgotten to hang the Do Not Disturb card on my door handle. I lay there sure that the cleaning lady would go away. Of course, there were more knocks, and I heard Julie's voice telling me that it was time to get up.

"Morning." I opened the door.

"Good morning, Mitch." She looked me up and down. I realized that she might have mistakenly thought that it was out of the ordinary for me to sleep with my clothes on, but my excuse, "Oh, I do it all the time," might have been worse than the assumption, so I quickly stepped aside and let her enter.

She wore purple pajama bottoms, white fuzzy slippers and a purple tank top. I was charmed that she let me see her in her pajamas, especially since she had gained my respect so thoroughly the day before.

"So, do you want to share some breakfast?" She sat down on my bed.

We decided that two complete breakfasts would be too expensive and time consuming, so I ordered one American-style breakfast with a carafe of orange juice and began to brew some coffee in the machine on top of the mini bar.

"I didn't come to give you orders, but why don't you get ready for the day while we wait." She looked at my eye. "I think it would be a good idea if I put some make-up on that bruise. We don't want to scare away any volunteers today."

I thought for a moment. "Well, it's hot; don't you think I might sweat it off?" I liked Rick's idea better than wearing make-up.

She shook her head no. "You look pretty shady."

I took a shower and dressed in a formal blue shirt, minus a tie, and one of my three pair of slacks, which were grey. Both of these articles were so wrinkled that I might as well have picked them out of a hamper. There was an ironing board in the closet, but Julie, much to my relief, didn't make mention of it. Instead, we split all of the food, even the orange marmalade for the toast, and while I took the tray outside, she retrieved a compact from her room.

I placed the desk chair in front of the mirror in the bathroom where Julie thought the light was most true. She held my right cheek to steady my head and began to apply the façade. Very instinctively I took quick glances down her shirt, noticing the tops of her breasts and just a tinge of pink skin. After a minute or two, the bruise was not unnoticeable, but the obvious fact that I had been in a fight recently was obscured. I touched it.

"No, Mitch; don't touch it," she said, applying more where I laid my fingertips. "Now leave it."

"Everyone's gonna know I'm wearing make-up."

"Only in this light. I can cover the rest of your face if you want."

"No, we'll go with this." I touched my face again.

"Ugh! Mitch, stop touching your face."

She dabbed again and stood upright. "Well, I guess I better get ready. Wait for me?"

I nodded.

After she left I looked into the mirror for a long time, slightly turning my face from side to side. My stomach turned with anxiety. I hadn't had to worry about maintaining my appearance since high school, but even then I didn't have to worry about wearing make-up, not even when my face looked like a cranberry marsh.

For about fifteen minutes, I watched part of a rerun of Sports Center that I had seen the night before, checked the TV menu to see what was served for lunch that day, drooled as if I hadn't just eaten breakfast, and turned off the

TV, turned off the lamp beside my bed, closed my door, and instinctively tested the handle to make sure it was locked, even though it locked automatically. I paced up and down the hall, looking into pictures of people in Victorian garb picnicking in a park, men in red jackets fox hunting on horseback, and a tree growing in moss-covered soil beside a small stream until I heard Julie's door open.

She poked her head out to make sure I was there, and when she saw me, she smiled and pulled the door shut. She wore a white short-sleeved sweater with a maroon stripe around the bust, very tight black slacks, and black high heels with no stockings. I noticed she had painted her toenails red. Her glasses and tightly pulled hair made her look serious, but I had never had a boss who applied make-up to my face, nor had I seen one in her pajamas, so I laughed inside feeling closer to her than a subordinate should. For some reason I had the urge to carry her to the elevator. I didn't want her feet to touch the ground. This romantic impulse could have been the result of the way she touched my face, or maybe it was the previous night's beer disturbing my morning judgment once again.

Instead of carrying her, we walked shoulder to shoulder silently and businesslike. I had to force myself to believe that none of this was sexual; she wanted to rid me of a black eye that might smudge her career. I realized, as we walked through the ballroom, that because I was her assistant, she was obligated to take me seriously. That suddenly made me less inspired. Consequently, I began to wonder what Ilo was doing at that very moment. Probably lying in bed with her beautiful brown legs curled toward her perfect bottom, I thought, as if I had to be thinking of one girl or another all the time in order to feel alive.

As we stepped into the street in approach to the office building, I began to get nervous out of a sort of fear to perform. In the seconds, approximately, that we remained outdoors, I sweated through my shirt and, in turn, moved each elbow aside to notice significant wet spots underneath each armpit.

"I'm sweating," I told Julie as we rode the elevator up to the office, and I lifted up my arms to show her.

"Don't worry about it. It looks like you've been working."

"But..." I gestured toward my face.

She shook her head and gently pushed my hand away from my eye. "How would you feel if I or Ted walked around town with a black eye?"

I didn't say anything as the elevator doors opened.

"Don't take this the wrong way, but you're not a sophomore in college anymore; you can't wear your wounds like badges. Besides that, I don't know how you see yourself, but on first impression people think you're good inside. That's golden in politics. Furthermore, when people hear you're from Battle Creek, they think of idyllic villages where Tony the Tiger comes out every morning, with Toucan Sam on his shoulder, and spreads sunshine and rainbows across the sky. We cannot have you running around with the imprint of someone's fist on your face."

She looked at me as I waited for her to exit the elevator, and then she walked. I followed her with a little more confidence than I had before I met her.

The aroma of scalding coffee pervaded the office, overpowering the ink, cigarette smoke, and musty carpet smell of the day before. P.J., already hard at work, turned to see who arrived, and Ted was talking on his cell phone and looking out the window. He might have watched us cross the street. As usual he wore jeans, blue this time, and the usual black cowboy boots. He had rolled the sleeves of his black dress shirt in a careless way, and he looked at his watch three quick times in a row as if his vision were deteriorating. I knew a lot depended on a certain amount of volunteers showing up within a half an hour, and I guessed that he was nervous.

Teresa sat at Reggie's desk working on some sort of spreadsheet, as if preparing something for him when he finally arrived at his station. Julie sat down at her desk and booted her computer, and I made for the long table, on the middle of which sat the coffee maker and Styrofoam cups.

"Julie, you wanna cup?" I asked.

She glanced my way.

"Julie, come and tell me what you think of these," P.J. said.

I poured her a cup anyway.

"Hey, Mitch," Ted said as he turned from the window.

I smirked and raised my eyebrows in greeting.

"Hey, Mitch, good morning!" Teresa said ebulliently.

"Morning!" I tried to match her enthusiasm. "How many do you think will show?" I leaned against the table, giving away the naïve assumption that I didn't think I had much to do that day.

"I have no idea, Mitch," she replied in a singsong voice. "I've never done this before."

"Hey, Ted, I've got an idea for those T-shirts," I said with a confidence that made me feel as though I had breached a rule of conversation.

"Awesome," he turned slightly away from the window. "You can tell us

173

about it at the meeting tonight."

I walked over to P.J.'s station, handed Julie her cup of coffee and handed P.J. the cup I had poured for myself.

"Mitch, what are you doing?" Julie asked.

I shrugged.

"Well, you should be seeing this too."

I pushed my chair over to P.J.'s desk so that Julie and I could sit on either side of her. The new web site had been organized by political topics as internal links, along with one to an online voter registration page, which was actually the key because the stacks upon stacks of blue and black flyers under and beside P.J.'s desk and along the far wall simply read "Register to Vote," followed by the page's URL.

I checked the time on the computer screen, which read 7:47. P.J. and Julie discussed improvements to the content of the pages, which were written in a very direct style, each short paragraph began with a question that was answered as thoroughly as possible in four or five very lively and rhythmic sentences. The visuals on each page featured very good-looking young women, striking inquisitive poses as if they asked the questions listed, and svelte young men who did the same. I thought they all probably worked for Kevin. As I listened intently, I noticed that Ted had not stopped pacing as seven minutes passed since I last looked at the clock. I watched him for a moment, and then I studied Julie's face. I tried to use it to inspire some focus and commitment inside myself, but nothing was there.

After my meditation I happened to glance toward the doorway to spot two mousy-looking girls standing there, as if waiting for a table at a restaurant.

"Hi," I said too loudly. My colleagues whipped their heads toward the door.

"Come in; come in," Ted said walking briskly across the room with his arm extended to shake their hands. Relief exuded from his pores in a volume that could almost be heard.

The girls looked uncertain and young enough to make me wonder if their parents knew where they were, and they spoke in soft voices as if afraid to be heard. Their faces turned red as we asked them questions like where do you go to school? How did you hear about us? Are you ready to get started? until a few more arrivals took the heat off from them.

We all greeted the newcomers as kindly as possible, trying not to size them up just yet as first impressions mean nothing when working with people who donate their time, and we went to our stations and waited as Ted showed them what each of us was doing (or was supposed to be doing in my case).

PIZZA PIE AND POLITICS
HOW MITCHELL MOON LOST HIS CHILDHOOD

More wandered in as complacent as the first five or six until we had almost fifteen by ten after eight.

At that point Ted called our attention to himself as he took a position in front of the row of windows. The volunteers sat at the long table and miscellaneous folding chairs that Ted had placed around the room as needed. After introducing us and concisely explaining the overall philosophy of his campaign, he asked who was willing to travel the suburbs for at least a week. Since most of our help consisted of college students, that is all he could ask. Only one boy raised his hand. We laughed despite the fact that it presented a huge obstacle. Instead of looking worried, he explained the roles available to them in Chicago and asked who would like to work the phones and answer e-mail in the office and who would like to do some footwork in the city. Most chose to do footwork in the city and shifted themselves and chairs toward Julie's desk. Three chose to stay in the office; this included the two girls who arrived first. My handful of volunteers and I shook hands, and we stood by my desk while Julie seemed to pull a small group aside. She talked to them for a few minutes, and they moved our way.

Ted followed them to my desk with some chairs, and I began to admit to my five volunteers that I only had a plan, I would never pretend to know how it would develop, and that I thought we had a chance to begin a political movement if we all honestly reached out to as many people as possible. This was a total romance, but it seemed to get their attention.

I brought up a map of Illinois that contained stars of colleges and universities with their names and their towns above and below them, and then I asked them which direction they would like to take. I received blank stares until one of them, hiding his eyes beneath the crescent-shaped brim of a baseball cap, told me that he wanted to head toward the Urbana-Champagne area. Then all of them decided that they would go to Champagne. I said okay, because of course we would make it to Champagne sooner or later. I thought that I made it clear that we would cover the suburbs first, but their enthusiasm began to make me consider the possibility that I had not been clear at all.

When one of them whispered that they were going to party with the "Get the fuck off my balls dude," I began to sweat, my head throbbed, and my face flushed with anxiety. My solution was to pull a car salesman trick by claiming that before the trip was final, I must first check with Ted.

I approached Ted, who, with calculator in hand, was counting the stacks of flyers and registration cards that lined the back wall. I tapped him on the shoulder and whispered, "I think I just screwed up."

"How's that?" he didn't look at me.

"They think we're going to party in Champagne tonight."

"Tell them no."

"They think I said yes." I paused as he shifted his eyes nervously. "Could you just shake your head no to me and then look at them and shake your head no?"

He looked me in the eyes, shook his head no, and continued counting the flyers.

I walked back to my desk, sat down and said, "Uh, no, we're gonna cover the suburbs first. We won't make it to Champagne until this weekend." They were not impressed. "Nobody's there now anyways, guys."

Two volunteers walked out on me at that moment, and I very apologetically told the other three that we would definitely have a good time in Champagne on *Friday*. This was my first half hour on the job in politics.

After I explained, more accurately, the actual plan and the fact that we would be distributing information and registering voters before classes started, Teresa brought stacks of flyers, fact sheets, and a Sterilite box in which to store them. She gave me the keys to her Volvo station wagon, showed me, on a map, a couple of key neighborhoods in Elmhurst, and wrote directions to Elmhurst on a sheet of paper. I printed a map of the city; the four of us made our way to the parking garage, piled into the vehicle with our papers stored inside the plastic box, which barely fit behind the back seat, and I found Elmhurst with much assistance from the map and the young lady, Tabby, who sat in the passenger seat.

We did some cold calling until around 12:00, when I decided that we should hand out information in the downtown area during lunchtime, and then we had lunch at the mall at around 2:00 and did some campaigning there. We went back to the neighborhoods and beat the streets until 8:00, our predetermined time to meet at Teresa's car. As I drove back to Chicago, I really thought we should have done something to get to know each other better, but we decided to work opposite streets all day, only sharing names and small talk during lunch. I asked if anyone wanted to get some pizza after our 8:30 meeting; no one seemed interested, so we picked up some fast food on our way back.

I parked Teresa's car on the street, very close to the entrance of the office building, and retrieved the empty box from behind the seat. We rode the elevator up to the office and seated ourselves in the same chairs we had used near my desk in the morning. We were the last to arrive, naturally since we were the travelers, and everyone seemed very interested in how everything went. I showed my reply by picking up the empty box, taking off the top, turning it upside down and shaking it.

"No one in Elmhurst told you to get off their property?" Ted asked.

"Not in so many words, no," I answered as everyone laughed. "They were very polite about their reservations toward your party. Of course, we did leave several fact sheets underneath windshield wipers, and we did a lot of running away before anyone noticed, but that's normal isn't it?"

"I have no idea," replied Ted, as everyone chuckled.

He reiterated his thanks and our purpose for being there and asked everyone to return at 10:00 the next morning, later because we would have to work later, and to consider recruiting anyone they knew to volunteer, and our teams sporadically left the office. I noticed that members of Julie's crew were much less reluctant to leave than mine, a handful of them talking to her for at least twenty minutes as if they had known her like a big sister. As soon as everyone left, Ted sat us down to take care of a few matters of business, the first being how we would find more people to travel.

Julie said that she would go to the chair of her old department at Northwestern in the morning to see if she could gather a few poly sci students. Secondly, he mentioned that I had an idea for the T-shirts, and I described it. Julie and Teresa had strong reservations about it, but Reggie liked it. P.J. withheld her opinion until Julie and Teresa finished explaining the ways that it would further offend people who would be on the fence concerning their votes in November. However, she supported my idea with a rebuttal that included the fact that it was a simple idea, therefore less expensive; it was a design that people would actually wear; and it did embrace the almost unconsciously collective attitude of almost everyone in America; What she said certainly beat the pants off from my desperate rebuttal, which was to be, "The cock is offensive to people, not the balls." Ted made a motion for P.J. and me to create the design immediately and to get it to the screen printer Kevin had contracted Monday morning.

P.J. and I began to work. Basically, P.J. who as it turned out, had artistic talent as well as writing proficiency, began to draw the design on her computer, asking me every minute or so if that's what I had in mind. Reggie, Ted, and Teresa left, and Julie stayed for a while to work on something. She finished well before P.J. had finished drawing and scanning the design that matched my imagination, walked over, and sat down. She put her hand on my knee and watched P.J. for a moment, and then she asked me if I would go to the campus with her in the morning. I agreed. She touched my face and mentioned that, besides a little bit of purple showing through, the make-up worked well.

"No drinking tonight, Mitch," she said as she left the office. "I saw those Heineken bottles on your nightstand."

I threw up my left hand to let her know that what she said had reached my ears.

Chapter 24

P.J. and I walked across the street, into the Palmer, through the Great Hall to which I could not help but pay tribute by cocking my head back as far as it would go to take in its decorum every time I passed through, and to the elevators. We stopped at her door and said goodbye as she ran her card key through the lock. As I stepped toward my room, I heard the latch release, but I didn't hear the door open. I looked back.

"How are you?" she asked looking straight into my eyes.

"I'm great. I mean it's…ah…nice to be a part of all of this. You know, I never really knew what really went on. I'm learning a lot." Being an inexperienced liar, I spit every word out as if they were rotten Brussels sprouts.

"No, I mean how do you feel? Things didn't go so well at first," she coaxed.

I nodded and looked at my shoes.

"You did well today. I…um…shouldn't say this, but we were afraid Ted was going to fire you."

"What do you mean?" My face must have been red from anger.

"He was pretty mad at you when you left this morning."

I shrugged.

"And we can tell that you don't wanna be here."

I raised my eyebrows and shifted my eyes back and forth as if wondering where they got that idea.

"You don't even act like you wanna be here."

I looked down, pulled my card key out of my pocket and said, "Thanks for noticing." I walked to my room as quickly as possible in case I lost my temper.

Once inside, I realized that I was shaking, mainly because she was right. I didn't want to be there, and my stoic nature prevented me from even attempting to act as though I did. I really didn't want to be wandering around the suburbs pushing flyers as much as I wanted to party with all of the college kids. Of course, my response to this revelation was to immediately check the mini bar. I got on my knees and peered in to see that the four I drank the night before had been replaced, and for some strange reason, this gave me the incentive to drink eight that night. After the sixth lonely twelve ounces, I became too full of myself and decided to call the apartment, sure that Charlie would love to talk to me no matter what time it was. The phone rang several times before Charlie picked up.

"Charlie!"

"Ah shit! Hey, Mitch." I heard his voice muffle as he told someone that it was just I.

"What's up, buddy?"

"Not a whole lot. What's up with you?"

"I'm just drinkin' some beers outta the mini bar. What's with you?"

"Well, Mitch, we fell asleep in front of the TV."

"What were you watchin'?"

"We didn't quite make it through *Bird*."

"You know what happens don't you?"

"Yeah, it's not the first…"

"…His sax turns into a beautiful woman, and they live happily ever after in a land where nobody expects him to do the same thing twice, and every night people gather outside their window to hear them making…"

"…Ah, c'mon, Mitch. You got the wrong number. You need to save that shit for Ilo."

"Nah, it's late and I ah…if every day's like today, I guess I won't be seeing her until the middle of November."

"See, if you can't just pick up the phone and call her by now, you've got a problem, my friend."

"I don't think she'd be too impressed to know I'm on number seven right now."

"Ah, I see. Well, you should call her tomorrow, dude. Today she asked me if you're still going to be able to make it to the wedding."

"You...talked to her?"

"Yeah."

"Where?" I was extremely jealous, so much so that my face burned from the inside out.

"At Drew's."

"What? You gotta be kidding me. You weren't working there?"

"Yeah, well it's just until school starts."

I said nothing for a long moment as my jealously turned to rage. I covered the phone and hit the wall twice, shaking the picture above the bed and creating a wide and increasingly crimson scrape across my index, middle, and ring fingers. I wanted to hang up, call Drew and abuse him for letting Charlie work there after telling me not to come back. I was strangely angry with Charlie, too, for working there without me and for being able to see Ilo.

"Mitch? Mitch? What's wrong? It's late, and I..."

"I thought you said you weren't going to grad school," I said in a vibrato that hinted at my frustration.

No answer.

"What? Did you and Keely break up?"

"No! She's right here beside me." His tone became serious. "It's just that her parents have some suspicions about me and their money, so..."

"...Ah shit! I get it; never mind, man." I paused and gathered more composure. "Hey, have you talked to Neil?"

"No, Mandy has though."

"No shit?"

"Like every damn day, dude. And she's over here all the time, even when Keely's not here.

"She doesn't have anyplace to go."

"*She* broke up with *him*."

"I'm sure she didn't want it to end that way though."

"You're stickin' up for her again. I wanna know what happened between you two when I was in Wisconsin. It's like..."

Someone knocked sharply on my door, and I carelessly threw the phone onto the bed. I opened the door to see Julie's drowsy face.

"Why were you pounding on my wall?"

I looked down at my bloody knuckles. "Um, news from home," I pointed at the phone on the bed.

She jerked her head away from me slightly and made a face, as if she could actually see toxic fumes exuding from my nostrils, ears, and mouth.

"Oh! You're not coming with me to Northwestern tomorrow. And, as you'll be happy to hear, you can just forget about the make-up."

I looked into her eyes and almost asked her why not, but then I remembered that I didn't care, waited for her to turn away and slowly and gently shut the door. I picked up the phone again, only to hear a soberingly negative dial tone, instead of the voice of my best friend.

After a wake-up call woke me at 8:00, I ate some shortbread and guzzled a bottle of water from the mini bar and lay down again, hoping five more minutes with my eyes shut would clear my groggy head. I lifted it and looked at my knuckles; the wounds had scabbed along the edges, leaving slimy red skin exposed. I decided that they only thing that would sober me up was to get onto my feet and stay on my feet for the rest of the day.

In the bathroom mirror, I saw that all of Julie's make-up had dissolved or rubbed away. The bruise near my eye still bloomed, but the swelling was completely gone and with it some of the purple coloration, maybe just enough, I thought, so that it wouldn't capture people's curiosity so much. With some doubt about that, I hurried through my shower and grooming and hurried over to make sure Ted saw my condition as soon as possible, just in case my appearance made a difference as to where he was sending me that day. Also, I had the urge to persuade him that our time would be better spent that day registering people to vote instead of flinging flyers.

Unimpressed that I arrived an hour early, his answers were: "Your face still looks like hell. I thought that you were supposed to go with Julie today, and there is no place in Joliet to just sit and register voters. That's why the flyers have the web address which links to online registration."

I guessed that I was going to Joliet, as Teresa put a quick coat of beige chamois on my face. While she did Ted came over to my desk and briefed me with the information I was supposed to have already planned, which consisted of telling me exactly where he wanted me to spread flyers, trusting his directions to my memory as I could not write anything down while Teresa held my face.

He also expressed his suspicions about the fact that I didn't have scrapes on my knuckles the previous night in relation to the fact that I was not with Julie (which he hoped would be a learning experience for me) and the fact that P.J. and I worked late together prompted him to ask:

"You don't have a problem working with women do you?"

PIZZA PIE AND POLITICS
HOW MITCHELL MOON LOST HIS CHILDHOOD

"No!"

"I might as well make up with my father and bring the Dreisbachs into the campaign if my man has a problem working with women."

"No, look, ah…" Since he said what was on his mind, I tried to do the same. "I called Charlie last night, and I feel like I'm being forgotten or something."

He had a look of incomprehension on his face. "It's Tuesday, Mitch."

"And I already feel like I can never go back there again."

"Hey, if you gotta go, let me know now, but I'll just tell you this: you can't control what goes on in Battle Creek, even when you're in Battle Creek, so why not stay here and see how things turn out?" He moved to the windows to wait again, anxiously, for the volunteers.

All of Julie's crew came through the door, raided the coffee and cinnamon rolls and seated themselves by 9:50. Julie arrived and sent them out to their districts before my crew even showed. By the way, my "crew" now consisted of Tabby, just Tabby and me. That is the second time that I seriously considered retrieving my car and returning to Michigan. I stewed until almost 11:00, almost completely ignoring Tabby, if not for a few statements like, "I can't believe this." And "Didn't we tell them 10:00?" and "We'll give them another ten minutes." I began to take the situation very personally, convinced that they didn't come back because they didn't think much of me, and becoming confused by my inability to gracefully accept work, purpose, dreams and identity as incoherent elements that would only combine sporadically and in due time.

The gist of it is that Julie went to follow up on a list of possible volunteers. As Ted began to see my annoyance, he told me that one had to help P.J. with e-mail, but the other four, assuming they were available to us, would be assisting me and Tabby the following day and for at least the rest of the week until school started. With more courage Tabby and I began to load the flyers.

It took us a few trips to Teresa's Volvo since we ambitiously decided to fill the rear compartment and the backseat with flyers, and we drove to Joliet, stopping first at the junior college near the expressway. Though the third week of August did fall between summer and fall semesters, we found small gatherings of people near and inside of the bookstore and cafeteria where we ate lunch. And there were hundreds of corkboards throughout the building to litter with flyers, as it was to be a speaking venue for Ted in September.

Of course the fact that our car, with the bulk of our flyers inside of it, was parked two hundred yards away from the classroom buildings meant that we could only hit so many corkboards, but we did cover a lot of square yardage there. Instead of splitting up, Tabby (an entering freshman with a journalism major at the University of Chicago) and I stayed together. We posted flyers sometimes alternately, sometimes simultaneously ducking into classrooms while maintaining a rather boisterous conversation about whether or not Michael Moore supported his thesis as well as he could have, where the argumentative holes were in his new documentary and what we would have done to bolster them, if we weren't posting flyers in empty classrooms for a political party with a very uncertain future.

In the car we continued a conversation about whether or not modern conditions are really better than the human condition in medieval Europe, considering the factors of war, murder, poverty, famine and disease. (She decided to count chemical and substance addiction as diseases and concluded that we are slightly worse off. I concluded that we are much better off simply because we were able to discuss it, as we drove to the Empress Casino.)

Here we ventured in for approximately five minutes before we realized that we could staple flyers to the back of the gamblers without gaining much more attention than the occasional mosquito and before two security guards escorted us right out the doors we entered. We did remain on the sidewalk, pushing flyers and saying "Vote for Dreisbach," for approximately an hour before a young lady kindly informed us that we were, in fact, slightly interfering with her normal business proceedings.

After that we posted more flyers at a private university and hoped to empty the multitude of remaining information at the mall near the expressway. For safety and to entertain each other, we stayed together at the mall too, standing near the food court, talking about our athletic inclinations in between our "Vote for Dreisbach's" and pursuing the question she posed—What really constitutes sport: As a society of leisure, have we stretched the definition too far?

On the way back to the office, she brought up another question that seemed well rehearsed:

"If someone deeply understands the consequences of her decisions, the repercussions of her actions, and the long-term meaning of everything she does, is she not as religious as any man, even though she hasn't stepped foot in a church since she was thirteen?" Needless to say, I loved working with her, and even though the questions might seem annoying to some, it was rare to interact with someone who would freely and honestly talk to me about anything academic. Now, it all has to be pertinent and practical, as if there is

PIZZA PIE AND POLITICS
HOW MITCHELL MOON LOST HIS CHILDHOOD

no time for exploring ideas. In fact, after we had unloaded our empty boxes, I decided that I wanted to work with her only for the rest of the week, barring the possible volunteers to come.

Only Julie remained in the office by the time we returned, which must have been close to 10:00. She talked on the phone and entered some information into her PDA at the same time. When she saw us come in, she smiled, held up her left index finger and mouthed, "Wait a minute."

After she hung up, she thanked Tabby profusely and told me that I'd have three more people to help the next day.

"Tell 'em to help P.J," I joked. "Tabby and I have everything under control."

Julie hadn't eaten yet, so the three of us went for pizza down the street.

"Full for a Tuesday night," I mentioned as I sat down. I could not quite process the fact that it was only Tuesday. My routine had changed so much that I might have thought that I was a different person, a soul who knew everything about my past but had not yet lived inside my body.

When the waiter came to take our drink order, I began to ask him what was on tap, but Julie told him that I would share a carafe of water with her. This did not offend me, mainly because I only began to answer his question this way out of sheer habit. She looked at me with a smirk to see my reaction, and as if to say, "There are other purposes for taking fluids into your body." However, she eventually ordered our pizza too, which was a tremendous slight to my years of expertise.

The same waiter returned to give us our drinks and to slide a pizza onto the silver pedestal platter of our neighbor's table. The rich scent of garlic, mozzarella and red sauce, now combined with the scent of Julie and Tabby, which was a mixture of sweet perfume and stale perspiration, made me strangely ravenous. Tabby's voice, like a bell, shook me out of this morbid state.

"What are we gonna do tomorrow, Mitch?"

"We're gonna pass out flyers, and we're gonna philosophize, Tabby, just like we did today."

Julie asked what we philosophized about in the tone of a mother asking her children what they learned in school that day. After we told her exactly what we discussed, she asked me if Ilo and I ever talked about those things. Her use of the name "Ilo" struck me dumb, and I noticed that she played with the sticker around her silverware as she said this, making eye contact with only the red and white checkered table covering. My heart began to beat rapidly, and I actually became a bit confused. Stupidly, I took the literal route in answering her question, saying something like, "Uh, I guess not now that I think of it."

"Then how did you entertain yourselves if you didn't talk to each other?" she asked and smiled at Tabby.

I searched her eyes, as if searching for the professional I just saw in the office. Noticing her glance at Tabby, I took a moment to swear to myself that I would never go out alone with two women again. And again I answered the question deliberately.

"We really didn't get the chance to spend much time by ourselves," I mumbled.

"So you're in love with a girl whom you've never really gone out with?" She smiled at Tabby again and took a drink of water.

Though she chose to merely tease me for some reason, I naturally felt attacked.

"I knew you were romantic," Tabby tried to save me.

"That's one way to look at it," Julie returned. "Another way to look at it is that you have a little bit of tunnel vision because you can't understand why she won't fall down at your feet."

"That's not true," I replied.

"Then list three things that make you love her, besides the fact that you want a conquest."

I thought for a moment, shoving my straw into my glass of water several times.

"Wherever she goes she draws attention," I finally said. "She just has this charisma."

"So she's hot. You're one reason closer to proving my point."

I could have said that I loved her because she was gentle, intelligent, positive, and ambitious, but by that time, I felt too insulted to share much truth with her.

"Why are you picking on me? This is why guys never admit to this shit," I said to Tabby.

"I'm willing to bet that you haven't had sex with her yet. That's the only reason you think about her at all."

"Well, that's awful cynical of you."

"Cynicism isn't bad if it's true."

As we made a slight dent in the enormous three layers of pizza on our table, our conversation became more lighthearted. In fact, I made a successful attempt at turning the conversation toward Tabby. I certainly did not want to alienate the only volunteer who seemed to enjoy handing out flyers with me.

We walked Tabby to her car in the parking garage and returned to our rooms. As we rode the elevator, Julie persuaded me to explain exactly why I beat on the wall the night before. She seemed to understand, though she didn't say anything or look at me. However, as we walked to our rooms, she asked how many days in a row since I turned twenty-one was I able to remain sober. Of course, just before I left Battle Creek I must have been dry for close to a week, and that was my answer.

"Why don't you just stop drinking for a few days, just until your bruises and scrapes heal." She paused. "It would've been nice to bring you with me this morning." She looked into my eyes.

I averted mine, shook my head "okay" and opened my door. Of course, the first stop, before I even put my card key down, was the mini bar. To my indignation, no one had replaced the alcohol I drank the night before. Confused and somewhat embarrassed, I called the maitre d' to inquire about the cause of this.

"That was Mr. Dreisbach's request," he answered.

I hung up and, although I was stung by the fact that someone thought I had a problem, I began to head for one of the bars downstairs.

"I can't charge anything to that room sir," the bartender in the lounge said. "No, I can't accept that either," as I put my last bill (a ten) on the bar.

I decided not to try the Old Downtowner, afraid to look like a desperate drunkard. I did, however, have a bellhop begin to hail a cab until I reasoned that I didn't have enough cash for the ride. I felt small after that, and I felt trapped. I wonder if I really wanted a drink that much or if just had to prove to myself that I was still at liberty to get one whenever I wanted.

As I sat on a couch watching well-dressed people coming in from a night on the town or the dinner cruise, I accepted it and went to bed, thinking about drinking the two small bottles of Southern Comfort that remained in the mini. I had trouble sleeping though; instead, I rolled around and frothed with sweat for at least two hours until I finally dropped off.

The next morning Julie woke me early, asking me if it wasn't nice to wake up without cottonmouth and a violent stomach. She put a quick coat of make-up on my face (The purple circle had reduced itself to one dark red crescent under my eye), and we went to breakfast with P.J., who informed me that Rick, the reporter, would be tagging along with me, Tabby and the four students Julie garnered up the previous morning.

Chapter 25

Rick, who would take his own car, helped us load the Volvo and took two volunteers with him to meet us in Schaumburg, where we split up again and worked in the neighborhoods Ted told us to visit. Rick, Tabby and I stayed together for a short time, going door to door and providing our pitch to whomever would leave their front door open for long enough. After accompanying me to a few households, Rick even set out on his own to help Tabby cover a few streets while I made sure the other four guys were covering some ground.

At around 2:30 we headed to the mall to get some lunch and distribute some flyers. Rick spent much of his time wandering back and forth between our three groups of two, asking bio questions, taking sound bites about the E Party from shoppers, and notes about a day in the life of a campaign volunteer. He brought a camera, which he wore around his neck, but he didn't use this until our last stop of the day, a mall in Mt. Prospect.

Tabby and I wandered around this mall handing flyers to passersby while another group of two stood outside the main entrance; the third group stationed themselves near a few of the more trendy clothing stores. Rick took a long break, and everything went well: Tabby and I discussed the colleges we

PIZZA PIE AND POLITICS
HOW MITCHELL MOON LOST HIS CHILDHOOD

would visit on Thursday in between conversations about the fact that popular music had become merely an exercise in vanity among citizens in an affluent culture. We hypothesized that those whose only goal is to be the center of attention, whether or not they have musical talent or vision, will always gain the marketing power in America over the truly influential musicians of our generation. As we traded categorical examples of this, I saw Rick running towards us and stopping to look around until I flagged him down.

"Mitch!" he yelled with his loafers clapping against the shiny tiles as he approached me. "Come quick. Your volunteers are in a fight at the main entrance."

I ran with him and Tabby for a moment and then ran full speed toward the entrance at Rick's insistence. What I saw as I neared the wall of doors was one of my volunteers being held down by two young men; another young man held my other volunteer in a full nelson while a fourth boy gave him half-hearted body blows. I charged through the doors and threw my body at the latter three. We all fell to the ground in a tangle, and in a scramble to gain our legs, I held the "hit man" down while my bloody volunteer struggled to escape the awkward grasp of the one who had him in a full nelson.

I felt a tennis shoe connect with my forehead, which caused a severe burning sensation, followed by several swift, short punches to the back of my head. Despite that and the fact that the "hit man" was now trying to hold *me* down, I managed to stand, hoping to at least protect my back. Two of them proceeded to swing at me as the other two held my volunteers. I tried to protect my face as punches flew at me, and I began to swing as one lunged to the ground and attempted to lift me off from my feet. I shuffled away from him, kicked him quite squarely in the nose and looked for some help. All I could see were my volunteers wrestling with the other two assailants, Tabby calling for help to people who tried their best to ignore the situation, and Rick taking photos. I managed to lock up with the "hit man," preventing any more punches until finally a rather enormous cleaning lady from the food court ended the whole scuffle by yelling obscenities at us and informing everyone that our identities were being documented, not only by Rick's camera but also the video monitors outside of the front doors. It took all of us a minute to decide who would let go of whom and when, but once we compromised, the four young men walked away into the parking lot as if it were all in a day's work.

Tabby went to get the other two volunteers, and while we waited a security guard finally came out to tell us that we weren't allowed to campaign there anymore, and when we finally got into the Volvo (I write finally because we were all so disoriented that it took us about ten minutes to remember where we parked), I asked why they were attacked.

"We didn't even do anything. I think they were mad at that reporter," one replied.

"What did he do?" I paused. "What did he say?"

"I dunno, just a bunch of shit about their stereo being too loud while he was taking an interview."

"That's it? That's all it takes around here to get in a fight?"

"Well, he chased them halfway through the parking lot," the other chimed in.

"And then they chased after him?"

"No. They got out of their car, just like normal and walked up to the doors, just like they didn't see us. And then, Bam! It was on."

I turned right out of the mall's parking area and into the street traffic. As I made the turn, I realized that the scabs on my knuckles had been reopened, and blood oozed down the back of my hand. The volunteer who had been hit held to his face a wedge of napkins that Tabby found in the glove compartment. It appeared to me that his nose and his lips had taken the brunt of it all.

"Don't you want to press charges?" I looked in the rearview mirror. "We can stop at the police station?"

He shook his head no and looked out the window.

"We should go to the hospital. You might have a concussion."

He shook his head no and mentioned that he had only been hit in the face a few times before I came out.

"It looked a lot worse than that."

"They pushed us around for a while and threw our papers in the parking lot; then they grabbed us and started hitting him," the other said tersely. I knew he must have felt guilty.

As minutes passed I became infuriated with Rick, who took pictures while I thought someone was seconds away from being killed. And then I felt as though an electric switch had been tripped in my mind; I was so consumed with rage against Rick that I almost had to pull the car over before we reached the expressway. At a stoplight I had to consciously lie to myself, mentally claiming that Rick was just doing his job, and I could not jump to conclusions about anything until I calmed down. That allowed me to safely deliver everyone to the parking garage, but I remember thinking several times that he planned the whole thing.

PIZZA PIE AND POLITICS
HOW MITCHELL MOON LOST HIS CHILDHOOD

As Tabby and I came through the office doors, two hours early with a surplus of flyers, Teresa was the first to see me.

"Mitch! What happened this time?"

In all of the confusion, I forgot about the sneaker burn that nearly ran the length of my forehead. I shook my head and looked around for Ted, hoping that he wasn't there. One volunteer sat at a phone; P.J. worked at her desk, and her volunteers remained occupied at the other monitors in the room, showing no reaction to Teresa's worried voice. I couldn't focus on the point where the whole incident began, so I started with:

"Rick just stood there taking pictures while my volunteer got his ass beat."

Teresa looked wide-eyed at Tabby, who explained the whole incident from the time Rick found us to the time we asked them to file a police report. Teresa wasted no time in calling Ted, who told me and Tabby to wait there after Teresa gave me the phone. By the time he and his bodyguard arrived, about an hour later, I was cogent enough to tell him all of the facts. (He immediately called the boys and their parents.) And I stressed once more that we should have called the police. He looked at Teresa, called Rick, wandered toward the door, and brushed his hand toward the hallway, signaling that he wanted Teresa to follow him.

When they returned he told me that no police would be called. Then, he began to explain the consequences if we told anyone what really happened, and when he began to aim veiled threats toward Tabby and me, Teresa stopped him, and again they went outside. I became quietly irate. I felt that Ted's true nature had come out in his panic, and I was just as disillusioned by his loss of control when I needed him to do something as I was by the fact that he threatened us. I looked at Tabby for a long time without speaking, and she put her arm around my shoulders. Mistaking this gesture for sympathy instead of camaraderie, I said without thinking, "I don't know if I'll be here tomorrow."

She released her arm, stuffed it in her lap and brooded. As if she wasn't hurt too, I pushed further:

"I'm going back to Battle Creek tonight."

She was silent as I looked for her next reaction.

"Go ahead then," she said coldly, stood up and walked out the door.

Not more than a second later, Ted and Teresa returned.

"What the hell was that?" Ted asked.

I shrugged my shoulders and looked at him dumbly. He waited, losing his temper in correlation to my silence.

"I think you've got a problem working with women, Mitch," he finally said. "If she isn't back here tomorrow, you're not back here tomorrow."

"You know what? That's fine with me. I've got seven dollars in my pocket and no credit. I don't even know when you're supposed to pay me." I looked at him and waited. Then I stood. "I guess I'm done here then."

Teresa followed me to the elevator, saying, "You can't make this decision when you're angry, Mitch. Wait 'til tomorrow; Ted didn't mean what he said either." And as the elevator doors closed, "If you leave now you'll never know why you're here."

In my room, I packed my duffel bag quickly, removed my cell phone from my belt, left it on the desk as if it were a tether, and opened my door to leave. As I did I saw Julie entering her door. I quickly put my head down, hoping to avoid any questions about my brand-new injury. She threw her head in my direction.

"Hey, Mitch. Have you eaten?"

"Uh, yeah, I was just…"

"…On your way to the bar?" she asked in a mock interrogative tone.

"Well…"

"…You really should get some rest. You know what's in store tomorrow."

I pretended to ponder the notion and to come around to her way of thinking, said "night," shut my door and waited until I heard her TV. In the meantime, I remembered to retrieve my cell phone and check for any messages, possibly out of determination to clear the room and the whole miserable experience of anything that was mine.

There were two messages:

"Hey, Mitch, this is Ilo. Thanks for the call last night. I'm glad you called my cell; my mom would have freaked if she heard the phone ring that late. My brother just left for Iraq. Anyways, it's nice to know you were in the mood to talk to me—you seemed to have a lot to say. I wish I could get you to talk that much when you're sober. Call me sometime when you are."

The second message was from Tabby:

"Hello, Mitch, you were a jerk tonight. I know you got your feathers ruffled a little bit, but you didn't have to take it out on me." Although she was serious, I remember laughing a bit because she talked as if she had known me for years. "I can't believe you're just gonna go back to Battle Creek. I wanna quit too, but I can't. At orientation I told my editor that my first story would be done before Labor Day, and I just don't have enough information about the

PIZZA PIE AND POLITICS
HOW MITCHELL MOON LOST HIS CHILDHOOD

campaign yet." She paused for a moment as if she thought I would pick up. "Well," she said in a tone of retirement. "If you're ever in the area again, don't be a jerk—call me okay. Call me soon. Bye."

I didn't call her, nor did I return to Battle Creek. Instead I lay on my bed and fell asleep, not waking until Julie knocked on my door at 6:30 the next morning. She didn't make a comment about the burn on my forehead, although I knew she saw it; she merely held up a folded page from the newspaper to my eye level. I saw a picture of me with the open hand of one of the attackers seeming to make contact with my mouth. The left fist of another was swinging toward my face. (Rick had to have been in good position to get that shot.) The headline posted the words: "Fist Fighting for Democracy," and the caption read, "Two young assailants try to arrest Moon's first amendment rights." The story that followed, which I read with trembling hands, was dishonest, stating that the scuffle ensued when seven skinheads tried to arrest our freedom of speech near the parking lot of that mall. Rick eventually lied about the facts, writing that our volunteers were bullied by the assailants, who first tossed our flyers into the parking lot and then proceeded to beat all of them mercilessly while shouting anti-liberal propaganda and simultaneously threatening several people who attempted to stop the onslaught.

He spent three paragraphs explaining the way I came from the other end of the mall to throw my body into the fight, taking control of a seemingly uncontrollable situation. He listed me as the co-director of the campaign and made certain to mention, in a one-line paragraph, that I was the same individual who put a drunk and belligerent reporter in his place at the CAC in July. He followed this with two ridiculous quotes:

"Every day is a fight out here. I wake up every morning ready for it." And, "This is no longer a grass-roots campaign; [There are people] who don't want a three-party race; they've got their blades sharpened, and they're ready to mow us down before the people have a chance to speak at the polls in November."

It didn't stop there. Apparently, he had plenty of space to review and highlight Ted's political agenda and to list a number of clubs at which he would appear later that night.

Five minutes earlier I had answered Julie's knock promptly, resigned to the fact that I wouldn't be able to back out, especially since I was going to be paid the next day, and somewhat ready to go out and spread the messages I still believed, if not the person who symbolized them. Now someone was trying to make me fist fight for the E Party, and that was not what I signed on to do. I wasn't even completely sure that I wanted to be there, so I certainly wasn't going to fight every day, which would be the result of Rick's dime-novel western technique. Basically, I felt trapped as if someone would be following me from then on, and no matter how I chose to handle it, a misdirected and egomaniacal journalist would revise my actions for me. I wasn't going to live a lie; that's what I thought at 6:35 in the morning anyway.

Still standing in the doorway, I flipped to the inside page of that section.

"I'm calling the editor of this shit rag right now." I bounded to the desk and retrieved the phone book.

"You can't do that," Julie said as I rifled through the bulky index.

I told her that the story was false. He was making a liar out of me.

"I will talk to Ted. This is between him and Rick now, and I know he doesn't like Rick's ethics, but he needs the media." She struggled with me to get the phone book away and back into the desk. "Have some faith, Mitchell Moon!"

"I suppose you want to try to cover this with make-up too." I pointed to my forehead. (Of course, a purple line near my nose still remained from my black eye.)

"Not this time, sweetie. By noon a lot of people are gonna know where that came from."

Tabby and I had loaded the Volvo by 7:30 and sat in the office to wait for any signs of volunteers. (Being exceedingly hungry, I gorged on cinnamon buns during the interim. With seven dollars left in my pocket, breakfast had to carry me through until dinner.) Eight o'clock came and went as we concluded that the four volunteers from the day before would not be joining us.. After loading Teresa's car with flyers and driving out to spend to usual fifty minutes stuck in traffic on the Stevenson, Tabby and I covered some more ground, quickly placing flyers on windshields at business parks, and stapling more to corkboards inside buildings of a couple of community colleges. The previous plan for the day was to cover parts of the neighborhoods off from Cicero Avenue, from Chicago Heights to Oak Park. It was typical of the whole week: a huge plan based on a miscalculated projection of free help. That's why Ted didn't come to the office, though I wanted to have an actual dialogue with him about Rick's story. He and Teresa decided to cover some of that area themselves that day and on into the weekend, along with securing funds from Kevin to advertise on several billboards in the densely populated suburban areas that only an army of volunteers could cover.

PIZZA PIE AND POLITICS
HOW MITCHELL MOON LOST HIS CHILDHOOD

Though my day began with confusion and the will for sabotage, Tabby, after I spilled my guts to her, put me in better spirits as we drove. Like a Zen master, she warned me that if I acted on my frustration, I would move in an unnatural direction, incongruent with my true character.

"Just be yourself," she said, "and let people think what they want. They'll figure out the truth sooner or later as long as you don't let the lies change you."

To substantiate my anger, I showed her the article. After reading it she shook her head and looked out of the window for a few minutes.

"It's Rick's lie, not yours."

"But aren't I lying just by passing out flyers and connecting myself with this campaign?"

"You think you're going along with it by not saying anything?"

"Yeah, I am aren't I?"

"But you are saying something…to me."

I shrugged off this statement as if she just didn't understand.

"Toni Morrison was eighteen years old once too," she said.

I silently accepted her point with inspiration. The song playing sounded as perfect as lines from Yeats, and I thought of great things on the horizon as though everything I had done, the terrible and the terrific, led me to that point in my life

Our work that day turned into play, and since that night after Memorial Day with Drew, Neil, and Charlie on St. Mary's Lake, I had never been so content with the thought that I would be spending the evening with someone who made me feel alive. Somehow I had earned another great friend in my life.

Chapter 26

At around 8:00 p.m., we stopped for a bite to eat (I had $1.21 left after this.) and returned to headquarters for our second assignment for Thursday, August 17. Everyone had gone home by the time we arrived, except for Julie and a small group of about ten volunteers. (Ted was not present.) Julie provided instructions to us for a plan she and Ted had developed, which basically involved campaigning (or at least passing out flyers and interacting with every lonely soul we could meet) at many drinking establishments in the city. She had divided us into groups corresponding to regions of nightlife hot spots, and then she brought out champagne to thank everyone for a successful week.

We all cheered and gave cheers to those around us, and after one plastic glass full, everyone disappeared as if programmed. I filled my glass again and drank and filled again as Julie approached Tabby and me near my desk.

"I don't think I can send you out tonight, sweetie," she said very directly to Tabby. "You'll have a hard time getting into those bars."

"We don't have to go in," I argued. "If we get there before 10:00, we'll be able to meet most people at the door."

"That might work once, but I need you to cover more ground than that."

"Well, who did you pair me with then?"

"Me."

"Okay, Tabby, do you want to come with us?"

"I guess so." She looked at Julie and me as if she wasn't sure.

"You might have to stand outside," Julie warned.

"Which means she can get 'em comin' in and comin' out," I asserted.

Julie looked irritated. "I don't think this is a good idea."

"She's my partner; she has been all week," I began to get adamant. I poured myself another glass, drained it and poured another.

"All right," Julie gave in. "I'm gonna call your parents though."

Tabby looked at her as if she had just been slapped.

"Yeah, why don't you call my mom at Buffalo Style's. I'm sure she'd love to talk to you while she's trying to run a restaurant at 9:00 on a Thursday night."

"She should know where you're going to…"

"…Let's go there first," I interrupted.

Julie saw some sense in this and made a quick call to a pair of volunteers who were heading toward N. Lincoln.

As Julie turned onto Lincoln, I recognized the neighborhood and realized that I could easily jump out, find my car, and return to my bed in the Crimson Rouge by 1:00 a.m.. I checked my pocket for my car keys, and then I inhaled the scent of two beautiful women, felt the little buzz of champagne, and saw the rest of the night as a bar crawl with them on either side of me.

The parking place that Julie chose was closer to my car and Teresa's house than it was to Buffalo Style's. We walked there quickly, but there was a small line outside. As we approached, Tabby said "Hi" to the bouncer at the door and walked up to him. They talked for a moment until he shook his head yes, looked at Julie and me, and waved us through. I walked to the front of the line, remembered my backpack full of flyers, and hesitated.

"Come on, Mitch!" Tabby yelled from the doorway.

I looked at her and shook my head no.

"Go ahead," I yelled to her and Julie. "I can wait in line just like everybody else."

I took off my pack and passed some flyers around, saying "make sure to register, and vote Dreisbach for U.S. Senate." Once I took my place at the end of the line I began to wonder if my choice was a good one. However, around 10:00 the line began to grow. I lost my place by passing out more flyers and striking up conversations with bored people who asked things like "Who's

Dreisbach? Are you the guy that got his ass beat at the mall? Why are you campaigning at the bar?" And "Hey, aren't you the 'get the fuck off my balls' guy?" They seemed antagonistic, but I knew how they felt waiting in line just to get a drink at their favorite bar; most of them were probably half in the bag from pre-partying, so I humored them the best I could and began to entertain them a little until the line began to move. Those who were there to eat were leaving, allowing room for those who came to drink.

At around 10:30 Tabby and Julie came out looking for me.

"What are you doing, Mitch? I wanted you to meet my mom."

"I'm doin' my job. How 'bout you two?"

They laughed. "Yeah, her mom let me get on the PA," Julie answered.

"Huh?"

"Number 201, your order's up. Be sure to vote for Ted Dreisbach in November. That's Ted Dreisbach for Senate." They laughed again.

I actually felt bad that I missed that. It made me thirsty for a cold draught of Bell's. Although Julie got us back on track, making sure that we hit two more bars on N. Lincoln. Sad Paradise was to play at one of these venues at midnight, and Ted would be there. We went to the other first.

Again, although there was no line here, Tabby knew the doorman, who also worked at Buffalo Style's. The benefits of this were that he let Tabby into the bar; he told us we could pass out flyers as long as we didn't bother the people eating dinner (He looked at me when he said this), and he bought drinks for all three of us. Tabby had a margarita; Julie had a Tom Collins, and I decided on a pint of Guinness. The girl who prepared our drinks wore a tiny black skirt, platform sandals, and a shiny purple top about the size of an Ace bandage to cover her chest. She told me that she liked my shirt and, after looking at my forehead, asked me if I played hockey. I said yes, not specifying which type of hockey. And as quick as a face-off, I put my $1 in her tip jar, thought again, dug the change out of my pocket, and dropped that in also. I was officially broke.

The downstairs of this bar was busy, but not quite full. As we walked upstairs, I noticed that the TVs played a Manchester United game that must have been taped by the owner. (No one paid any immediate attention to it.) Upstairs we found another bar, several tables matching the wooden tables downstairs and a few couches. The three of us sipped our drinks and decided that Julie would stay upstairs to schmooze and buy drinks for people. Tabby and I left our backpacks near her as she sat on the couch, and we went downstairs. Though it was not a quiet bar, the atmosphere was so controlled that I felt awkward, and after trying to strike up two conversations and bumbling into the same waitress twice, I concluded that this was not the place to campaign. However, Tabby seemed to have more luck at certain tables, receiving much more attention than I could have, so I got out of the way completely. This meant sitting at the bar and going through the embarrassment of trying to make my beer last as long as possible, saying no to the bartender every time she asked me if I wanted another, and watching at least three groups of men buy Tabby a drink while she sat and talked to them.

As 11:45 (bar time) rolled around, I concluded that I was the only one watching the clock, so I went upstairs to find Julie, stopping at the end of the bar to get Tabby's attention. She sat with a gentleman of at least thirty years who wore black slacks and a white dress shirt. Evidently, he had bought her a bottle of beer and was in the middle of his own campaign when I told her that I thought it was time to go. He shot me a glance that might have gotten me into my third fight of the week had I not turned toward the stairs immediately, mentally castigating anyone of his age who would hit on an eighteen-year-old and simultaneously wishing she would follow me and share that beer he bought her. She tried to introduce me to him, but I started to walk without looking back. I began to curse him as the typical urban pantywaist who dresses up to go to the bar until I caught a glimpse of myself in a mirror near the stairs. I could have been his twin in the clothes I put on that morning.

Julie sat on the same couch between two men who feigned deep interest. I began to wonder why I even had to leave Monroe Street that evening. I couldn't get that attention if I walked up and down Lake Michigan Avenue wearing a sandwich board and screaming as if tomorrow were doomsday. After I mentioned the time to her, we went to a third bar on N. Lincoln. This time the doorman was not an acquaintance of Tabby, and after Julie tried to explicate her into the bar to no avail, she went in to find Ted. I stayed outside with her. I could hear the hollow sound of a live band playing inside, but I didn't recognize them as Sad Paradise, judging by the lead singer's voice. Tabby acted a little drunk, shoving flyers at passersby and saying things like: "Hey! Where you goin'? The party's in here," and "You're goin' the wrong way, people."

I laughed and looked at the bouncer who was also laughing.

"I hope she's a marketing major," he said.

"Nope, we recruited her from Coney Island."

"So you're here with Dreisbach?"

"Yup."

"Well, he's in there. He showed up with some big dude. I hope I don't have to fight him tonight."

I pursed my lips and shook my head no.

"The owner warned us about you guys. Said you like to fight."

"Not really; Not me; I guess it depends on who else shows up." I thought of Rick.

"Well, I'd hate to throw you outta here."

I looked at him expecting some hint that he was joking, but looked me straight in the eyes, as if looking for an excuse to show me how serious he was. I started to get the feeling that he wanted to beat me up, so I looked away. Tabby talked to a small group of guys, as Ted came to the door and introduced me to the owner of the bar. I asked them to watch Tabby campaign for a moment, and they laughed.

"Who is that?" the owner asked.

"It's Tabby Cannon," I answered.

"Ha! Is that Shirley's daughter?"

"I have no idea, sir."

Ted called her over, and the owner led us through a crowd that did not end at the bar. It was a warm night, and that particular bar felt swampy. He ordered a pint for Ted and me and a Coke for Tabby.

"This one's too young," he screamed to the bartender. "Sorry, sweetheart," he yelled to Tabby. "Your mom would kill me."

She agreed.

"Go ahead and get those flyers around," Ted bellowed. "I'll see ya in a minute."

"Wait," I screamed, remembering what I had wanted to talk to him about for the last seventeen hours. "Rick isn't here, is he?"

He nodded his head yes and nodded his head down the bar, as if he saw him.

"Well, look…" I began to order him to make sure Rick didn't get near me, because I sensed that there would be a few people willing to send me to the hospital in order to make a big hit in the morning paper. As I explained my issue to Ted, not really knowing if he heard a word I said over the cacophony, Rick appeared at my side, handing me a tumbler of scotch.

"I saw you come in," he said. "I owe you one for yesterday, Mitch."

I took it from him without a word. Ted scowled at him and punched his shoulder firmly. Then he made a motion for him to follow, and they disappeared into the adjacent room where the band played.

PIZZA PIE AND POLITICS
HOW MITCHELL MOON LOST HIS CHILDHOOD

Tabby stood with me at the bar while I downed the scotch. We took some flyers out of our packs: I put the pint in my left hand, and we spread the word for a while. I remember feeling comfortable there for a few minutes, despite my initial instincts. It was a simple college bar with a lot of friendly people. I felt that a fight was imminent, but I couldn't see myself getting into a tangle with anyone there. The crowd was heavy, but the tone was easy until S.P. started to play. Some of the drinkers gave Tabby and me cheers and clinked glasses with us; some of them told me, facetiously, to get the fuck off their balls when I placed flyers on their tables. I heard Ted on the P.A. after the first band's set. Though the crowd became silent, he didn't speak of politics. Instead he told a story about his first time at that bar, drinking on a fake ID and getting an MIP after walking out with a full bottle of beer in his hand.

About a half an hour passed until Sad Paradise took the stage. By this time I had finished my first and last pint of the night while I pushed flyers, when S.P. began giving directions to their soundman. Tabby and I stood just inside of the second room, taking a long break when Teresa and P.J. entered, deciding to stand in front of us. As Ted introduced Sad Paradise, I noticed that there seemed to be no way to get back to the other room because of the crowd that had formed behind us. People also congregated in the street outside of the room we were in, ignoring the threats of the two bouncers. I started to sweat through my shirt and wiped my forehead with my sleeves.

I thought I knew chaos until the drummer, after tapping the high hat a few times and kicking the bass, hit the snare to begin the first song. The crowd released a collective scream, as if some kind of rage had been bottled up inside of them for years. It was startling to see the twisted faces and fists pumping in the air to the back beat. I could feel myself inching closer to Tabby, and I put my left arm around her waist. We were in a precarious situation if only one person decided to apply his violence toward another. The song, called "Whores on Capitol Hill," was not the jukebox music I was used to at Rikki Tikki's. To contain my panic, I began to plan an escape route for Tabby and me. As I mapped it out, the song ended, and the singer began to acknowledge us campaign workers, asking us to raise our hands, and told the crowd to take home a flyer if they hadn't received one. Tabby and I pulled out our backpacks and merely handed them over. As they passed around the room, Ted's bodyguard put seven cardboard boxes on the stage. The singer pulled out a T-shirt and held it up to the crowd. It was the one I helped design. The black shirt had a rattlesnake on the front; its rattle painted red, white, and blue; and below the snake were, of course, the words "Get off my balls." The crowd roared. The singer turned the shirt around to show that the back contained red letters that made the suggestion to "Vote Dreisbach for Senate."

"Who wants one?" he asked and threw it into the crowd. "Wear it with pride, my man. Don't get rough now. Everyone gets one before the set is over."

I had seen free T-shirt giveaways at crowded venues before, and I had seen a few end with police and ambulances at the scene, so before the singer could open his mouth to sing the next song, I asked Tabby if she wanted to get out of there. As she said yes, I held her close and made a way for us out of the crowd and toward the door that we entered.

Just before we reached the door, I felt an enormous hand squeeze my shoulder. I stopped, turned around and had to look up slightly to see whom it was. I figured that Rick sent this guy, and I tried to shake myself free.

While grabbing my other shoulder, the stranger said, "That guy wants to buy you a drink."

I looked to see Kevin, staring solemnly over the bar, an empty bar stool on either side of him, obviously cleared when he arrived. The man who grabbed me helped us to get through the crowd. We stopped just to the right of Kevin, and he turned to look at us slowly.

"Hello, Mitchell," I think he said (I could hardly hear anything.), and he put out his hand to shake as I introduced him to Tabby.

"Well, aren't you pretty," he said loud enough for us to hear.

She shrugged and looked toward the door. I didn't blame her. He hadn't said one word to me since a "hello" at Grant Park, but I stuck with it for the free drink.

"Hey, put them on his tab," the stranger yelled at the very preoccupied bartender. "Whatever they want."

I ordered a Bushmills. Tabby declined, and we sat at the only two open chairs at the bar, Tabby to his left and I to his right. The stranger stood with his thighs about twelve inches from Kevin's stool.

"I hear you're doing some good work," Kevin said.

"What?"

He repeated himself.

I thanked him, and we tried to talk about what we had been doing all week, but the music prevented it. Tabby repeatedly looked at me over his head and flicked her eyes toward him as if he had a bomb in his shoes. As it turned out, we sat almost silently until I abruptly slugged my drink and made a motion to leave. Kevin elbowed the stranger and made a tipping signal toward his mouth.

"Sir, two more please," the stranger yelled.

Tabby stood and yelled that she had to go. She seemed to wait for me to get off from my stool.

"Oh no, stay with us. We'll go to after-hours," Kevin said.

I nodded my head yes. "I'll see ya tomorrow," I yelled to Tabby.

"No, you won't. You're going to Champagne," she returned.

"I'll call you."

She shook her head slowly from side to side, and then she was gone.

"Have you seen her naked?" Kevin asked after she was gone, almost pressing his lips to my ears.

I shook my head no.

"She's very pretty."

I shook my head and lifted my eyebrows to add emphasis. And then it all hit me. She would start school Monday as I went on the road. That was our last hour working together, and since I planned to take one more shot at a relationship with Ilo at Drew's wedding, I might not return to Chicago in September, if everything went well. That was the last time I would see her.

The bartender placed another Bushmills in front of me, and I sipped, feeling a tingle at the top of my head and a numbness in my spine.

"Have you even been to any of the after-hour clubs in Chicago?" he asked in my ear.

I shook my head no and took another sip of the whiskey.

"I can introduce you to some girls. You can be my drinking buddy tonight."

I raised my eyebrows again and smiled very enthusiastically, pretending that it was a good idea, but it didn't sit well with me while Tabby was out on the street all by herself. I had met plenty of girls and had drunk until six o'clock too many times. Tabby was my friend.

"I'd love to under normal circumstances," I yelled. "But I've been up since 6:30 in the morning, and I gotta wake up in about six hours. Will you give me a rain check on that?"

He nodded and looked agreeable. We shook hands.

As I entered the outdoors, the streetlights and headlights looked blurry, and I felt the slight presence of a whiskey buzz in my eyes as I looked for a short girl wearing a blue backpack. I didn't believe that she got away that fast, but I couldn't see her on the sidewalk as far as I looked. I surmised that she either took a cab or went back to Buffalo Style's, so I began to jog toward the bar.

"Hello, aren't you a pretty girl," I said.

"Oh my God! That was the biggest pornographer in North America." She squeezed my hand.

"Oh yeah, I know."

"Is that how Ted can…"

"…I don't know for sure."

"What does that make me, if I've been pushing his cause all week long?"

"That's what I've been wondering."

"I quit."

"Me too."

"Are you serious?"

"No. I haven't been paid yet."

"You're gonna accept money from them?"

"Yes."

"They're creeps."

"Kevin and Rick are creeps, but you know what, Kevin hasn't lied to anyone about how he made his first million. And Ted isn't pushing pornography or anything else. With someone like Kevin on his side, he doesn't have to do any favors for anyone. If he had to use his father's money, they'd make him dance like a marionette." She let go of my hand, and I felt embarrassed for turning her off.

"You wouldn't have said that this morning," she reminded me.

"You kinda cheered me up."

She made a face to show that she might have regretted that. "The people deserve to know how Ted's campaign is being funded."

"Then they need to know exactly how all campaigns are funded."

As we reached the door of Buffalo Style's, we were trying to piece together the facts that we had about Kevin without arguing, and I digressed by mentioning that my car was not far away and explaining to her how it got there. She listened carefully and asked when I might be back in the area after Friday. I repeated the information about my car.

"Oh, you didn't think I was going to…" She stopped herself.

I didn't say anything, and I nervously felt my pocket for the car keys.

"I don't think that's a good idea. I mean guys get all weird after…you know, and I don't want you to be all weird with me. You're my friend."

"No, I wasn't thinking of…I don't think we need to…I've spent the night with girls I liked before, and we didn't…I'm just gonna go now."

"No, Mitch. I don't want you to think that…"

"…No, no, not at all. I'll come see you when all of this is over."

PIZZA PIE AND POLITICS
HOW MITCHELL MOON LOST HIS CHILDHOOD

"In November?"

"Ah, maybe earlier than that. I don't know."

As I walked away to find my car, I left a message on Julie's cell, explaining my early departure from the bar as a fear of getting too loaded (as if I were really making some progress in that area). I felt obligated because the campaigning was to continue at a couple of after-hours clubs on N. Sheridan and N. Clark.

I drove back to the parking garage near the Palmer and returned to my room, castigating myself for thinking that Tabby would have come with me and stewing in embarrassment for letting her know that's what I wanted. If I had any money, I certainly would have met Julie at the Oasis since S.P. would have been finished, and they would have been moving on by then. But I didn't see the logic in putting myself back into the situation after all. I wanted to call Tabby to invite her to lunch on Friday, but all I would do by pursuing the whole urge is to embarrass myself all over again. Then, as my mind wandered while flipping through the television channels, I thought about how good the next two months would be if she could come with me, not just because I was horny but also because I felt better about the whole process when she was around me. When she sat beside me in Teresa's car, I felt as though it didn't matter where we turned or what time it was; it always seemed as though we were going in the right direction at the proper pace. I wondered what it would be like to bring her to Drew's wedding with me, and then I reveled at the thought of going home in seven days, imagining the wedding as one last party with my best friends before we all went our separate ways, one more memory to add to the volume that suspended our souls in a state of eternal youth.

I wondered what they would think of Tabby, and I felt very inclined to introduce her to Charlie and Neil. Oddly enough it was the same feeling I had when I was little after finding an important football card in my bubble gum package, someone like Ed "Too Tall" Jones or "Mean" Joe Green. I had to run to their houses just to show them, even though it probably didn't mean anything to them. So I acted on an impulse. I went to the desk, found the phone number for Buffalo Style's, and called for Tabby.

She said "hello" after the person who answered found her. The lack of background noise made me imagine her sitting in her mom's office.

"Hey, Tabby, I'm wondering about something."

"Yeah?"

"I don't really want to wait until November to see you again."

"Okay," she laughed.

"Well…so there's a wedding next weekend, and I'm wondering if you'll go with me."

"Ah…next…weekend. Um…I don't know," she said very slowly. "My mom's gonna wanna meet you first."

"Okay!" I said. "Uh, Tabby?"

"Yeah?"

"Is that a yes?"

"Um…I guess so. Yes."

"I'll call you tomorrow."

She gave me her cell phone number, and I hung up feeling very positive. I felt as though I had just wiped everything away in order to begin something new. I saw a clean solid foundation onto which I could build anything. I sensed that I could have a friendship where I didn't feel as though I always had to fix something or go back and try to make it right, which always happened when Charlie and Neil were involved. Then I started to wonder why it took her so long to agree to go. I didn't want her to feel obligated just because she had already rejected me that night. I thought of calling her back to ask her if she felt obligated, but then I started to think of Ilo and how she looked in those tiny dresses she wore to weddings. I thought it would be nice to actually sleep with her in a bed, if that were possible; everything felt forced with her. Then I started to panic because I couldn't remember if I had invited her to be my date. I honestly thought that I might have, so I spent at least an hour going through everything I thought I ever said to her, trying to recreate different scenarios that might not have happened at all. I fell asleep while imagining these, making myself feel guilty about inviting Tabby and convincing myself that she would feel uncomfortable in Battle Creek.

Chapter 27

In the morning I put my comb, razor and toothbrush into the duffel bag I had packed on Wednesday night, checked out of the Palmer in a nervous state due to an assumption that I would be responsible for the mini bar charges (This turned out to be false, as I never even saw the bill), and went to the office for instructions and to pack my car full of all the campaign materials that would fit. I guessed that I would be traveling alone, and after speaking with Julie, this turned out to be true. (The volunteers we had would be starting school on Monday, meaning they could help Julie cover Chicagoland and the Northeastern part of Illinois, and Ted was going to begin the Herculean task of garnering support from the destitute class and the over-forty crowd.) She quickly and unconvincingly mentioned something about hiring someone within a week or two, but even though I felt that they were taking advantage of me, I didn't want another partner. I foolishly thought that I could do everything by myself, even after she assured me that I would have help at many campuses that I was to visit.

Julie also gave me a quick verbal quiz about where we stood on the issues, just in case someone wanted to corner me. We went to the empty office across the hall and sat down, facing each other across a dusty table. She played a combative college student, and though she assured me that my job was to register voters and give them information about the Dreisbach ticket, she wanted to make sure I was prepared to answer questions whenever and wherever they were asked.

"Okay, so what's your party's stance on fossil fuels, the lack thereof?"

"Well, car companies, individual scientists and oil companies themselves are working to develop alternatives in the form of petroleum and diesel substitutes, electric hybrids, and fuel cells. It will take at least twenty years to put the logistics in place for the fuel cell, if we're talking about automobiles. If we're talking about HVAC issues in households, the fuel cell alternative is a great one right now. Because of the logistics problem of fuel cells, the E Party strongly supports ethanol and biodiesel. They both have the potential to help Illinois farmers, and they can be used while we add fuel cell service to our existing gas stations and service plazas. The E Party suggests a combination of alternatives, instead of relying on just one. Either way it will be a very difficult transition if the government and American society continue to be loyal to fossil fuels."

"Okay, what about Medicare and the fact that a large percentage of individuals have no health insurance?"

"These are both huge issues. As far as Medicare goes, if the doctors and hospitals didn't have to pay so much for liability insurance, the cost of quality healthcare could decrease, taking some pressure of from the state's budget. The E Party wants to make it more difficult for individuals to sue doctors, but that will only be effective if hospitals, doctors, and specialists agree to reduce their rates. For that to happen, insurance companies all have to agree to reduce their rates. So if this idea is to be made into a bill, there has to be the written stipulation that these groups all agree to increase their rates only according to the rate of inflation.

"As far as health insurance goes, the reason that a lot of people aren't covered goes right back to the personal-injury-lawsuit problem. Insurance rates are high because it costs so much to cover the doctors' legal expenses. Employers can't afford it. Also, we've lost millions of manufacturing jobs to other countries in the last decade. A lot of people who have lost these jobs have no health insurance. The Democrats and Republicans believe that technology training will lead to job placement for those people, but the E Party doesn't see that as an effective solution. As technology continues to increase at an exponential rate, following Moore's law, it will be a case of one person doing the job that several people used to do. That's common sense. We need to preserve the manufacturing jobs that we have, not only in Illinois, but also all over the U.S. In the long run, it is regressive to send them overseas. Someone needs to draw the line now, and that is one of Ted Dreisbach's priorities. According to our statistics, people will pay a few dollars more if they know what they buy was made in America."

"You're all over this stuff," Julie said. "I feel like I'm talking to Ted. Have you been studying?"

"Uh, no, maybe Ted and I are on the same wavelength after all, huh?"

"Okay, okay, okay, umm, I'm gonna assume that you have an answer for the education issue, so…"

"…Well, the government's been pissing on the fourteenth amendment for I don't know how long, and that's something that I…"

"…Okay!" she stopped me. "Pissing? Come on, Mitch. What about stem cell research?"

"The current Senate has stifled the funding of this development with ethical arguments, and although the ethical dilemma is serious, scientists have made leaps and bounds in their research, solving many of the ethical problems as the Senate argues about methods that are now obsolete. We need more scientific literacy among all elected officials, and we need better communication between our government and our scientists if we are to progress as a nation."

"Mitch!" she exclaimed. "That was awesome. I'm sorry but I didn't think you had anything to say. I know you're a hard worker, but I thought I was just going to grill you. I need to talk to Ted about letting you write some things for P.J. on some of those lonely nights you're about to endure."

When we returned to the office, she had a short discussion with Ted in which she apparently raved about our little quiz. Ted beamed as I hadn't seen him do all week, and he said, "I told ya. He can talk about that shit for hours too. If he had any debating skills, he'd be dangerous."

From my desk I saw him go to move to Reggie's desk, and I saw Reggie open the check register on his computer and load the paper. A moment later Ted came to me with my week's pay. I looked at it, and it was twice as much as I expected. Then I looked up at Ted suspiciously and asked, "Is this for my expenses this week too?"

"Nope, you can charge anything within reason. I'll have Reggie explain 'within reason' to you before you leave." He handed me a credit card.

"The check is all mine then?"

"Yeah, you can cash it at my bank," he gave me directions. "I'd get some traveler's checks too, and open a checking account. Have them send your debit card and register to my P.O. box," he paused. "But this isn't just for pushing flyers. Julie's gonna contact the student newspapers at the colleges you'll visit to see if they'll let you write a column while you're there."

After Reggie talked to me, I retrieved my car from the garage and filled it so full of T-shirt boxes that they blocked the back windows. I put a few boxes of voter-registration cards and flyers in the front seat. After I made my last trip up to the office, Ted handed me a new notebook computer.

"This is a little gift from the E Party. You'll need it for those articles... Quit staring at it, and get outta here."

I wanted to tell him about my leave of absence for the wedding, but he was in such a good mood that I didn't want to spoil it. I did say goodbye to P.J., and Julie walked me to my car, giving me the address of my volunteer at U of I, and telling me to call her every day, even if I didn't have anything to talk about. She gave me a huge hug, and I was off to the bank. I thought of calling Tabby, but I remembered what she said about meeting her mom. It was already 9:30, and I thought that it would take three hours to drive to Champagne. I decided there was no way I could try to find her apartment, chat with her mom and still make any progress at the U of I. Also, I maintained the impression that she didn't really want to go to the wedding. She'd call me if she did.

I arrived in Champagne in just over two hours, but it took me almost another hour to find my volunteer's apartment. He wasn't ready yet when he opened the door, so we didn't actually start working until close to 2:00. He suggested that we begin at the bookstore on the Champagne campus, explaining that we should do the dorms on Saturday and Sunday since everyone was busy moving in on Friday. Since we had no table behind which to sit and no chairs regardless, we gave students clipboards on which to fill out registration cards once we really started making progress. At first we approached everyone who entered the building, but most passed us by until we decided to wear the T-shirts and gave them to the students before we asked them to register. Even if they were already registered, we let them keep the shirts. This worked well, and we used this method for all of the bookstores that we visited until we stopped at around 7:00 out of hunger.

I dropped him off at 8:00, asking if he wanted to go grab a beer. He declined, so I made copies of the flyer and registration cards, checked into my hotel room, and called Julie, who told me that I had a meeting with the editor and the faculty advisor of the newspaper at 9:00 the next morning. I set my alarm and walked to the nearest bar, overwhelmingly pleased by the cash in my pocket.

A line of students stood here, but it moved fast, and I found myself ordering a light beer and a Bushmills by 10:00. The room was absolutely packed, so I hovered near the bar for over an hour until a seat opened. I said hello to two girls who sat next to me with their backs to the bar. We had a short conversation that ended when the one closest to me said she was thirsty, pretending to need advice about what to order: water or a rum and Coke. I told her that she should stick with water, and she said something about me to her friend. They relocated as soon as they found two more empty stools.

I ordered a beer every fifteen minutes for a couple of hours, and at first the bartender appeased me by saying, "Sometimes they just go down good." However, not long after that, he asked me if I was going to make it home all right, and then he told me that he couldn't serve me anymore. I tried to go to a bar down the street, but the doorman wouldn't even let me inside. I found my way back to the hotel after going in the wrong direction twice and passed out on the covers until my alarm woke me at 8:00. I took off the clothes I had worn the night before, ran an iron over them, put them back on, washed my face, and brushed my teeth; then I was off to the meeting where I was allowed to write an op-ed column about the E Party in general, and I picked up my helper at around 10:00.

The hangover hit me at about noon when the temperature rose to about ninety degrees. The only thing I could do was buy about four bottles of water and a few candy bars at the snack machine in one of the dorms. I worked slowly for a few hours, often sitting in the shade trying to call people over to me while my help ran back and forth between dorms, coming back to my car to get boxes of T-shirts every now and then. I wanted to crawl inside and sleep on one of the couches in the lounge until about four o' clock when I began to feel somewhat healthy again. We moved to another set of dorms, and when we began to double our efforts, I noticed that we were running extremely low on T-shirts. We only had about five left when the day ended.

I called Ted on my way to the hotel, and he said that someone would bring more to me by midnight. I took that opportunity to tell him that I needed Friday, Saturday, and Sunday off so that I could go to Drew's wedding.

"Are you crazy?" he replied. "You're not flipping burgers for me, Mitch. That would set us back three days. Do you know we have every single day planned out until election day?"

I knew that, but I explained my situation anyway.

"Look, Mitch. You'll be in Springfield on Friday. If you can leave for Battle Creek on Friday night and return to Springfield at 9:00 Sunday morning, we'll figure something out."

"There's no way I can do that."

"Otherwise, you better tell them that you're not gonna make it. I definitely don't want it to come to this, but we'll find somebody to take your position before we'll set the schedule back three days."

Before I even hung up, I decided that I would call his bluff. I didn't think there was any way I would miss that rehearsal dinner.

That night I decided to avoid the embarrassment of going to the bar alone, but I did pick up a six-pack after I ate dinner and drank them while I wrote my article. After that night I had no time to be drunk or hungover. On Sunday I made copies of the flyers, visited a community college in Champagne, and drove to Decatur. On Monday I worked at a community college there and two small colleges in Lincoln. I stayed in Lincoln on Monday night, stayed up until close to 3:00 a.m. writing articles for two of the colleges I visited that day, and I woke up at 6:00 a.m. on Tuesday and traveled to Bloomington to visit a community college. In the afternoon on Tuesday, I registered some voters at one community college in Normal and posted flyers in a second C.C. there until the security guards closed the buildings at around 9:30. That night I received another shipment of T-shirts at a motel in Normal and stayed up very late writing an article for the student paper in Bloomington, conscientiously trying not to repeat myself. I hadn't thought of beer since Saturday night, preferring the in-room coffee to keep myself awake long enough to prepare myself for the next day. On Wednesday I woke early for more of the same, a small college in Eureka, a community college in East Peoria, and a community college in Peoria. All of this paved the way for Ted's visits for speeches and occasional debates in September and October.

That night I made more copies and began another article for the community college in Peoria when my cell phone rang, which hadn't happened since Julie's call on Friday. Based on what she mentioned just before I left, I thought I would die of loneliness, but I was so busy that I didn't even care to take that call, checking for a message instead at around 11:30 after I finished and e-mailed my article.

Tabby left the message. In a hurry she tried to tell me more about her first days of college than a short message could contain, and she asked why I hadn't called her. I felt obliged to call her immediately, and although I could tell that I woke her, she claimed that she was just lying in bed reading her psychology book. I found it easy to tell her everything I had been doing and writing, and before I knew it, the clock next to the bed read 1:00 a.m. I told her that we should go to bed, never guessing why she really called, but she reminded me of the wedding before I could escape.

I hadn't thought about the wedding since Thursday night. In a flash I saw the whole trip back to Battle Creek as a burden, and making a date of it, or having someone to entertain the whole time, seemed impossible. The result of this happened to be a panicked sort of decision-making process.

"Ah...ah...ah...I ah, don't even know if I'm gonna make it now," I sputtered. Then I told her what Ted said and predicted that it wouldn't be any fun for her if I was under so much duress in trying to make it there and back in a little more than twenty-four hours. She didn't buy it. She asked if Ilo would be there. I said that I really didn't know, and of course she didn't believe that.

"Mitch, do you want me to go or not?" She waited. "Hello? This isn't a life-or-death decision."

I was stumped, but I couldn't remain silent for long either, remembering how I felt when it took her so long to agree to go with me.

"Of course I *want* you to go," I replied before silence spoke for me. "I'm not gonna be quite right though."

"Well, that hasn't bothered me yet."

She could make me feel pretty good about things with just one well-timed sentence like that. I didn't know if it was because she was so smart or that we shared the same insecurities, but she knew exactly what to say sometimes.

After I told her that I would pick her up on Friday night, I called Charlie because, for the life of me, I could not remember if Ilo would be there or not. He was absolutely lit, answering the phone on the first ring yelling, "Car 54, Car 54, where are you?" and laughing in a sloppy manner.

"Charlie! Turn the music down."

"No, you turn your hearing aid up, dick!"

"Dammit, Charlie! I have to ask you something."

"Oh no no no guy guy guy. I have to ask you. Hey, Mitch?"

"Yeah?"

"Ya want some sketti?" I didn't hear anything after that but a squeaking sound.

"Oh, Charlie!" I heard Keely's voice say. "He just wrapped spaghetti around the phone," she said to me. "Just a second." I heard the same squeaking sound.

"Hey, Keely, I have to ask you something."

"What's up?"

"Is Ilo gonna be at the wedding?"

"Oh yeah, don't worry about that."

"I didn't…"

"…invite her? No, she got an invitation though. She's wondering why you haven't called her."

"Well, we didn't part ways on the best of terms. I'm really not sure if I can deal with that stuff right now."

"She's not mad at you anymore." She paused to tell Charlie to stop whatever he was doing. "She wants to go to the rehearsal dinner, Mitch. Ya know what I mean?"

"No, but I know there might be an open seat for her because I don't think I'm gonna make it to the rehearsal dinner."

"Oh…well okay, I'll tell her," she said right before hanging up on me.

I spent Thursday at Western Illinois University in Macomb. I had three people help me there, and we covered as much ground as we could before we ran out of T-shirts. I stayed in Macomb that night, received another shipment of T-shirts, and sent the same article I had written the night before, not really caring anymore if I repeated myself. My phone rang three or four times while I wrote, and when I finished, I checked for messages. The first was from Charlie, saying "You, Ilo, me, Keely, Neil, Mandy, St. Mary's Lake, Friday, one last time, dude. We'll have a blast. I can't believe you've gotta come in on Friday. You can't let your job run your life, man."

The second was from Neil, saying "If you're not there on Friday morning, and if you don't get up the balls to ask Ilo to the rehearsal dinner, I'm gonna find you and break things over your head. I mean it, Mitch."

The third was from a perturbed Drew: "Hey, Mitch, will you call me and tell me exactly what the hell is going on?"

The fourth was from Ted: "Mitch, Ted here, I'd like to meet you at the medical school in Springfield on Saturday. I wanna introduce you to some people over lunch, so if you're going to that wedding on Saturday, please let me know ASAP."

All of the sudden pressure directed me toward making the compromise that couldn't be avoided. Although I wanted that Labor Day weekend to be a legendary bon voyage for us into adulthood, that ship had set sail. There was no way I could leave right then and there in order to reach Battle Creek later that morning when I had so much to do on Sunday. Also, I didn't see myself having any fun if I worried about having to find a new job, considering Ted's threat. So I called Drew, and I called Ted, telling both of them that I would be in Battle Creek on Saturday only.

Very early Friday morning, I started at the U of I in Springfield, and not long after I started working outside of a classroom building, a telecommunications major asked me if he could do a quick interview with me for the local PBS station. I guessed this was spontaneous on his part because he said he needed to get the camera, and of course I agreed although I hurried all morning planning to cover this interview, the U of I and a community college before 6:00 so that I could get to Battle Creek at a decent time. He told me that he would be back in a half an hour, but after forty-five minutes I had to move on. I didn't see him again for almost two hours when he caught me outside of a computer lab. The interview consisted of him filming me registering voters and asking a few questions to orient the viewers to the E Party. The one good question that he asked had to do with what set the E Party apart from the Democrats and Republicans, and I said, "Accountability and communication."

"Right now very few people can tell you who's a good politician and why. They vote a straight ticket more often than not, without knowing anything about the people for whom they vote. This means that our so-called democracy is based on people voting for the group that endorses a candidate rather than the individual. This means that every major election is decided based on one criteria: Which of the two major parties had more supporters show up at the polls? There's no logic there, and there's no individual accountability, which means there is no conscience. The E Party strives to give the government a conscience and the people of the United States some credit for having the intelligence to make informed decisions, on the condition that they are not left in the dark.

"By the time Dreisbach is finished with his career, people will be analyzing and voting for individuals based on a set of simple benchmarks that will gauge their political effectiveness. If there is one thing the E Party can and will do, it is to establish a universal way for the citizens of the United States to evaluate their elected officials and those running for office whenever it's time to vote. Now, we certainly don't strive to be a source of information about other political parties. (They have to decide whether or not they'll communicate with the people.) We'll just give the people a logical way to decide who's gonna make the rules. I mean, you have a grade-the-profs web site on this campus; America's gonna grade the politicians, and the E Party will create the report card to be used for generations.

"Basically, the E Party wants to bring competition back to politics because the best politicians must succeed in our political system. And our best leaders from all parts of society should be encouraged to involve themselves. That doesn't happen a lot right now because of the sloppy way in which our government has been conducting itself."

This was completely off the cuff, but I hoped that it would become a self-fulfilling prophecy. If accountability wasn't the one thing that distinguished the E Party from the others, if Ted couldn't stand by it, then we would never really make a difference anyway. Of course, I neglected to tell him about this later, when I arrived in Battle Creek, because of a more serious complication.

At the community college in Springfield, I slung more flyers, and after around 3:30 when the campus became more sparsely populated, I posted more in the classrooms. I sat down in the cafeteria to check my banking account online, became absolutely delighted that Reggie put more money in, and wrote a column for their newspaper over dinner. I made for Battle Creek as soon as I finished and e-mailed it, which was close to 6:30.

I didn't take me long to decide that I wasn't going to stop for Tabby. I could tell from the messages that Charlie and Neil left that they would not react well to my bringing her. Of course I should have told them about her, but what would they say after I pined for Ilo for almost two months? It would be a travesty to bring an outsider to Drew's wedding after everything that we went through together, and I was well aware of the hypocrisy. However, I couldn't think of a way to explain the situation to her in any way that would make sense, so as I turned off from 55 onto I-80, I called Julie for advice. Of course, after I explained the situation, she gave me the old adage that I should have expected: "If they're really your friends, and you really want to bring Tabby, they'll understand."

"They are really my friends, and they won't understand," I answered. "I just wanna know what I should say to Tabby."

"I don't think there's anything you can say that would make any sense of this to her. Honestly, Mitch, any excuse that you make now, even if she pretends to understand, will change everything between you. You don't invite a girl to a wedding and then disappoint her. You'd be lucky if she ever talked to you again."

At the moment, as I drove up 55 going eighty-five mph I decided that I could deal with that. Although I hadn't been able to befriend someone so

PIZZA PIE AND POLITICS
HOW MITCHELL MOON LOST HIS CHILDHOOD

easily in years, I wouldn't have to talk to her again if I just plain forgot to stop for her. I could make a big mistake out of loyalty to my friends, but I did not want to explain myself if I ever broke someone's heart.

By the time I saw the sign for I-80 west, I had made incredible time. If I followed 55 to Chicago in order to get Tabby, it would cost me at least an hour more. I imagined myself cruising up to the landing at St. Mary's lake with a case of beer in my hand by 12:00, honking my horn, the hero of the night, arriving to join Drew on his last cruise as a single man. I turned onto I-80 and decided that I would have to forget about Tabby.

However, as I-80 turned into 80/294, the construction traffic stopped me dead in my tracks. I began to get frustrated, cursing the civil engineers and city planners for creating such a perpetual bottleneck at the gateway to the east. After traveling approximately four miles in fifty minutes, surrounded by a wall of trucks trying to get Friday's orders delivered by Saturday morning, my frustration turned toward myself. I started to look at the map for routes that I should have taken. At least two or three could have delivered me from the mess into which I drove myself. One would have been to follow 55 to 90, only ten miles from Tabby's apartment. I should have been there by now (she would have thought so anyway), and I wondered about the reality of betraying someone I admired. At first I became conceited that I was capable of such a thing, but then I started to wonder how long I could be proud of myself for consciously making a mistake in order to avoid disappointing my friends.

With all of my adrenaline spent, and with the clock proving to me that I would no longer be able to make it to Battle Creek in heroic time, I knew that I could not appreciate Drew's wedding if I felt guilty. In fact, I could see myself having a bad drunk and ruining everyone's evening. So I very timidly pulled to the right lane and drove onto the first ramp I saw. In doing this I did everyone a favor, even if they wouldn't see it.

I took a road north through Calumet and found I-94 north after about fifteen minutes, and I arrived at Tabby's apartment at around 10:30. She wore her usual wide-legged jeans, T-shirt and flip-flops and appeared to have been lounging on the couch, but besides the moment it took her to fetch her bags from her bedroom, I could tell that she was ready to go. While I stood in front of the doorway, next to the tiny kitchen, the scuffed wooden floors, and the exposed plywood on the furniture in the minuscule living room told me that her mom was not the owner of Buffalo Style's as I had assumed. This conclusion comforted me for some reason as we took a quick walk down the street to meet her, after I loaded Tabby's suitcase and garment bag into my car. Apparently Tabby had already told her who I was because after I shook her hand, she told me that she went to Albion College, just east of Battle Creek. She also told me to stay on 90 to 94 west in order to avoid any traffic at that time of night, and I did.

The first thing Tabby said to me as we crossed the Indiana border was, "I'm glad you asked me to come. I couldn't wait to get out of the city."

We talked about every little thing we did in the last eight days, right down to what we ate during our meals. I had forgotten how talking to someone in such a flowing and easy manner could make me forget about my worries, and I felt elation when I thought about being with her for two more days. Unfortunately, just across the Michigan border, we had a small argument after I pried a little too far into her job at the school's paper. It seems that one of the reasons she was given a feature article in her first weeks as a student happened to be the fact that she was about to begin working on the Dreisbach campaign. At first her attention was to be on Ted only and the strategies he had used to turn everyone's attention toward the Senate race. However, the event at the mall disturbed her so much that she decided to put the screws to Rick. She couldn't stand the fact that Ted basically had his own reporter while claiming to be a pioneer in fair campaign strategy. I told her that was a mistake, and she told me that Rick could potentially ruin the campaign, Ted's career and my career all at once. I snickered when she referred to what I was doing as a career, but to show her that I was serious, I mentioned the careers she would ruin if the story were released, namely those of Julie and P.J., even if she could prevent Ted and me from taking further responsibility for Rick's deviations. I rambled on about how far out of her league she was until she silenced me with one statement: The "reporter" at the CAC, a recent grad of Loyola and a regular at the bars on Lincoln, verified that Rick contrived the whole thing to get Ted's name on TV when coverage started to sway away from him before the primaries. She also thought that he planned the fight at the mall for a similar reason, but she had to find one of those "thugs" to prove it. Furthermore, since June, he had consistently and blatantly used statistical fallacies to project the foregone conclusion that Ted would win the election based solely on the votes of the state's impoverished class in combination with votes from the state's population of "Generation Xers." Basically, he used his rhetoric to convince companies to give him special-interest funding because of his influence on Ted, who would not accept it.

I couldn't contain my anger enough to keep the car on the road. (I was just as angry with her as I was at Rick.) I pulled off at the first rest area and sat with

PIZZA PIE AND POLITICS
HOW MITCHELL MOON LOST HIS CHILDHOOD

my hands on the wheel for a few minutes after parking, considering whether or not to drive her home. Finally, I took a deep breath and spoke:

"If you publish this story about Rick, the E Party's finished." I paused. "Don't you realize what a chance we have here? We could put a foot in the door for a third party that's not dependent on special-interest funding. Without that financial pressure on him, he could set an example for generations. You can't ruin it, Tabby."

"Ted doesn't know what Rick's done," she replied.

"Then let's just call him right now. Let's tell him. You don't have to publish it to everyone."

"I didn't go out looking for trouble, Mitch. But I'm the only one who knows as of right now, and if I don't blow the whistle on Rick, someone else will soon enough. I'm involved in this, and I'm not going to let my name come up in someone else's story. If I don't publish what I know, *I'm* finished. I'll never be able to make a living doing what I love."

"I have to tell Ted."

"Of course, you should."

"You'll cut our throats."

"I'm sorry. You can take me home now…if you want to."

The statement I made before about "*our* throats" bothered me, as the car continued to run in park. A week before I never would have said "our." Only three months out of college and I was already a full-grown hypocrite.

"Do you wanna go home?"

"If you wanna take me back, I'll understand." She paused. "I'm gonna publish the story either way."

I nodded, backed out, put the car in drive and continued on I-94 west, not stopping until exit 97 in Battle Creek. I didn't talk to her much for the remainder of the drive, just enough to reassure her that I blamed Rick and didn't like Kevin much either.

Taking her back to the Crimson Rouge would have only added to the turmoil at 1:00 a.m. I supposed Neil and Charlie would return from the lake at around 3:00 a.m., probably with Keely and Mandy, and if I explained the situation to them then, I would only have to explain it to them all over again on Saturday afternoon.

I decided to take —66 north into downtown where we could stay at the nicest hotel in Battle Creek. (It was also where the reception was to be held anyway, so we were supposed to stay there on Saturday too.) Still avoiding conversation with Tabby, I parked in front, pulled our bags out of the trunk, and marched to the door, which was locked. I rang the buzzer and waited; I pushed it excessively and waited again. Finally, a security guard poked his head out of a side door with a cigarette dangling from his mouth.

"There's no vacancy," he yelled.

"We're here for the Van Diemen-Nelson wedding."

He nodded.

A moment later he opened the door for us from the inside. I could smell chlorine from the pool, and I heard a distant thumping coming from the dance club on the other end of the building. Once inside the doors, Tabby looked around at the spotless lobby and sitting room where the lighting made the woodwork and marble sparkle. It wasn't the Palmer House Hilton, but her smile made me believe that it was more than she expected. The night clerk asked us if we had a reservation. I guessed that it would be under Moon, Van Diemen, Waters, or Casteele.

"Well, you can't have the wedding suite, and all of those reservations are for Saturday. Did you make a reservation for tonight?"

I looked worried and told her that I thought the groom had arranged everything.

"Just give me your name, and we'll go from there," she laughed.

She welcomed us to Battle Creek and handed the card keys to me. We took the elevator to the ninth floor and entered our room. Under the circumstances I think we were both relieved to see two double beds. Tabby actually unpacked, placing the few articles of clothing she brought into a drawer under the television and hanging her garment bag. While she took a smaller bag into the bathroom to prepare for bed, I decided to call Ted.

He answered in a groggy voice.

"Hey, Ted, Mitch here. Where you at?"

"East St. Louis."

"How's it going there?"

"It's all right; what's up, Mitch?"

"Uh...I just got word that someone's writing a little article about Rick and his ethics."

"Yeah."

"You need to break all ties with him and Kevin as soon as you can."

"Look, Mitch, I know you don't like the guy, but you don't need to play games with me, all right. I'll take care of it in my own way. You leave him out of your articles, man."

"It's not mine. Someone else is gonna have the pleasure of makin' him look like a clown. Do you know what he's done, by the way?"

"Ah, shit, Mitch; it's 1:30 in the morning."

"He's lied so much that he's about to undermine you without even trying, Ted. And I wouldn't doubt it if the parents of those volunteers that were with me at the mall slap a lawsuit on your ass. Haven't you been reading him?"

"Mitch."

"You better get used to that question, man. The first thing you need to do in the morning, before you even get out of bed, is call his editor and tell him that Rick had no authorization to report on your campaign. Then, you need to go public with the same statement."

"Listen, Mitch; don't tell me what to do, and sober up will ya? I can tell you been drinkin'."

"Just tell Teresa to look into it if you don't believe me." My anger made my voice tremble. I hung up on him and threw the phone at the heater on the other end of the room. The "clang" must have startled Tabby because she stepped out of the bathroom door, wearing only a T-shirt and red underwear.

"What was that?"

"Ted doesn't believe me." My voice still quavered.

"Oh, he will," she said before going back to the sink.

We both slept into the latest hour of morning on Saturday, and she woke to let some late August sunshine into our room. We ate lunch in our room and decided to go for a swim downstairs. A large group of people had beaten us there, and as she took off her T-shirt and soccer shorts to expose her bikini, no one gawked at her as they would when Ilo came into a room, except me.

I should have taken those few hours to buy some new clothes (I had been wearing the same three combinations for two weeks), but I wasn't certain that I would be wanted back in Illinois. Instead we went to the mall to pick up my tux, and I drove around, showing her where my parents lived, where I went to school, where I worked and where we played field hockey. (I still felt miserable about missing those last games, and I told her so.) We returned to the hotel at around 3:00 to get ready for the wedding. She used the bathroom first, while I stared out the window at the Episcopal church. I wished Tabby and I could just stay in the hotel together until those bells rang on Sunday morning.

When she came out of the bathroom, she mentioned that I looked sick, but she stunned me so much in her silver dress that I didn't acknowledge it. She wore silver high-heeled sandals that drew my attention toward her shapely calves. I didn't think that she used any make-up, and she wore her glasses because contacts irritated her eyes, but she let her hair down, and the way the red, yellow and light brown fell, just slightly kissing the tops of her brown, freckled shoulders, made me look forward to a change of seasons.

Chapter 28

I put myself into the tux, and we walked to the Episcopal church, arriving about an hour before "kick-off." Mandy was there, along with the families and Keely, who stood at the front door with the other bridesmaids. She said, "Hey, Mitch," as my eyes adjusted to the light, and I introduced her to Tabby. She said, "Oh...hi." I could tell she tried not to act confused, and her eyes scanned Tabby up and down in a catty manner.

"I didn't know you were bringing a date, Mitch."

Tabby looked at me.

"Well, here she is!"

The other three bridesmaids laughed, but Keely didn't break a smile.

A lady from the church gave me directions to the minister's office, and I introduced Tabby to Mandy before I said goodbye. Mandy showed much more cordiality than Keely, but as I walked away, she looked at me as if she had my head in the center of crosshairs.

"Mitch!" Charlie yelled as I opened the door to the office. We shook hands and bumped shoulders.

"Is this the other one?" the minister asked Drew. "Are you sure you know how to do this?" he joked and shook my hand.

"Oh yeah. I know the procedure. You don't have to go to the bullpen just yet."

Drew and his brother greeted me, but Neil didn't even look my way. We waited for an hour, celebrating with a shot of Jack Daniels when word of the bride's arrival came. I checked Tabby from the wing every fifteen minutes or so, delighted to see that she got along with Mandy. And as the organ began to play, Neil decided to voice his issue with me.

When the minister asked us to line up near the entrance to the chapel, Neil took me aside and said, "Do you now what I had to do to get here yesterday? I lost half of a paycheck and maybe even my job, but you couldn't make it."

"I was…"

"…I don't wanna hear it. You're gonna do shots until you puke tonight."

The minister heard this and shot a glance our way.

"Gentlemen, do you mind?" He swept his right hand toward the others, and we fell in line.

As we entered and turned to face the congregation, I saw Tabby sitting next to Mandy in the second row of the bride's side. We smiled at each other. And as I scanned the congregation, I spotted Ilo sitting next to Kenny toward the back of the groom's side. We also smiled at each other. As we waited for the bride, I couldn't stop looking at Ilo, and at one point, she stood to take a picture. Neil made very obvious gestures toward Mandy, trying to find out who sat next to her. When he made a conclusion, he glared at me over his left shoulder.

"You jackass, why didn't you say something?" he whispered.

The wedding turned out to be the most emotional of the summer. Before being pronounced man and wife, Jenn's father brought Charlie his guitar, and he sang a very slow and unique version of "If I Ever Lose My Faith in You." He belted it out so clearly that no microphone could do his lungs justice, and it proved so powerful that even some of the men in the congregation wept. I was just surprised to see him perform in front of people; he had always been so shy before Keely.

In the receiving line, and even on our way to take pictures, no one mentioned my date, partly out of respect for Drew and Jenn, and I think partially our of a new sense of awe in Charlie. No one had seen him sing so seriously and with such feeling before. (No one had seen him sing since he fell in love with Keely.) While we rode in the limo to the hotel for the reception, Keely said she wondered what her parents thought about him now.

PIZZA PIE AND POLITICS
HOW MITCHELL MOON LOST HIS CHILDHOOD

Over a quiet dinner in the ballroom, Neil, who unfortunately sat next to me, tore into me again.

"What the hell were you thinkin' bringin' that baby here when you knew Ilo was comin'?"

"I didn't invite Ilo."

"No shit, you stupid ass."

"I didn't want to."

"Well, how long are you gonna wait to tell her that? There she is."

We looked at the table below us and to the left, next to the dance floor. She saw us and waved. I didn't wave back because Tabby sat at the same table, between Mandy and Kenny.

"Look at her," Neil referred to Ilo. "There's no comparison. Did you lose your eyesight in Illinois or somethin'? You could be bangin' a swimsuit model tonight," he aphorized Ilo.

"You're goin' too far, Neil."

"You've gone too far. You come into town whenever you want with some flavor of the day after you whined and whined about Ilo all damn summer. Then Mandy and Keely talk her into giving you one more chance, and you blow it before you even come through the church doors."

"No one asked me if I wanted another chance." I paused. "Ilo's too difficult."

"You and your talk about how there's no Miss Right, no Miss Perfect, and then you go and rob the cradle 'cause someone's too much of a challenge."

Until that point Charlie had been trying to act as though he paid no mind to our spat, but he choked on a drink of beer in an attempt not to laugh, and his chest shook as he internalized it.

"I'm not robbing any cradle. She's eighteen."

"Oh, she's legal. Is that what you're sayin'? Well good job, buddy." He stuck out his right hand to shake.

This time Charlie couldn't hold it in any longer, and many of the guests looked up from their meals, hoping to see the source of joviality. Neil threw down his napkin, grabbed the remainder of his prime rib as if it were a piece of beef jerky, and walked away to talk with Mandy. She caught him before he got too close to the table, and they left the ballroom.

"What the hell was that?" I asked Charlie.

"Neil's been all wound up since he got here. He's nervous about Mandy; he knows he fucked up." He sopped au jus with a broken dinner roll and shoved it in his mouth. "You should have told us though," he mumbled.

"I tried to. You were too damn drunk!"
"You called?"
I nodded. He returned to his meal.

As the dinner hour subsided, Charlie asked, "Don't you think you should go down there and break the tension?" Without Mandy there only an empty chair stood between Ilo and Tabby.

I walked down and said "Hi" to Ilo first, which I shouldn't have done: I sat in the empty chair while we talked about what I had been doing since she saw me last. With Tabby listening she asked me why I only called her once, as if she forgot what she told me right before I left for Chicago, and if I was going to dance with her later. Sensing Tabby's eyes on me, I shrugged my shoulders, turned away from her and asked Tabby if she wanted to go for a walk.

"I'm not exactly wanted here, am I?" she asked as we reached a small smoking lounge in the hallway next to one of the portable bars. We both sat.

"You just wait. We'll get a few shots in them, and you won't even remember how this all began."

"Can we stay here until then?"

We did just that for most of the early part of the reception, except when I left her to join the wedding party's dance. The mood of the table had transformed since we left. Neil seemed his normal self again after his "walk" with Mandy, ordering pitchers of beer from the waiter and sending Kenny for rounds of shots. In fact that table had quickly become the center of the party: In the short time I was there, drinks were chugged, drinks were spilled, cigars were smoked, stories were told, and cheers were given on a frequent basis. I wanted to stay there, and I might have if Neil didn't break the mood by castigating the DJ with vulgarities for not playing "Electric Avenue."

After I sat with Tabby for maybe an hour more, Mandy and Keely walked by us once to visit the bathroom, but they didn't notice us, and at around 9:00, Charlie did the same but stopped on his way back.

"It's after nine o'clock, Mitch. Would you beer yourself please? You're bringin' me down, man."

I didn't smile, so he tried a different approach: sitting and talking to Tabby, and making her laugh. She brightened up a bit from the enthusiastic attention and agreed to let Charlie buy her a drink. He returned with it and Neil, and as soon as she saw him coming, she excused herself to the ladies' room.

"You're just gonna sit out here?" Neil asked.

"You're not helping me much at all, Neil. Ya know what I mean?"

PIZZA PIE AND POLITICS
HOW MITCHELL MOON LOST HIS CHILDHOOD

"Well, you're not helpin' yourself much either, are ya, buddy? I know you. I know you wanna get crazy."

I agreed but explained to him, in more base terms, that he hadn't done much to make that transition achievable. He understood but mocked me by adjusting his bow tie, licking his middle fingers, which he used to smooth his eyebrows, and making a pompous face. When Tabby returned Neil handed her the drink that Charlie bought and asked her to come and sit at the table with us, if she could stand our shortcomings in the social skills department. This worked, and I felt proud to bring her back into the party.

Neil brought us two chairs, and we sat near the table, almost behind Charlie and Keely. However, the longer we sat, the quieter everyone grew, until Charlie brought us shots. We called Drew and Jenn over and gave cheers to something, but after that, everyone became solemn again. It was different when I visited the table without Tabby, and I started to feel a bit of anger toward everyone there. Neil blamed it on the DJ, who did act as if he had somewhere else to be, and he had a "talk" with him, yelling that if he played Journey or Creed one more time he was going to run him through with a swizzle stick. This proved effective as the ballroom erupted with laughter and applause for Neil's suggestions, and the DJ changed the tempo by playing some keyboard, bass and hi-hat driven dance music. I didn't think that was anyone's favorite, but it was enough to fill the dance floor. Mandy dragged Neil to the planks and returned for Tabby and me. We danced to this song, more energetic club music, and a decent remix of a Charlie Parker tune. Charlie managed to convince the DJ that everyone would like to hear some Clifton Chenier Zydeco music, and after he produced something similar from his collection, we all formed a circle. Charlie performed first, completing a maneuver that looked something like the running man, flowing into the sprinkler, segueing into a single spin, the splits, and finishing with the helicopter. Neil and Mandy took the center, swing dancing very drunkenly, and all the guys cheered when Neil tossed her into the air and held her at chest level for a moment because her flimsy skirt flew to her waist, showing only a skin-colored thong. They disappeared after that, leaving the center open. People started chanting, "Mitch, Mitch, Mitch." I held up my hand as if to say "no thanks," and I began to lead Tabby back to our seats. Someone caught my arm.

"Come on, Mitch!" Ilo yelled. "Let's get crazy."

I looked at Tabby apologetically, and she screamed that it was okay, as she returned to her seat. Everyone cheered as Ilo and I took the center. She wiggled in a circle waving her index finger. I couldn't just stand there while everyone cheered, so I strutted around as Mick Jagger might have done. She stopped me with her right arm, pushed me behind her, and proceeded to bump and grind her backside into my cummerbund. Everyone cheered except Drew, who yelled, "Take it easy; my grandparents are here!"

The song ended soon after that, and embarrassed, I walked quickly toward Tabby, hoping she hadn't seen what happened through the circle. The DJ changed the tempo for a slow dance, and before I could leave the floor, Ilo grabbed me again and asked me to stay. I looked at Tabby, who gave me a weak smile, and I danced with Ilo, making sure to make eye contact with Tabby periodically and to wave at her once or twice. The song ended, and the DJ had the audacity to play Journey again. Immediately, I could hear Neil yelling at him and then at Drew to pull the plug on him. Ilo held me closer and said, "Just one more dance." Neil stormed around the ballroom, throwing up his arms and screaming "Pull the Plug!, Pull the plug!" It didn't take long before the chanting crowd overwhelmed the music: "Pull the plug! Pull the plug!" they yelled. We stopped dancing, and Ilo kissed my neck, then my cheek. I didn't mind, but then she flicked my ear lobe with her tongue and squeezed it between her lips. I jerked my head away, slowly shook my head no, and released my grip on her waist.

"If you want to you should," she said.

The DJ and Neil were at a standoff over the amp cord and one of the electrical outlets.

"You don't touch my stuff, man," I heard the DJ yell.

"I shouldn't," I said and waited for her to reply for some reason.

"So what are you gonna do, go back to your little girlfriend?"

That's all I needed to hear from her. The problem was that by the time I reached the table, Kenny pointed toward the doors out of which Tabby ran. I followed, but she was out of sight before I exited the ballroom. I assumed that she either went to the ladies' room or up to our room. I decided to check our room quickly and fly back to the first floor if I didn't find her there. So I rode the elevator up to the ninth floor, ran to the room, and put my card into the lock. When I saw green, I pushed the door frantically; the inner latch stopped it with a reverberating bang and kicked it back into my face.

"Tabby, I'm only here to see my friends; I'm not here for Ilo. I didn't even know that she'd be here when I asked you."

The room was lit but silent.

PIZZA PIE AND POLITICS
HOW MITCHELL MOON LOST HIS CHILDHOOD

"Tabby, let me in, and I'll stay with you for the rest of the night. That's all I really wanted to do when we woke up this morning."

She didn't answer.

"I'm just gonna stay here then."

I slumped against the door, my weight keeping it slightly open against the latch, until I fell asleep.

Mandy woke me almost an hour later.

"Go downstairs," she said after shaking me awake. "I'll see what I can do."

I returned to the ballroom to hear a Dave Matthews song. I thought the disc jockey must have somehow avoided his termination until I saw Charlie on the dance floor with two microphones and his guitar. The guests sat silent but attentive. I returned to the table and noticed that Ilo wasn't there. I asked Neil where she went, and he told me to be quiet. Keely informed me that she went home. Charlie followed with a Jimmy Buffet song that brought people to the dance floor, and I got up to sit at the bar, just outside of the ballroom. In disbelief I watched him perform, wondering how Keely got him to come out of his shell like that, hoping that Neil and I didn't stifle him, considering the possibility that we had always stifled each other. It wasn't more than twenty minutes after that when I felt a small hand on my shoulder.

I turned to see Mandy.

"She's looking for you," she said, pointing toward the table.

I rose immediately, but she stopped me.

"I'm gonna miss the hell out of you," she said looking up into my eyes.

"What do you mean?"

She started to cry.

I hugged her as if I had never hugged anyone.

"Neil would die for you, you and Charlie both," she said as I held her, never wanting to let her go for what she represented to me—my first love and all the passion of my childhood. "He should tell you that before you leave for Washington tomorrow, but he won't."

She let me go.

"He doesn't need to tell me. That's why I put up with his bullshit all the time."

"Me too," she said as I kissed her cheek and took a long look into her eyes before walking away to Tabby.

She stood near the table looking every which way including in my direction without seeing me, until I was ten feet from her.

"I can't believe this," Tabby pointed toward Charlie. "Does Neil always get his way?"

Neil heard this and picked his head up from whatever trance held his attention.

"Neil gets his way every now and then." We smiled at him, and he smiled back at us dreamily. Then I said something like, "Look, I just got caught up in …"

"…no, I don't even know you that…"

"…I mean I'd rather have my ear lobe in your …"

"…and you guys are like family, so…"

"…if you wanna go back to the room…"

"…no, let's just see what happens and then…"

"…Do you wanna dance?"

"Yes," she said.

"Play some Bob Marley already, will ya?" Neil bellowed coarsely.

I danced with Tabby; Drew danced with Jenn; Keely danced with her father; and Mandy danced in front of Neil, turning to lift the back of her skirt, showing him her underwear and the garter belt he had caught, and turning again to stick out her tongue at him. And of course Charlie sang, until they wheeled away our alcohol and kicked us out into the rest of our lives.

Printed in the United States
74893LV00003B/227